About the Author

Hugh Bellamy spends his winters skiing and living in Pra Loup with his wife, Jane. His summers are spent on various projects renovating and refurbishing his home in Devon. He is a keen cricketer playing for a local club and an avid watcher of Somerset County Cricket Club. He lives at the foot of Dartmoor and is often seen walking his two black Labradors across the moor.

Snowfall

Hugh Bellamy

Snowfall

Olympia Publishers
London

www.olympiapublishers.com
OLYMPIA PAPERBACK EDITION

A CIP catalogue record for this title is
available from the British Library.

ISBN: 978-1-80074-644-2

This is a work of fiction.
Names, characters, places and incidents originate from the writer's imagination. Any resemblance to actual persons, living or dead, is purely
coincidental.

First Published in 2023

Olympia Publishers
Tallis House
2 Tallis Street
London
EC4Y 0AB

Printed in Great Britain

Dedication

For my three girls.

Acknowledgements

I would like to thank Jane, Charlotte, Harriet and Jamie for their help and advice.

1
Snow Fall
Presage

'In winter with warm tears I'll melt the snow
And keep eternal springtime on thy face.'
- *William Shakespeare (Titus and Andronicus, Act III,*
Scene I)

Large downy flakes fluttered delicately through the cold night. They pitched gently on the boughs of the pine trees and nestled briefly upon the tarmac, dissolving into aqueous spots that silently intermingled their brief and intricate existences, before melting into the night.

The carving knife arced into the point where his neck and shoulder met. It scythed downwards, cutting through sinew and muscle, seemingly meeting no resistance, such was the force of the blow the blade sliced into his carotid artery. He gasped in shock and surprise and sank to his knees; confusion playing across his ever-clouding eyes; the phone he was speaking into spilled from his hand to the ground as he spluttered one final word. A powdery crystal of snow landed momentarily on the bright screen before it liquefied and ran in a diminutive rivulet from the phone to the ground. The knife was jerked sharply back out of the gaping wound and a blue trainer ground the splintered cell phone into the rough bitumen surface. His life blood pumped out, mixing in scarlet splashes with the thawing snow, each surge bringing the darkness closer.

Had he really deserved this; did he deserve to die?

He was feeling cold, so cold,

What had happened to him? There was so much more he wanted to do.

Blood was pooling around his right knee, he looked up and saw his friend standing over him. He called out his name but could not hear a reply. He could feel his life force, his energy, his being ebbing away, the darkness was swallowing him and the light was fading.

Chapter One

Michael stood contemplating the fourteen heads that spread in rows across the room. He nodded to the two invigilators who quietly patrolled the exam room. Michael looked down at thirteen bowed heads furiously focussed on their Geography scripts and the one face which appeared to be upturned to catch the warm rays of the Devon sunshine spilling in through the window. The upturned face was adorned with opaque sunglasses and a black, woollen beanie hat. Pens scurried across exam booklets and brows furrowed in anxious concentration hovered over the thirteen desks. At the fourteenth, the disinterested Dylan stared disconsolately into space. He had not written a single word. Michael felt a growing frustration tightening his chest as he thought about the hours that had been spent supporting Dylan. All that time going through the terminology of 'igneous intrusions' to make sure he understood and now, when it really mattered, Dylan had not bothered to put pen to paper – not even to doodle! His future was disappearing and his opportunities evaporating as the clock hands swept round their numeral studded kingdom and the examination plodded towards its conclusion.

Not that Dylan's future had been that bright before he entered the exam room. Years of poor parenting, through a childhood best described as 'free range', had prepared him well to fail. Hard work was an anathema to him but his father had paid for him to go on all of the expensive trips: to the mountains skiing and kayaking on the water during the Ardèche adventure holiday, Dylan had been ever present.

The challenge had not changed throughout the thirty-five years of Michael's teaching career. Even at this rural comprehensive in a pretty market town populated with antique shops and quirky clothes boutiques the tensions remained. Teachers were still exhorting their charges to make greater efforts and to believe in themselves in the face of so many parents who seemed to care little and do even less for their offspring.

Michael stood, battling the growing tension that tightened his body and rose in his throat. He sought solace in the thought that this was the last summer season of exams for him. The end of the perpetual cycle, the production line of school year upon school year was almost – tantalisingly – within his grasp. He flicked at an errant crumb from his breakfast toast that had snared on his suit-trousers his eyes playing over the fine check that patterned the dark green material. That would be a blessing – no more suits and ties. He mused; no more reports; no more marking; no more meetings; no more spoilt, angry, disadvantaged, demotivated, egocentric, arrogant teenagers and their whinging parents. No more making a difference!

Michael had been a devoted headteacher, caring towards both students and staff. In-fact his easy smile and quiet self-assurance had made him very popular with most. He made principled decisions and fought hard for what he believed to be right. He had always fought hardest for the Dylan's of this world. Now though, he felt like a spent force, his self-confidence and humour a thin facade that hid uncertainty, irritability, scepticism and a sense of futility that was often prowling in his subconscious ready to engulf him.

Michael's attention refocussed upon the classroom as

Dylan's feet began to beat a virtually silent tattoo on the linoleum floor, the tedium of inactivity tickling at his consciousness and plucking at his nerve ends. Dylan was the epitome of so many teenagers; the vanity and ignorance of their youth proving to be impenetrable to wisdom.

Teaching had been Michael's passion but now he just felt an all-encompassing fatigue, a fatigue that gnawed at his soul and dragged him into huge troughs of despair. The truth was it was not the Dylan's of this world or their parents or even the ever-changing diktats of misguided education ministers that had brought him to this place. Teaching had been Michael's passion, but it had been a passion he shared with his wife. They had trained together, he had taught in secondary and she in primary. Through unrelenting hard work they had become headteachers, their school communities replacing the children they had never been able to have. Now she was gone, and his life seemed utterly pointless. He felt cut adrift in a sea of purposelessness. Sitting on the sofa with Georgie, the trials of the school day; the plight of angst-riven teenagers; the flaws and failings of some colleagues; the commitment and courage of others had all been dissected and defused. On the sofa or laying in their king-sized bed they would talk for hours about their schools, their staff and the pupils in their care. Georgie almost cared too much about the children in her schools – so many times she had suggested they should adopt a particular child who was having a difficult time. It was the usual conclusion to her monologues of concern but one that she knew was unrealistic and unachievable.

Michael often felt he knew the children at Georgie's school better than he did those at his own; such was the passion and detail of her outpourings. Some of her tales of dysfunctional nativity plays and idiosyncratic children had passed into the couples' own folklore and would resurface regularly when they were with friends or would be referenced in their daily banter. One of the more shocking and most often referred to from early in Georgie's career was the tale of young Andrew Parry, a five-year-old who faced significant behavioural challenges. He had been brought to school by a distraught mother who had explained to Georgie that she felt her darling son needed to see the educational psychologist again. Apparently, he had killed the family cat by putting it in the freezer. Georgie agreed wholeheartedly with the mother that such an act was extreme by any measure. Later in the day, she spoke to Andrew about the cat's demise, hoping to hear it was in some way unintentional. She asked the child why he had put the cat in the freezer and received the prompt reply that he put it in the freezer because he knew the fridge would not be cold enough. Whenever Georgie and Michael drove across Dartmoor and passed the prison at Princetown Andrew's tale would emerge and postulations were shared as to whether he had grown up and reformed or was possibly a resident in the bleak grey stoned institution. The couple had woven their own history, sharing ups and downs together. His beautiful Georgie had met every challenge head on and had encouraged and cuddled him through the darkest times and the best. Hot chocolate, red wine, the Western Morning News crossword, and the woman he loved were all the support that Michael had needed, all he needed to bolster his resilience and help him head back to school the next day... The next week... The next term... The next school year. Now the backbone of that support was gone and with it the mantle and anchor of Michael's Devon world.

He could remember very clearly sitting with the consultant as she told them that the test results had come back positive; he remembered clinging to Georgie in that moment, he remembered crying together on the way home as their hopes and dreams disappeared to be replaced by drug regimes, nausea, pain, and a dark chasm of fear. Even in such a dreadful situation, Georgie was determined to be positive and hopeful. Even when it became clear that the cancer was not going to be beaten; she had smiled at Michael, her paper-thin cheeks still dimpling mischievously, as she said,

"Come on look at the bright side, if I am going to die young at least I will never have to deal with saggy boobs and you chasing off after younger perter models!"

With an inaudible sigh, Michael's mind returned to the room. He glanced across at Dylan again, still, he had produced nothing. Michael walked quietly to stand beside Dylan's desk. The boy did not know the invigilators, who were only employed to work in the school at exam times, but a word from the headteacher might possibly, just possibly, have some positive impact and stimulate some sort of effort. Michael leant down to speak in hushed tones to the disaffected youth.

"Come on Dylan, you can do this. You know your Geography. Go on, have a go at the paper. You're here; you might as well get something out of it."

Dylan glared through his sunglasses at Michael's pleading face. For a moment, he did not speak and Michael wondered if Dylan was going to completely ignore his gentle encouragement, but he did not.

"Mate, this is a crock of shit, you just don't get it do you, I don't need exams. Geography is bollocks. All you lot want to do is to control us, stop us being people. School's not about the kids it's all about the adults and making them feel good about themselves and you are the worst, you arrogant smarmy bastard."

Michael suddenly wished Dylan had just ignored him as the lad pushed his desk away and tipped up his chair as he stormed from the room. Dylan turned back as he reached the door to hold his middle finger up in a mutinous salute. They were actions that seemed planned to cause Michael maximum embarrassment and distress and they had hit their mark. Michael turned to all the other students in the room whose concentration upon their scripts had been completely decimated by the outburst.

"I am very sorry you have been disturbed, please refocus upon your exam and be assured the exam board will be informed about the disruption." Michael informed the thirteen remaining students. He marvelled that his voice sounded reasonably calm when he felt in absolute turmoil. His pride was severely bruised but what he really struggled to deal with was Dylan's self-destruction.

Michael paced around the room, frustration tightening every sinew. Suddenly he was forced to sit down as a wave of dizziness came over him, a dull ache beat in his jaw and a vice seemed to grip his chest forcing his breathing into short gasps.

Chapter Two

During his recuperation, from what had been a classic heart attack, it became even clearer to Michael that most of his friends over the years were not actually his friends at all but Georgie's. The huge outpouring of grief when she had died had passed now and with it much of his contact with the circle of people with whom they had shared skiing holidays, curries and days on the beach. He had received the odd 'get well soon' text in hospital, but few visits. Without Georgie it seemed he was not quite worth the effort. Deep down he supposed he had always known that it was she who was popular and gregarious whilst he was more likely to be opinionated and make humorous comments that were just a little too personal. He had always told himself that it was difficult for Secondary headteachers to strike up friendships; there was some distance between his professional and private personas. Friendly with staff and parents but never friends was his rule, or perhaps, his awkward reality.

Michael sat in his Devon long house looking out at the October rain drilling down from the opaque slate sky. He knew that he needed to do something with his life, but a deep malaise had enveloped him. The cricket season was over, at least during the summer he could watch his beloved Somerset play. Michael had been born and brought up in Taunton at a time when cricket was dominated by the superhuman feats of Ian Botham, Viv Richards and Joel Garner and the 'cider county' had dominated the one-day competitions. He had relished dashing to the ground after school and squeezing under the wire behind the stand at the River End to see his heroes play for a couple of hours before trudging away with the prospect of homework to be completed. He loved watching the superstars, but his real favourite was Brian Rose, the tall blond left-hander who opened the batting and seemed able to stroke and caress boundaries at will. It had always been his dream to play for Somerset, but he had had to face the fact that he simply wasn't good enough. The closest he had come as a boy was to be invited to an indoor net by the county. It had been a 'trial' for local boys and the coach of the time, had overseen the session. Michael had not covered himself in glory, finding some of the older lads bowling rather quicker than he had faced previously and in a time before helmets, he did not enjoy the ball zipping around his ears. Nothing, though, could disrupt Michael's love of cricket. The summertime of his youth was spent at Taunton Deane Cricket Club, the team his father had played for in the fifties. The ground sat behind Vivary Park in Taunton, two sides were flanked by roads and the other two sides by trees. The pitch was the love child of Cecil Buttle, the retired county groundsman. He could be seen throughout the summer, sporting his string vest, sitting on his mower cutting the outfield or on the antique roller ironing the wicket to a marble finish. Michael missed the old man who had died years ago now. He had always greeted him the same way, 'all right my son and heir?' and Cecil always had a tale of his days as a county player to tell. Michael had played for the club since he was eleven years old and whilst there had been a number of breaks in between, as work dragged him around the country, he still played for them nearly fifty years later. He had played with one or two members in the club for the entire time and they were true friends but, and it had always been that way, they were friends who existed in the summer bubble and only tended to be seen outside of the season at the club Annual General Meeting or Annual Awards Dinner.

That was also not likely to change now as Michael lived in Devon an hour away from Taunton, which made socialising difficult. He still enjoyed playing and despite his heart issues had managed to play a few games towards the backend of the season. It was probably the teacher in him but being the elder statesman in the side was fun, and he loved scoring runs and feeling bat on ball. The one area of the game he battled with was his lack of flexibility in the field, but he intended to do something about that for the coming season. He had thought about moving back to Taunton but his closest friend, James, was in Devon and so was Georgie.

He looked around at his ancient home, nestled in its peaceful valley overlooking the Ludbrook. It was listed in the Domesday book and had been home to humans and animals alike for over a thousand years and for much of that time had hosted both together. Georgie and Michael had breathed new life into the old building, renovating and refurbishing throughout but ensuring curiosities like the butter store, a small box shaped recess with a wooden door set into the external wall, were preserved. It had been a labour of love and it would have been as Georgie had often said, 'A great place to grow old together.'

The sturdy stonewalls were over three feet thick. Huge timbers supported the first floor and spanned the fireplaces. The house exuded an air of permanence as it moved from generation to generation; resisting storms and strife; sitting solidly as human triumphs and tragedies were played out in its interior; ecstasy and adversity seeping into its lime-mortar veins and disappearing from human memory.

Photographs depicting their lives adorned the walls; smiling faces on mountaintops; Georgie clutching her wedding bouquet; Michael completing the London Marathon with his great friend James at his shoulder. The couple had always thought they had too many photographs of themselves on display. They had worried that they had been a bit narcissistic, but now Michael just felt comforted by smiling faces of the images. His eyes flitted from picture to picture and landed upon one of Georgie with her parents. Her mother had died some years ago from breast cancer; they should have taken that as a warning. Georgie's father had died only just before the daughter he so doted upon.

Michael had always considered that it had been a blessing for her father as he had died believing that his beautiful daughter was recovering. For Georgie it was a hammer blow. She had always been very close to her father and often talked about how she cherished their family holidays to the south of France in their VW campervan. Her eyes would light up as she recounted tales of swimming in the surf or playing tennis with him or getting lost on a walk to find the local boulangerie. She treasured her time with her father and was bereft when she lost him and it.

The timings of their deaths meant that Michael was now a wealthy man. He had inherited Georgie's death in service benefits and half of her father's estate. He sat with no mortgage, a healthy pension and several hundred thousand pounds in the bank. He had plenty of money but had lost everything he actually valued.

He sat entirely alone, his own parents had died shortly after Georgie and Michael had married.

Michael's mother, Anne, had been in her mid-forties when she had finally, and unexpectedly, conceived and his father was twelve years her senior. Having older parents was sometimes tricky for Michael when he was growing up, his father was often mistaken for his grandfather and was certainly not a force in the dad's race at Sports Day. There were many upsides too. His father was a wise man, a successful architect, who felt very fortunate to be a father and, having retired before Michael started school, invested huge amounts of time in him. He was always there at sports fixtures, threw thousands of cricket balls for Michael to hit and provided unstinting help and support with homework. His mother referred to him as her 'little miracle', which was a little embarrassing at times when he was a teenager but actually reflected how she felt about him. The couple were utterly devoted to each other and to Michael and he often thought about how lucky he was to have grown up in such a loving home. They had felt like a team and Michael had had a wonderful childhood and what his parents lacked in youth they made up for in time, patience and effort. Their holidays together were always adventures and often under canvas. Michael's father, William, was fascinated by history and read history books and historic novels voraciously. His reading would be reflected in their holiday destinations as he chose interesting and intriguing places for them to visit. Whilst he had been an architect, he was far more interested in the stories old buildings told rather than the development of new ones. They would often walk around old churches working out from the arches and masonry the periods when the building was constructed and extended. William would be thrilled to find a Saxon or Norman arch and his enthusiasm was infectious. They would also try to understand significant times for the local community from the dates on tombs, gravestones and memorials. The two world wars were usually notable but often significant numbers of deaths between 1347 to 1353 period indicated the prevalence of the Black Death which was estimated to have cost up to two hundred million people their lives worldwide. Their camping trips to France had been among Michael's favourites, like many young boys he was fascinated by the 1914 to 1918 and the 1939 to 1945 conflicts. Their trips to the Normandy beaches, Pegasus Bridge and Vimy Ridge had all been memorable but William had been careful to ensure his son did not glorify the wars and insisted that they also visited a number of the War Cemeteries. The myriad of rows of white crosses at the Bayeux Cemetery, where nearly five thousand men were buried, provided a further and very sobering memory for Michael. When Michael was in his late teens the family holidayed in the French city of Strasbourg. William had given up on camping, feeling that a man in his mid-seventies needed a few creature comforts and they had stayed in the Hotel Gutenberg in the city centre. William had taken them on a day trip to Natzweiler-Struthof in the Vosges Mountains. It was the site of a Nazi concentration camp that had operated from 1941 to 1944 and had mainly housed resistance fighters from occupied Europe. Fifty-two thousand had been imprisoned there twenty-two thousand of them dying either in the gas chamber or due to the exertions of the enforced labour they undertook. The museum on the site had only just reopened after it had been burnt down by neo-Nazis in May 1976. It included the shocking details of the 'Jewish skeleton collection' which was an experiment carried out on eighty-six Jews by August Hirst. It was an attempt to demonstrate that Jews were racially inferior to Arians and cost the eighty-six men and women their lives. William was visibly upset by what they had seen and talked for hours with Michael about man's inhumanity to man and the absolute sanctity of life. Michael had never seen William so emotional or passionate and listened intently. Michael could not disagree with his father, and shared his sense of outrage, but was also staggered as much by the fact that the museum had been burnt down just a few years before. The realisation grew that Nazis were not just a blip in history but still very much a feature of current society.

One of the wonderful things about William was that even in such a heightened emotional state he was still able to debate and discuss issues without taking personal affront. As Michael would discover in life this was a rare trait- so many people found it impossible to separate criticism of their ideas from criticism of them as people. Once Michael had put forward the argument that the state had the right to take the lives of murderers or terrorists and that perhaps sanctity of life was not an absolute. William had gently taken him through just a few of the miscarriages of justice in the United Kingdom that had cost innocent people their lives; Timothy Evans who was executed for killing his wife and child when the perpetrator was actually the serial killer John Christie; George Kelly who was executed for murdering a Cinema Manager in 1949 when the actual killer was Donald Johnson and the really shocking case of Derek Bentley who had already been arrested when Christopher Craig shot and killed a policeman. Michael's arguments had begun to crumble, and his world view was nudged by his father's morality.

It had taken all his mother's subtle skills to save the holiday from the troughs of despair that William and Michael had slipped into but she knew her husband and her son and had gently brought them back into the sunshine. A photograph of the three of them drinking coffee, taken by the café owner in Strasbourg at the end of the holiday sat on the mantlepiece in the lounge, broad smiles radiated out into the room. William had passed away in his sleep in his early eighties. It was completely unexpected and, like everything in William's life, totally without fuss. Anne had been devastated and she seemed to deflate; her energy and vitality seeping away with each passing day. Even though she was so much younger than William she had died just a few short months later, the doctors said it was an aneurysm, but Michael felt that his mother just didn't want to live without her doting husband at her side. He missed his father's counsel and wisdom and his mother's tender love, but Georgie had filled the void they had left and the focus of his emotions had soon rested entirely upon her. His world was Georgie, their existences were inextricably intertwined. They worked together, played together, laughed together and ultimately, when they were given her terminal prognosis, they cried together. She cried because she knew he would be lost without her. He cried because he felt so utterly impotent; he could do nothing to save his precious wife. As the waves of gulping tears abated they still clung to each other, scared of letting go. Georgie whispered reassurance to Michael,

"Michael, everything in the universe is made of atoms, I am made of atoms, you are made of atoms. Atoms don't go away, they are just rearranged. My atoms will be rearranged but I will always be here, a part of the universe, part of your universe. I won't ever leave you, but you must live on. You must overcome your grief and do the things that you love. If I know that you will continue to run, to ski, to laugh then perhaps I can rest easy!"

Michael had sobbed a barely audible reply,

"But I need those atoms in just the form that they are now. How can I do anything … be anything without you? How can I live, breathe, be, without you?"

Just next to the television, hanging on the wall was one of Michael's favourite mementos. Throughout all the years he and Georgie had skied together, since before the introduction of electronic lift pass systems, they had kept their lift passes, each with a tiny photograph of the holder. Twenty years' worth of passport sized photographs stared out at Michael attached to ski passes from a plethora of ski resorts. Michael looked anew at the frame. Resort names and memories crowded in; Tignes, Val Thorens, St Martin, Altenmarkt, Flachau, Saalbach, Flaine, Puy St Vincent, Val Cenis and their favourite of them all… Pra Loup. Michael and Georgie were never happier than when they were skiing and never happier skiing than when they were in Pra Loup.

They had discovered the resort by chance on a school skiing inspection trip and had fallen in love with it. The one hundred and eighty kilometres of pistes were reputedly the sunniest in the Alps, which was no surprise as Pra Loup sat in the Haute Provence only an hour and a half by road from Nice and the Cote d'Azur. Whilst the skies were often a blanket of blue, the snow record was excellent and the pistes always beautifully groomed. They had always skied at least twice a year.

Michael used to joke that the only reason to go to work was to be able to afford to go skiing and often Pra Loup had been their destination. For a moment Michael's mind wandered to the slopes; to their dream of owning an apartment in their retirement and skiing for the entire winter with fresh croissants and vin chaud. For the first time since Georgie's death, eighteen months before, a glimmer of excitement wormed its way into his consciousness. He had money; he had nothing in the UK that he'd rather be doing during the winter months, in fact, nothing he wanted to do at all. If he bought a large enough apartment, Georgie's friends, their friends, might actually come and see him. It had to be a better option for them than visiting a taciturn retiree in this memorial of a house sitting in damp Devon.

Chapter Three

Full of anticipation, Michael pulled out his android mobile phone and typed into the search engine *'Pra Loup properties for sale'*. Thoughts cascaded through his mind; which part of Pra Loup? How big? How much? For a moment a pang of guilt swept over him. How could he be so excited about their dream without Georgie? But the realisation was taking root; she was gone, and he needed to live. The website Loup Immobilier flashed up on his screen and he tapped the screen inputting the fast-evolving criteria for his search; Pra Loup 1600, close to the lifts, two bedrooms, balcony, good views. A blue circle rotated in the centre of his screen and five search results appeared. He thumbed through the selections. Prices varied from 227,000 euros to 255,000 euros, all easily affordable. After half an hour of studying the online information about each apartment Michael pressed the 'Email Us' link and typed a message to the estate agent.

I am interested in purchasing a two-bedroom apartment in Pra Loup 1600. I live in England but can be at the resort next week. Is it possible to show me what you have available? I am a cash buyer.

> *Best wishes,*
> *Michael White.*

He sat back and took a deep breath, was he really doing this? He had no time to generate an answer as his phone pinged signalling the arrival of an email. The email notification icon appeared, and he opened his message.

Dear Monsieur White,

I am available on Tuesday at ten a.m. to meet you at the office of Pra Loup Immobilier in Pra Loup 1600.

Sincères amities, Francesca

Chapter Four

Booking a tunnel crossing and weeklong hotel stay in France did not take Michael long. He decided to stay in the valley town of Barcelonnette which sat at the base of the mountain road to Pra Loup. It would only be a ten-minute drive up to the resort but there were no hotels open in the resort out of season. Staying in Barcelonnette would also give Michael the opportunity to explore the beautiful town which dated back to the thirteenth century but had been largely rebuilt in the eighteenth century following two major fires. With its mixture of miniature narrow streets in the centre and large opulent villas skirting its edge Barcelonnette had always attracted him. The town's wealth was founded upon the enterprise of the three Arnaud brothers who had travelled to Mexico from the town in search of a better life and had achieved huge success over there in the textile industry, opening a range of stores. They were followed by countless young men from Barcelonnette and the surrounding Ubaye Valley. More than fifty percent of the young men emigrated to Mexico in the second half of the nineteenth century. The 'Mexican Minotaur' was stealing the men of the valley.

However, many of the most successful men returned having made their fortunes in textiles, retail and manufacturing and built the huge villas that populated the valley as a sign of their wealth. As a history teacher Michael had always been fascinated by the local history and was looking forward to walking the narrow streets and sitting at cafés in the multiple squares watching the life of the two and a half thousand inhabitants unfold before his eyes.

The drive to the Alps had always been something Michael had enjoyed; emerging from the tunnel at Calais, changing the clocks and heading for the autoroute and this time was no different. He had delighted in ticking off the cities they passed as the kilometres clicked by, Arras, Reims, Dijon, Lyon. It was always thrilling when they reached Grenoble, the gateway to the Alps, and emerged from the city and travelled along the N85 towards Gap followed by the D900 to Barcelonnette. The complete change of scenery as the road swept up the Alps was always magical and filled with a sense of anticipation and excitement. Even now, as he made this journey on his own, the same feelings tingled through Michael's body. There was a dusting of snow on the mountaintops, but the trees that cascaded down the slopes into the valley below were a triumph of autumnal hues. The sky above was an unbroken cornflower blue, contrasting sharply with the white peaks. Intermittent villages straddled the road or sat on hilltops in the middle distance, all seemed to have an air of weathered permanence and to be marked by a church spire reaching upwards from their heart.

The two-hour drive to Gap evaporated into the scenery as Michael's Volvo dropped down towards the large town and then skirted its edge as the road headed on towards the Ubaye Valley and Barcelonnette. The whole area was drenched in heavily laden fruit trees and vines, which flanked the road, interrupted by the occasional stall advertising 'produits local'. At Espinasses the route crossed the foot of the Lac de Serre-Ponçon which sat calm and sparkling in the October sunshine. The deep turquoise of the reservoir stretched into the distance and dropped away to the left as the road climbed once more into the peaks. The narrow winding road afforded the odd glimpse of the lake below, which then transitioned into the Ubaye River. Michael knew he was close now but his exploration of Pra Loup and Barcelonnette would not begin until tomorrow. As the afternoon dissipated, he felt the fatigue from his early morning start and ten-hour drive wash over him.

However, as Barcelonnette came into view, a deep sense of calm and even of homecoming rested alongside his exhaustion. Michael parked his car in the market square and walked the short distance to the hotel he had booked. The 'Hotel de la Placette' sat in a small square just off the main street, Avenue de la Liberation. Michael entered the dark interior of the hotel, past its garish red exterior. As he attempted to book in he realised immediately that he would need to improve his French dramatically. Georgie had been fluent and had always spoken on the couple's behalf, translating for Michael as necessary. 'Une bière s'il vous plaît.' was simply not going to cut it if he really intended to spend his winters living in Pra Loup! Having dropped off his bag in the rather individually decorated black and white bedroom Michael walked out of the hotel turning left and then right. He headed to the Tandem bar which sold tapas and, unsurprisingly, cocktails. A couple of the tables were peopled with young French couples chatting animatedly. He sat quietly in the corner and attempted to order some food in his broken French. Fortunately, the waitress picking up on his accent smiled and spoke to him in fluent English. Michael ordered the 'planche de fromages' and, in the spirit of adventure, a 'Penicillin cocktail'. Another couple entered the bar and took the table opposite him. They both seemed on edge and were talking to each other in short bursts, interspersed with shrugs and sighs. They were older than the other customers. The man's dark hair was greying at the temples and his large frame looked incongruous, perched on the small bar stool. Initially the woman's face had been out of sight for Michael but when he did catch a glimpse of it he was taken off guard. Her face was framed by an auburn bob and her high cheek bones and full lips were incidental to the electric blue eyes that sparkled across the room. The lyrics of the Cranberries' hit flitted across Michael's consciousness. Her eyes flicked in his direction and locked with his. He realised he was staring and looked quickly away, seeking the waitress and the bill. Walking back to his hotel snatches of the Cranberries' song lyrics drifting around in his head,

'*Domine Domine Deus, electric blue eyes where did you come from?*'

Chapter Five

The following morning Michael awoke to another clear sky, a fresh croissant and strong chicory-scented coffee. He drove out of Barcelonnette and over the river. Tendrils of ephemeral mist rose from the river's tumbling surface and from the surrounding fields as the chill of the night receded amid the sun's probing fingers. The road snaked up the mountain. The long sweeping bends transported Michael from the valley floor at eleven hundred metres to Les Molanes, Pra Loup's lower station at fifteen hundred metres and then up into the heart of the resort at sixteen hundred metres. Seeing Pra Loup drenched in oranges, reds, yellows and greens rather than a blanket of white seemed incongruous to Michael but still breathtakingly beautiful. The road, which transformed into a one-way loop around the village before re-joining itself for the descent back down into the valley, climbed past tennis courts and apartment blocks before it widened to reveal the shops, hotels and ski lifts at its centre. Michael spotted the Loup Immobilier offices on his right and parked in front of the expansive glass frontage displaying rows of property details.

A wave of excitement washed over him as he climbed out of the Volvo and glanced down at his watch. Ten to ten. He was a little early. He paused and took a deep breath as his eyes played across the village and then upwards to the slopes and peaks above. The two main ski lifts sat antithetically against the tableau of grass and trees and climbed away up the mountainside. As he pushed through the glass door waves of excitement bubbled through him and emerged as a small smile crinkling across his lips, rivulets of excitement were effervescing through his veins. He was early but he could always sit and wait if Francesca was not ready.

Opposite the door was a large desk covered in faux black leather with a PC sitting on top. The chair behind the desk was empty, Michael's eyes travelled up the wall behind the desk which was dotted with a number of professional certificates. In the centre was a photograph of a female skier wearing the French national team ski kit, flying around a giant slalom gate with one ski in the air.

The inscription below read; *'Francesca Riehl – Équipe Française'*. Michael heard voices coming from a room to the rear and glanced to the right to see a woman emerging through the door whilst talking over her right shoulder. As she entered the room, she turned to face Michael. He was looking, once again, into a pair of sparkling blue eyes. *'Electric blue eyes who sent you?'*

Francesca smiled and spoke to him enquiringly

"Monsieur White?"

"Er... yes .... oui.... er .... sorry, sorry I am early Francesca," he stumbled in reply.

"Oui. Yes. It's OK. Bienvenue. Welcome to Pra Loup. I saw you yesterday, did I not... In the Tandem bar?"

"Yes. Yes. I am staying in Barcelonnette," Michael replied feeling flustered and disconcerted by the searching examination of her striking blue eyes. He wished he could be more assured and talk more coherently.

"So... Take a seat," Francesca directed, indicating the chair at the front of the desk. Michael sat down. "We will look at some suggestions I have on the computer and then, if you are happy, we will visit them."

How was it, Michael thought, that the French accent could turn such mundane sentences into poetry? Francesca turned the screen so that they could both see it and steadily scrolled through four apartments, all of which seemed to roughly fit the criteria he had emailed.

"Are you content to visit these ones?" Francesca asked.

Michael stroked his chin, which was a habit that a past headteacher had told him was a tell-tale sign of stress, and then nodded his agreement entranced by Francesca's lilting voice and dazzling eyes.

The first three apartments were all a little way from the lifts, sitting above the shops or next to the tennis courts. Michael could not imagine himself living in any of them, either because of their layouts, their poor views or the distance to walk to the skiing. He mused that if he was to live in a ski resort he wanted to see the mountains and have easy access to the slopes and be in a reasonably spacious apartment in order to host guests. However, the fourth, and most expensive by some margin, sat looking out onto the slopes a hundred yards from the Clappe ski lift and immediately seemed a much better prospect.

They approached the building from the main road at the rear of the property. The entrance hall of the apartment opened immediately onto a large, conjoined kitchen and living area with expansive picture windows that framed the slopes outside, and through which flooded the unbroken morning sunshine. Francesca stood back and smiled as she observed Michael's reaction to the panorama revealed through the glass. The bedrooms and bathroom led off from the left of the living room. One bedroom shared the magnificent view of the Bonnet and

Garmine pistes. Michael turned to Francesca as they stood by the window looking up at the mountain.

"It is fantastic, and I would like to buy it," he gabbled, his excitement thwarting any attempt he was making to appear calm and sophisticated in front of this beautiful woman.

"Bon, you don't waste time Monsieur White, are you sure you don't want some time to think or to see some more properties, perhaps at 1500?" she enquired looking a little taken aback at the pace of Michael's decision.

"No, I am certain, I love it and I want to buy it and I want to act fast, to make sure I don't lose it; there cannot be another such perfect property in Pra Loup!"

"Okay, that is good, the furniture is all included, and the price is three-hundred thousand euros a bit more than you wanted to pay. What suggestion will you make, or is it too much?" Francesca asked, looking rather amused by her client's almost childish excitement.

Michael had read that there was something of an expectation to make offers five percent lower than the asking price so, with a quick bit of mental maths, he put forward the figure two hundred and eighty-five thousand euros.

"Okay, I will phone the owners and give your suggestion; you may continue to look around the apartment."

She walked through the entrance hall pulling her mobile phone from her pocket.

Michael turned to survey the apartment noticing for the first time how well furnished it was. He knew he would pay the asking price if necessary. Indeed, he would happily pay even more to own this gorgeous apartment. Georgie would have loved it, he thought with a sigh.

Several minutes later Francesca swept back into the room,

her lips smiling and her eyes twinkling.

"They have said yes. You now have an apartment in Pra Loup! We will go and have lunch and then we can go back to the office to begin the paperwork."

Michael smiled, this was a good day and there had not been many of those for a long time. They walked companionably from 'Le Cheverny', Michael's new acquisition, to 'Le Coq Noir', one of the few restaurants open during the off-season. Michael and Francesca were shown to a seat by the window which looked out onto a grassy expanse which in the winter was the busy meeting point for the ski school and terminus for the four runs that dropped back down into the village. They looked at the menu and both chose the Salad Montagnard. Michael attempted to make small talk, which had never been one of his strengths.

"You skied for France and you speak perfect English?" he ventured.

"Mais oui. It is a long time ago now. When I was in my early twenties I had a ski scholarship at Dartmouth College in America, and following College, I skied for two seasons in the Europa Cup. I did quite well and had one and a half seasons in the World Cup. I skied slalom and giant slalom but I injured my knee twice which made it impossible to be very successful. Well, it was fun, but now when I ski there is no pressure. The only pressure in my life is… to sell apartments!"

"So, no pressure today, your job is done," Michael smiled.

"I hope so. You know about the local taxes, national taxes and the apartment service charge? You are okay with them?" Francesca enquired.

"Yes, no problem," he responded.

"What job do you do so that you can afford to be here all winter and in one of the best apartments in Pra Loup?" she probed.

"I am retired, and my wife died so I can do as I choose and money is not a problem. I will live in my house in England in the summer, watch cricket and probably do some consultancy work in schools. In the winter I will live in my apartment in Pra Loup. Hopefully lots of friends will come and visit me in Pra Loup – it would be lonely to ski by myself."

Michael found himself revealing rather more than he had intended to Francesca. His mind was racing. He was a lot older than her, and she clearly had a partner, if the evidence he had seen in the Tandem bar was to be believed. But was it usual for estate agents to go out for lunch with their clients? He looked into her startling blue eyes and decided just to enjoy the moment.

"Why is the resort called Pra Loup? Are there wolves here?" he asked wanting to make the conversation last for as long as possible.

"Ahh. Pra Loup was built in the 1960s, to develop the old village which was begun in the twelfth century by monks. Honore Bonnet, the coach of the French ski team at the time, helped to design it. The name comes from the patois 'Praloven' meaning; houses on their own in a field."

"So, nothing to do with wolves?" Michael interjected.

"No," Francesca smiled back, "that is a modern addition."

"So, there are no wolves in the Alps?"

"Well..." chuckled Francesca. "There are no *French* wolves in the Southern Alps but there are Italian wolves that immigrated in the last century which are now resident! So, we do have wolves, they are not just the resort logo."

The two finished their meal and then walked back to the Loup Immobilier offices. Francesca took note of Michael's details in order to complete the initial paperwork, which she said would be ready for signing the following afternoon. She explained that in France there was a three-month interregnum before the final signing, payment and exchange, all overseen by the local 'notaire', who also happened to be the Mayor of Barcelonnette. Francesca assured Michael that she would do everything she could to ensure the completion took place before Christmas as he was not keen to spend the festive season in Devon. He saw himself swooping down the slopes of Pra Loup and the Espace Lumière during the festive period.

Michael drove back down the mountain road to Barcelonnette; the valley was laid out before him stretching away to Jausiers in the distance. He looked forward to exploring it over the coming few days. He reflected on his morning. He didn't know why he had been so entranced by Francesca. She had to be fifteen years younger than him and in a relationship. Perhaps he was just enjoying some female company after nearly two years of solitude. He sighed; he needed to focus on the present and his new adventure in Pra Loup, the Ubaye valley and life in France.

The following morning, he received an email from Francesca informing him that the initial paperwork would not be ready for a couple of days as her colleague responsible for producing it was 'away from his desk'. This was not a problem for Michael who focussed his attentions on his explorations.

Chapter Six

Over the coming days Michael spent time wandering the bustling streets of Barcelonnette; spotting trinkets that he might purchase for his apartment and sitting in the cafés populating the squares, watching local life unfold. Georgie would have loved this place with the autumn sunshine softly brushing the shop fronts and the several floors of shuttered windows above them. He discovered a small restaurant, Le Gènèpi, which served beautiful home cooked food from the region. He had returned to it more than once enamoured by the muddle of eclectic tables and chairs and the delicious dish 'souris d'agneau'- a smile of lamb. It certainly made him smile, the tender meat falling succulently from the bone and disintegrating in saporous mouthfuls!

He also ventured up the valley, ignoring the route to the large ski resort of Vars, rather taking the right turn through St. Paul and the tiny villages beyond. In places the houses were so close together that his Volvo barely squeezed through the passage between them. More than once he found himself, utterly irrationally, breathing in as he passed though these pinch points. He stopped as he entered St. Paul and ventured into a rather ramshackle bar with a few plastic seats scattered outside and a very large mountain dog chained up, still growling at his approach. The whole place looked as though it had not been touched for generations. An elderly gentleman emerged from the dim exterior, slightly hunched but with a disarming smile chiselled on to his weather-beaten face. He moved towards

Michael's table. He looked as though he had been carving out his living here since before the formation of the mountains and like the local villages appeared to be chiselled out of the rocky slopes; his hands were clawed with arthritis and he shuffled, stiff kneed, to Michael's side and shrugged enquiringly as he asked what Michael would like to drink.

"Que est ce que vous voulez boire?"

"Un café, s'il vous plaît", Michael stumbled in response.

Although both the bar and the owner appeared to have seen rather better days the coffee was excellent, strong, black and almost treacly.

Whilst Michael was enchanted by the bar and its ancient owner the greatest joy of St Paul was a stone's throw away from where he had sat to sip on his espresso. It was an artisan brewery which Michael soon discovered, after partaking in a short tasting session, made a beautiful light beer. He sampled all the varieties and decided to pack the back of the Volvo with six boxes, each containing six bottles of La Sauvage Blanche. He harboured the fear that, as with so many previous occasions, the local alcohol which had tasted so delicious on holiday when it was accompanied by blue skies and stunning scenery, would turn out to be awful when drunk at home amidst a Devon deluge. He hoped he would not be adding this beer to his list, which was topped by a particularly poor limoncello!

The road beyond St. Paul led upward to the village of Maljasset where it ended, flanked by steep slopes and a beautiful village church. En route the road slid past the breath-taking Pont du Châtelet.

The bridge was awesome in the truest sense of the word. It spanned a gash in the rock hundreds of feet deep, scythed by the tumultuous mountain river that spumed through the base of the cut in the rocks. The Pont du Chatelet had linked the two rocky walls for over one hundred and thirty years, and yet still appeared transient despite having survived a mine explosion in 1944. Amongst the rocks, up to its left there were the concrete remains of the Maginot line – a series of concrete bunkers that were built to defend France against the Italians and the Germans in the 1930s and named after the minister of war Andre Maginot. As a history teacher Michael was always fascinated by such edifices and resolved to research the area more on his return home.

On the afternoon before his departure from Barcelonnette Michael returned to the Loup Immobilier and sat with one of Francesca's colleagues, Pierre, who took him through the documentation he had to sign. His English was excellent, as of course was his tan, and he took the time to explain everything clearly and answer all of Michael's questions. The role of the estate agent in France seemed far more thorough than in England. French estate agents appeared to be heavily involved in ensuring the legal process ran smoothly and were keen to help in any way they could. He even offered to help Michael sort out the internet in the apartment upon completion. Michael was disappointed not to have seen Francesca before his return home, but that disappointment dissipated against the waves of excitement that he felt about his purchase and his upcoming winter in the mountains. His mind was full of tweaks he could make to the apartment décor and purchases he would need to make in order to have it fully kitted out for the winter. The drive back to Calais, and then on to Devon, flashed by in a whirlwind of planning and anticipation.

Chapter Seven

Michael realised that the next two and a half months were going to be busy, but he relished the sense of purpose which he now felt. The deep void left by Georgie had not gone, however he was beginning to find that he could sometimes skirt around its edges rather than wallow in its depths. He had developed a plan: he needed to organise everything to kit out the apartment, he needed to get fit, he needed to improve his French and he needed to invite friends to come and ski with him. His first task, however, was to go online and buy a season lift pass. He expected this to be a considerable outlay but he was pleasantly surprised to find that the Pra Loup pass was only just over four hundred euros; the price of a lift pass for about ten days in many other ski resorts.

It did not take much research to establish an effective and accessible way to improve his French. Duolingo was a free online app that Michael could access on his phone. It was clearly American in origin as words such as 'toilettes' were translated as rest rooms and 'l'addition' as the cheque, however it was structured and required the users to speak and write the French being taught. It also included podcasts of native French speakers which Michael found useful as it was the pace at which the French spoke that he found particularly challenging. Listening to the podcasts, which used the vocabulary which he was learning in the accumulative exercises helped him to recognise the words in context and at pace.

Once he had compiled a detailed shopping list he spent a

couple of hours in Dunelm trawling through the aisles for soft furnishings. He wanted a red-check effect, something he always associated with mountain chalets. He managed to find bedding, curtains, cushions, throws for the sofas, armchair and lightshades that all met his criteria. He wheeled his finds to the checkout, alongside a mountain of pillows and duvets. His dream was becoming more of a reality by the moment. His life settled into something of a pattern as October and November disappeared into the autumn mists. Mornings he spent working through Duolingo and noting down new vocabulary to refer back to; afternoons revolved around a gentle run, with headphones on, listening to a French podcast.

Rebuilding his fitness was crucial for Michael. Before his heart attack he had run sub-four-hour marathons. Now he gently stumbled a few kilometres. The hills were the challenge, leaving him breathless and tight chested. Living in Devon meant that hills could not be avoided, particularly when you lived on the edge of Dartmoor and the view from the garden was up to Ugborough Beacon.

His days were also frequently punctuated by a growing addiction to checking the live webcams from Pra Loup to see what the weather was doing. October had seen spasmodic sprinklings of snow that had fallen prey to the gentle autumn sun. November saw more significant snow falls and the landscape gradually lost its green and orange hues as it became enveloped in a pristine white blanket. Michael's Pra Loup, webcam visits were compulsive and only increased in December when the resort's snow making facilities added to the natural snow fall, the pistes were clearly being prepared. Evenings were often rather quiet and lonely times, but they did provide the opportunity to source new sets of ski kit online. Even Michael, who was not one for a wardrobe full of clothes, was certain that one pair of salopettes and one jacket would not suffice for a season's skiing; and you could never have enough thermals or ski socks. He had to remember that all this gear would have to fit in his car… and in the apartment, so he did try to rein in some of his spending. He also spent time phoning round his friends and organising his calendar for when people might visit. Before Georgie's death he would always go running with his friend James on a Friday night and spend Saturday afternoon at the football. Since Georgie's death this had become a real highlight of his week. The two of them would spend Saturday afternoon watching a home game of one of the four local football teams: Plymouth Argyle, Exeter City, Torquay United or Ivybridge Town. Neither of them was a passionate supporter of any of the teams, they liked to see them all win; they just enjoyed the experience and the atmosphere. Their football watching began in November because James' motor cruiser only came out of the water at the end of October. When it was in the water James spent every weekend on his Parker Eight Hundred. He loved motoring around the South Devon coast; sometimes sleeping on board as he moored in Salcombe or Brixham. Other times, if he had just taken a day trip, returning to his flat which overlooked the Mayflower Marina.

Occasionally Michael joined him. This was often with James' younger brother Tim, who was a marine based in Plymouth. Tim was Michael's idea of an all-action hero. He was six inches taller than both other men and always had a story to tell. Michael soon realised though that the stories were never about Tim's active service, they tended to rotate around drinking, rugby and tales of foreign climes that didn't involve military action. Michael had asked Tim about his experiences in Afghanistan, but the big marine was always evasive and just talked about the people and conditions which just added to the air of mystery that surrounded him. Michael was never sure whether Tim was intentionally trying to create this aura, whether what he had been involved in was confidential or whether Tim really found the memories uncomfortable. The only occasion that Michael had heard about action in Afghanistan was when he had asked Tim about how he had received the two-inch scar, that creased his tanned forehead, running parallel to his left eyebrow. They had been sitting on James' boat, moored in Brixham harbour, watching the sun go down and supping on chilled Italian beers. Michael had asked about the scar which had provoked Tim into sitting forward to reply in a hushed conspiratorial voice. Michael had craned forward to hear the whispered confidence.

"We were dropped deep inside a Taliban held area in Afghanistan, me and six colleagues on a black op. Our objective was to neutralise a Taliban leader who, intelligence had told us, was visiting his dying mother in his home village. We knew which house she lived in and we were hoping he was not accompanied by too many of his Taliban fighters. We crept into the village under the cover of darkness using our night vision equipment to find our way to his parent's house. We managed to reach our target without raising the alarm. There were two heavily armed guards outside the house, but both were asleep. We silenced them permanently." Tim punctuated his story by drawing his forefinger across his own throat, "Then we slipped into the house, we searched room to room, the only sound was a rasping snore from the back of the property. We followed the noise and entered a bedroom with two single beds, an old woman was propped up on pillows in one, her rhythmical wheezing masking the noise of us moving. Our target was fast asleep in the other bed, one of my colleagues moved swiftly towards him with knife in hand. At that very moment the old woman stirred and was suddenly wide awake and staring straight at me, everything seemed to be moving in slow motion. She cried out to her son, but it was too late for him and then in one flowing movement she leant over the side of her bed and grabbed her chamber pot. Without hesitation her hand swept up and she threw the missile at me, it slammed into my head cutting deep into my brow and covering me in stinking urine. My first experience of chemical warfare."

Michael was rapt by the story, but his concentration had been broken by James laughing uncontrollably at his side. Michael had turned to him eyebrows raised enquiringly, more than a little surprised that his friend was being so openly disrespectful to someone who had clearly risked his life for his country. James spluttered and explained as Tim began to rock with silent mirth, "He's taking the piss literally, he got that scar from swimming into the side of the public swimming pool when we were children, blood everywhere. He was racing against me, looked up to see where the side was and found it was right there! Dad had to come and get us and cart Tim off to casualty where he cried like a baby when they stitched him up, not much of a hero really!"

Michael had been covered in embarrassment at his own gullibility but that had soon been washed away by another couple of Birra Morettis. Michael had learnt his lesson though and steered clear of asking Tim about areas of his life he clearly wasn't willing to share, sober or drunk.

It had also become very apparent over time that Tim could drink Michael and James under the table. His talents didn't end there, he was a very good man to have around in a crisis, he was always calm and was a practical problem solver. He was the one who had managed to get the boat unlocked and the engine running on the occasion that James had lost the keys when they had motored around to Salcombe. They had got there just before lunch and moored in the channel before going ashore for a fairly liquid lunch.

On their return to the boat James, who was famously awful with keys and could lose a set walking across a room, realised he had lost them. They had retraced their steps but despite a thorough search the keys could not be found. Tim had subsequently managed to break into the boat cab and get them on their way with little fuss but plenty of good-natured ribbing of his brother. Even though Michael did not have the greatest sea legs a weekend on the boat with these two was always a memorable event. Such weekends did not happen often as James was usually hosting a female acquaintance. Over the years different women had accompanied James but eventually the outcome was always the same when they realised that James was far more committed to his boat, his running and his school than he ever would be to them. Michael observed that James did not seem to mind when they left and actually appeared to enjoy the thrill of the more transient nature of his relationships. Michael had wondered, when he was first getting to know James, whether this was the behaviour of a man who didn't like responsibility but that was the antithesis of the man Michael saw at work. James never ducked a problem and was always happy to deal with a tricky situation and to accept blame when things had gone wrong even if it wasn't his fault. In that sense his shoulders were as broad as his brothers, he basked under the pressures of hard work and duty and his judgement could be trusted even in the trickiest of situations.

So, from November onwards, the weekend would begin on Friday night when James came over and they went for a run together. James was younger and fitter, some twelve years younger, but whilst Michael's hair had made the transition from jet black to grey his swarthy skin, chiselled features and muscular torso belied his age. James still had a shock of unruly dark hair and more boyish good looks which, it appeared, a fairly wide range of women found enticing. Both men stood over six feet tall, James was slighter but rippled with sinewy muscles. Michael was amazed at the hands that genetics had dealt James and his brother Tim, whilst facially one could never doubt they were related their body shapes and sizes were completely different, one a bulky man-mountain, the other slim and lithe. It was perhaps because of the contrasting physiques that the two had never really fallen into sibling rivalry, they tended not to bother to try and compete with each other as their physical skill sets were so utterly different. It was in character traits where they were much more closely aligned; what was obvious was that they were both natural leaders.

Michael and James had not just shared the pain of marathons but also those of management in a large secondary school. James had been Michael's deputy for eight years. He had appointed James to the role and subsequently guided and mentored him. James was an impressive leader and committed professional, and when Michael had taken the decision to step down the Governors had chosen James to succeed him as headteacher. He was the one exception to Michael's rule of 'friendly but never friends' with staff and he was thrilled for James that he had been appointed to the role he knew he was desperate to take on. Selfishly, Michael reflected, he was also relieved that someone he trusted implicitly would be taking on the school into which he had poured so much of himself and that someone shared many of his deeply held principles, a moral man.

Many school problems had been resolved during their long runs and a deep friendship had been moulded under the pressures of running a large comprehensive school. The dynamic had changed when Georgie fell ill and subsequently died and again with Michael's heart attack. It had been James who had supported Michael and who had provided both a shoulder to cry on and exhortations to face life again.

Since Georgie's death, following the Friday runs, the two had fallen into a comfortable routine of eating at the local pub, 'The Ship Inn'. Although they missed Georgie's home cooking, the food at The Ship Inn was always excellent. The Inn sat just off the square in Ugborough, a fifteen-minute walk from Michael's house. He always received a warm welcome and he and James would sit and discuss his winter plans and mull over the challenges James was facing at school. Michael hoped it was useful for James to have someone to talk to who understood the personalities and contexts of his work. Michael tried to listen carefully and ask clarifying questions but not to give advice or opinions, as he was only too aware that it was James' school now, and even after such a short time away he was out of touch. He also tried to keep the fact that it would be a very exciting time for James as a new head in the forefront of his mind. Even though it was a headship in a school James knew so well and had worked in for several years, being able to shape it in light of his own educational beliefs would be thrilling, challenging and at times more than a little overwhelming.

A running theme of their discussions was Mr Vines and his family. Mr Vines, Dylan's father, had three children, two of whom were still at the school. Talk of Mr Vines was usually kept for the pub as such a troubling subject seemed a little more palatable with a pint of mellow Doom Bar to lubricate the conversation

Mr Vines had been a thorn in Michael's side from the moment that Dylan had joined the school in year seven all the way through to GCSE results day. That final 'results day' had capped off five years of putrid hatred that Vines had spewed both on social media and in person. His stale whisky breath had been the backdrop to his irrational and very personal rants, which had often been punctuated by his forefinger being driven into Michael's chest. The face-to-face encounters were, in a way, more manageable and the damage could be contained, but the unrelenting social media attacks had proved a huge problem.

Vines' acid comments were in a public forum and open to students and parents alike, and as with so much on that platform, people took them at face value. The attacks were corrosive, but the site hosts refused to act despite the concerns raised by the school and the police. They were powerless, they explained. If Mr Vines did not actually threaten Michael, then there was nothing they could do. Of course, the wider problem was that this was part of the experience of leaders and teachers in schools across the breadth of the country. Social media had provided a platform for malcontents, with or without justification, and schools dared not, and often could not, respond.

Dylan's results day, Michael's final commitment as headteacher, had been classic Mr Vines.

Michael had been with colleagues handing out the envelopes that contained the examination outcomes that could impact so massively on the students' future. Whilst Michael's recuperation from his heart attack was not complete, he wanted to be there to close the final page on his career in education. The last student he expected to appear to collect results was Dylan Vines, after all he had not written a single word in any of his exams.

Nevertheless, here he was sullenly swaggering up to the desk with his father bristling on his shoulder. The eruption was instant as Vines screamed at Michael; his face puce and veins pulsing from his neck, his tufts of greying ginger hair jutting forward with each bellow, spittle torpedoing from his lips.

"Five years and he's got eight us. You're fucking useless. How much do you earn you bastard? You've destroyed this school and you've destroyed my son."

The rant had seemed interminable. It had been planned to cause maximum embarrassment and upset for Michael, a family trait, and had been fuelled by a significant early morning alcohol intake. He never really knew what he had done to provoke such behaviour from this man. Vines had been told after the exams that Dylan had written nothing on his papers. It was not surprise that had caused the outburst, it was just a great final opportunity to publicly denigrate Michael.

Staff and parents had stood paralysed with shock as Vines had bawled out his abuse. It had only come to an end when a large rugby playing parent, who was also an off-duty police officer, had ushered Vines out of the building. Michael had wanted to exact revenge on Vines on so many occasions. He had desperately wanted to run after him and beat him to a pulp. So often he had fantasised about what he wanted to do to this dreadful man, he would love to drive a fist into his fetid mouth but, as always, he took a deep breath and smiled at his colleagues trying to make light of Vines' behaviour.

It now appeared that it was not just Michael who was the focus of Vines' discontent. His attention had shifted seamlessly onto the new head, James. Michael could only listen to James' update on Mr Vines, he could offer no solace nor solution as he had none. Nothing he had tried had any beneficial impact, indeed, often his actions seemed not to smother the fire but to pour petrol on the flames. He felt his own headship had been blighted by the man and, perhaps irrationally, held him at least partly responsible for his heart attack. Michael could see James would have his work cut out as the youngest child was demonstrating very challenging behaviours and his misdemeanours were always supported by a father who really did not seem to grasp that indulging his son's deviant behaviours was hugely destructive. The staff were always wrong and his youngest son blameless, misunderstood and mistreated.

Chapter Eight

On one of the Friday night meals at The Ship Inn in mid-November, as James drew deeply on his beer with the light foam speckling his upper lip, Michael asked him when he would be able to come out to Pra Loup for a ski.

"Well," replied James as he returned his glass to the table its contents significantly diminished, "I don't break up until the twenty-first of December and you aren't sure when you'll complete."

Michael interjected, "Actually I've had the full contract through today, although understanding it might be a bit of a problem. The estate agents are suggesting completion on the twenty second of December."

James continued, "Ahh, right. But I'm seeing my parents for Christmas Day and then I'm going to my brother's for the New Year, so it had better be February half term, which I think is the fifteenth," he proffered whilst checking the calendar on his phone screen, "If you can fit me in then? I could come out at Easter too if you're not too bored of my company – or of me beating you down the slopes?"

Michael smiled. They both knew that whilst James was the quicker runner and the younger man, he was no match for Michael on the snow.

"That would be great. I'd better get some lessons so I can keep up, but in return can you keep an eye on my house, particularly if it gets really cold, just pop over every now and again?" Michael requested.

"No problem, that still seems like it's a good deal for a ski trip or trips!" James smiled as the two raised their glasses to each other sealing the contract with Doombar and a smile.

"And perhaps I'll ask Miriam to take a look at the contract for me. It'll be helpful to have a French speaker check it over." Michael mused.

Miriam was the Head of Modern Foreign Languages at the school and had dual French and English nationality. She had worked at the school long before Michael's arrival and had a quality to her that defied many attempts to guess her age, she appeared to be nearing the point when she might retire but, according to her colleagues, she had always looked like that. She had come to Devon from her native Paris to be with an English artist who had been studying at the Paris College of Art when they had met but had subsequently decided to return home to Totnes. The relationship floundered after a couple of years when Miriam discovered that her beau was apt to take a very hands-on approach with his models. By then though she had found another love; the school, but this was a love she was willing to share. She could be in her late forties or in her late sixties, it was quite impossible to say, her dyed orange hair, thick foundation and heavy-handed black eyeliner masked any hint of the woman who lay beneath. What was clear was that she was passionate about teaching French and utterly committed to the school and its students.

With the completion date now confirmed Michael spent time with Miriam the following week pouring over the wedge of documents trying to ensure he had a reasonable grasp of them. Miriam was very patient with him as, despite the many hours spent on Duolingo, his vocabulary did not stretch to legal terminology. She sat in her classroom, where they had agreed to meet, and used two of the students' tables pulled together to form a square, to spread the plethora of documents across. Michael was enveloped by her sweet lilac scented perfume and the stale nicotine that clung to her, the two aromas seemed to battle with each other for supremacy and had created a very individual fug in the room. She poured over the papers, her glasses perched on the end of her nose and much of her face obscured by her extraordinary hair, which Michael pondered, sitting next to her, could easily be a wig. She paused periodically to point at the text and explain to Michael, in her rasping cigarette forged voice; passages that she thought were particularly pertinent. After two hours of patient interpreting, disturbed only by the requirement for fresh coffee, Miriam sat back smiling, her task complete. Michael thanked her profusely and pulled a bottle of Salcombe Gin from his bag, which he was reliably informed was Miriam's tipple of choice. Given the broad smile that rearranged the myriad creases extending from the corners of her mouth, like the prongs of two grass rakes, Michael presumed his intelligence was accurate.

Having a fixed date for completion Michael found himself even more motivated to improve his French and his fitness. As James wryly observed, he was becoming obsessive. Michael planned to drive down to Barcelonnette and stay the night before the completion of the contract, on the twenty first, at the Hotel de la Placette. That meant leaving Devon on the twentieth and staying at the Ibis near the Folkestone to Calais tunnel that night. The Volvo was a large car, but Michael had planned carefully and assiduously. Soft furnishings, clothes, kitchen implements, and appliances, crockery and nick knacks were all shoe-horned into the vehicle along with a basic 'Do It Yourself' tool set and decorating kit. He didn't think he had forgotten anything. He had novels to read, his laptop and Bovril to drink and three months' worth of heart pill prescriptions in his suitcase. The boxes of spironolactone, lisinopril, clopidogrel, atorvastatin and bisoprolol took up quite a space in his luggage and also in his daily routine. Remembering to take them was a necessity not an option. Georgie would be proud of how meticulous he had been. He had even remembered his passport and phone charger! Finally, the time had come to begin his adventure. He walked around the house checking that everything was unplugged, windows were shut, and doors locked. The heating was set to come on for an hour each evening and James had undertaken to check the property regularly. As Michael walked to the front door his eyes rested on a beautiful black and white photograph of Georgie which was sitting on the bookshelf. Her eyes seemed to stare out of the picture deep into his and that gentle, almost rueful, smile played on her lips He looked at it and sighed, then picked it up and took it with him to the car. Suddenly he wasn't sure he could do this on his own. He had kept himself so busy that his inadequacies had slipped into the shadows but now, without Georgie by his side, their dark fingers began to pull at his inner thoughts. He physically shook himself, climbed into the driver's seat and turned the ignition key. What would Georgie think of him? He reversed the car off the drive and headed for the A38, allowing Ken Bruce and Radio Two's 'Pop Master' to fill his head.

Chapter Nine

By the time Michael reached Grenoble, and was faced with regimes of snowy white mountains, he was awash with excitement again. The prospect of skiing for a whole season was all consuming.

The Ubaye Valley had been transformed since his last visit and now, from the valley bottom to the mountain peaks, it was ensconced in a thick white blanket of fluffy concertinaed flakes. The villages he travelled through were all bedecked with sparkling Christmas lights and as he drove into Barcelonnette, he entered a Christmas scene of narrow streets cuffed with drifts of snow reminiscent of a pseudo-Dickensian greetings card minus the gentlemen in top hats. He parked his car and walked the few yards to his hotel. Traditional Christmas music played from the speakers suspended above the shopping streets which were thronged with people. All the shop windows glistened with Christmas wares and the cafés were serving vin chaud from steaming vats just outside their entrances. The night sky was dark, but Michael could just glimpse the lights of Pra Loup on the mountainside above.

He ate in the hotel bar, surrounded by its black and red décor, and carefully sorted through all the documentation needed for his meeting with the vendor and the notaire on the following morning; the day when he would complete the purchase of his slope-side apartment! He was due to meet Francesca and the vendors at Le Cheverny apartment at ten am. After checking that everything was in order and the meters read, they would all proceed down the mountain to meet with the notaire in his offices in Barcelonnette. He could hardly believe that it was really happening, but then his life had become shrouded in disbelief over the past couple of years, his reality – their reality – had been turned on its head. This though was a positive event; exciting, even thrilling and his body fizzed with anticipation. Sleep would be a challenge but, whether he slept or not, tomorrow would be the beginning of a whole new chapter in his life and it would be... must be... a good one.

Michael arrived at the apartment just before ten and was met by Francesca. Her face was wreathed in a welcoming smile and she bent forward and kissed him three times on alternate cheeks.

"Michael, bien venu."

He felt a frisson of excitement as her blue eyes met his. He could not help but wonder if it was usual for the estate agent to kiss her clients, and was there any significance in the three kisses... Or was he just being a foolish old man? Behind Francesca in the living room of the apartment stood an elderly couple who welcomed him with handshakes. The gentleman introduced himself and his wife. His wife was a small, neat looking, woman with a tidy bob of grey hair, fine features and a seemingly constant smile playing at the corners of her thin lips. He was a big man with a thatch of white hair and a large angular face completely dominated by an enormous nose which dwarfed his other features. It was difficult not to fixate on the bulbous protrusion but Michael had had a colleague who suffered from rhinophyma and presumed that this cruel disfigurement was another case of 'potato nose' as it was sometimes dubbed. Its owner was clearly used to people reacting to his condition and ignored Michael's hesitation as he spoke indicating himself and his wife in turn with his right hand.

"Monsieur Briatte et ma femme."

"Bonjour," intoned Michael in response, inclining his head in a slight bow and forcing himself not to stare at Monsieur Briatte's nose.

Francesca hurriedly intervened and picking up her iPad from the kitchen surface explained to Michael that they would go through the inventory, then check the condition of the fixtures and fittings and finally take the meter readings. She appeared to have been in the apartment before Michael arrived as she seemed to know where just about everything was stored. The whole process took little more than half an hour with Francesca switching between French and English effortlessly depending on whether she was talking to Monsieur and Madame Briatte or to Michael. Her language skills were impressive as she hardly tripped at all over any of the English terms or the grammar. As the inspection came to a close Michael stood for a few moments gazing out of the lounge window onto the pistes which swooped down among the trees towards him. He could not wait to carve through their gossamer veils which steepled down the mountainside. He grinned at the prospect and turned to leave the apartment and return to his car for the short journey down to Barcelonnette.

The notaire's office was on the ground floor of an austere but imposing building just outside the centre of the town in what appeared to have been the former military base. It was dominated by a substantial table that ran the length of the room, surrounded by chairs. All of the furniture was constructed in the same rich pine. The notaire and his assistant sat on one side of the table; Francesca, the Briattes and Michael sat on the other. This came as a relief to Michael as he was able to avert his eyes from

Monsieur Briatte's face and concentrate on the information being presented. The last thing he wanted was to appear gauche and rude on this his first day in the community, but it was very difficult not to be fascinated by the lumpy mass of nose, just as it was difficult not to rubber neck at a car accident as you drove past. You knew it was wrong but that didn't make it any easier. Michael kept his gaze fixed upon the notaire, whose dark hair was flecked with grey at the temples and extended down to form a trimmed beard that circumscribed his deeply tanned and lined face. He was wearing chinos and a tailored green velvet waistcoat over a white shirt that was open at the collar. He looked comfortable and relaxed in this setting but was clearly a man who spent a great deal of time outside in the sunshine of the Haute Provence. He cut a very different image to members of the legal profession that Michael had come into contact within the UK. They tended to be grey men in grey suits or earnest tweed clad women, both lacking any sense of humour and rarely available when you actually needed to speak to them – particularly when it was about your house conveyance. Frequent holidays and long lunches seemed to take priority. The notaire's assistant was young, blond and, like her boss, deeply tanned. She tapped at a laptop computer that was sitting on the table. On the wall to their left was a large television screen which displayed copies of the documents that Michael had been studying the night before. The notaire, who was one of those middle-aged men who simply exuded authority and confidence, talked through the documents using Francesca to check with Michael that he understood the points being made. Michael was relieved that he had spent the time with Miriam examining them as the notaire's approach was fairly forensic. Finally, Michael and the Briatte's signed a number of forms and the notaire confirmed that he had transferred the monies, which Michael had paid into the notaire's account previously, into the Briatte's bank. The Briattes passed Michael the keys and with smiles and handshakes all-round the transaction was complete. A sense of euphoria swept over Michael. He wanted to dash back up the mountain immediately to unpack all the items he had brought and organise the apartment. Luckily his English reserve prevented him from pushing past the other members of the meeting to get to the door. Besides, Francesca turned to him clearly keen to speak to him.

"Michael."

"Francesca, thank you. I am so happy with the apartment. Thank you so much for everything you have done."

"De rien mon ami, you are welcome. But if there is anything you need, you know where the office is, just ask. I will pop in on you on the twenty fourth, at the end of work to check you are all OK. Shall we say five o'clock?"

"That's very kind," Michael replied. "I'll look forward to it."

"Au revoir Michael. A bientôt."

She pecked him three times on his cheeks again and left to return to her car.

Michael was soon back in Pra Loup unpacking his car and sorting his belongings in the apartment. By the time the crockery, cutlery and clothes were packed away, beds made, and the curtains and pictures hung it was early evening. He realised, as he glanced at his watch, that he had not eaten since breakfast at the hotel, and he had not yet thought to do any shopping for food. He surveyed the apartment. The rooms looked more homely and the frame that now hung in the hall reminded him of all the ski holidays he had enjoyed with Georgie. It was the clear frame that contained all their lift passes from 1985 at Zauchensee to the early twenty first century at Les Deux Alpes. The gallery of photos documented their changing faces as the years had passed, wrinkles and grey hairs had appeared, but Georgie's mischievous smile and dimples were constant features. He decided to drive down to Barcelonnette and shop at the Carrefour there. He knew it would take longer than shopping at the little supermarket in the village, but it would give him more choice and save him some money. He also knew that Carrefour had a good wine and spirits selection, and he did not intend to face Christmas without a good stock of beverages, even if he was to be on his own.

Chapter Ten

Sitting at his dining table that evening, having polished off a bowl of ravioli followed by a coffee eclair which he washed down with half a bottle of Merlot that trickled its raspberry flavours across his palate, Michael pondered the day. He could not help wondering if the kisses on the cheeks and the offer of 'checking up' were in any way significant or merely the delusions of a lonely man. He wasn't sure how it happened but as the evening disappeared into the wee small hours, he found himself googling information on the significance of kisses on the cheeks. He read an article by a career diplomat that explained that the greeting was merely one of friendship in France, and that it dated back to peasant customs. Interestingly, in Paris two kisses was usual but in the south in Provence three was more customary. He felt rather foolish and turned his mind to the key task for the morning; the purchase of skis and boots.

Francesca had recommended Godille Sport whose shops were in the central arcade. There was one that specialised in clothing and one that focussed on ski equipment. Michael clambered into bed between his soft flannelette sheets, and exhausted he fell into a deep sleep.

In the morning, he woke with the sense of excitement and anticipation that were becoming part of a new reality for him. He decided that he deserved a fresh croissant and coffee in one of the nearby cafés before he made his way to Godille. He had decided to purchase his skis and boots in the resort in order that any problems or necessary adjustments could be resolved quickly by the same people that had sold them to him. He also hoped that the regular waxing and servicing of the skis throughout the season might then also be carried out at a preferential rate. Likewise, he hoped that this might also extend to a preferential rate for any friends that might come out and hire or buy equipment.

Godille sport was not busy when he walked into the shop. It was early in the season, midweek and (despite the excellent early snow) the resort was nowhere near capacity. Michael realised that this would all change by Christmas week; and Christmas Eve was only two days away. He was desperate to get out onto the slopes as soon as possible so that he could enjoy them before the Christmas crowds appeared.

Godille was packed with skis standing to attention in serried ranks; the rental section on one side and on the other all of the various makes and models were for sale. Another corner of the shop was set aside for ski boot sales and fittings. In his faltering French Michael introduced himself to the blond-haired Adonis who was unpacking new boots and putting them on the shelves. Michael explained what he was after – a good all-round mountain ski on which he could execute short turns as well as carve across the mountain and which would cope with some off-piste skiing. The assistant introduced himself as Gerard. He was sporting a tight white t-shirt that showed off his muscular physique to its best. He listened carefully to Michael's request and brought over a variety of skis for Michael to consider. Gerard explained the difference in performance of the skis, finding it necessary to illustrate the flex in each ski by pushing down on the tip of the vertical ski. These subtleties were a little lost on Michael who felt Gerard was just taking this opportunity to show off the flex of his biceps to the young female assistant on the other side of the shop. Michael was tempted by the Stocklis, but with a price tag of over a thousand euros he found it difficult to justify such expenditure with his standard of skiing. Ultimately, he settled on a pair of Rossignol Experience eighty-sixes which Gerard seemed to think would suit him and at just over seven hundred euros Michael could square the expenditure with his conscience. Selecting a pair of ski boots took a little longer. Michael told Gerard that he wanted "Les chaussures de ski qui resemble des pantoufles." Gerard just laughed at this request for ski boots that felt like slippers! After trying on eight different pairs he had a clear favourite; a pair of Rossignol All Track one hundred and twenties, which, even if they didn't feel quite like slippers were certainly the most comfortable ski boots Michael had ever worn. Having taken payment for the skis and boots Gerard told Michael to come back in half an hour when the skis would be prepared and the boot bindings would be attached. It was now eleven thirty so Michael headed back to the café where he had enjoyed breakfast and ordered another coffee.

Chapter Eleven

Shortly before one o'clock Michael finally set off from his apartment, ski kit on, skis and poles in hand. On the snow just in front of the apartment he clipped on his skis and skated across the snow to the Telemix Clappe – a ski lift that had both six seat chairs and cabins. He slid through the computer-controlled gates, proffering the left arm of his jacket where his pass was safely zipped away. He stepped onto the carpet and was soon scooped up onto a chair.

After a few minutes being carried through the path carved amongst the tree tops, he was deposited at the summit of the lift and quickly pushed himself off down the blue La Clappe run. He always worried at this point on ski holidays, as the first run loomed, that he would have forgotten how to ski. The excitement and anticipation of skiing was always replaced by that dry mouthed apprehension and then just as quickly the excitement would return. He knew from experience that being bold and attacking the slopes would jog his muscle memory into action. His new skis felt slick against the snow and for a moment he worried he would not be able to stop. As he linked his turns and carved down the piste he immediately felt at ease and whooped as the freedom of his movements touched his very soul.

He straightened his skis as he came to the bottom of the slope and flew down into the dip, thighs burning, and up the other side to the next lift, Peguieou. Peguieou took him up to the top of the mountain and as he came off the lift and turned to the right he smiled as he looked down across the panorama of the resort. This was a good place to be. Michael skied the runs above Pra Loup all afternoon, frequently returning to his favourite red – Honore Bonnet. The snow was pristine, the sky blue and the pistes far from busy- a perfect Pra Loup day. The next two days he spent revisiting the entire resort, including the linked ski area of Foux D'Allos and the wonderful Sources du Verdon run and its thrilling 'schuss', where you set your skis straight and crouched to achieve maximum speed for a couple of kilometres. It was a run that allowed the most mediocre skier to feel like a downhill racer, the wind tearing at their faces and goggles as they plunged down into the resort of Val d'Allos.

On Christmas Eve Michael finished skiing a little earlier than usual to ensure that the apartment was immaculate for Francesca's visit. She arrived at 5 p.m. on the dot. He had been so subsumed by the skiing and the beauty of the resort that he had not thought a great deal about his guest but now as he heard a knocking at the front door butterflies flapped in his stomach and he felt like an over excited teenager on a first date. He went to the front door and opened it to reveal his incredibly considerate estate agent. As she entered the flat and her sparkling blue eyes met his he felt a little in awe of her beauty and elegance. Her tailored jeans and fitted jacket showed off her stunning figure and Michael immediately regretted not having made more effort with his own attire.

Francesca greeted him with three kisses and a cheery

"Bon soir Michael, ça va?"

They walked round the apartment which had undergone a slight transformation, even although the furniture remained the same.

"Very good Michael," Francesca grinned. "Now you can buy

me a drink and perhaps we will watch the fireworks together before I go back to Barcelonnette to see my family?"

"Yes, of course," stammered Michael. "Where do you want to go?"

"Le Loup Blanc is close, and we can see the slopes from there."

"Okay."

Michael picked up his wallet and his jacket and they walked outside and across the snow to the bar. Michael was feeling very flattered with the time Francesca seemed willing to spend with him. If it was just professional customer-care it was amazing; if it was something more it was staggering.

Sitting in Le Loup Blanc, nursing their vin chauds Francesca explained the order of events. The 'animations' would begin at six, once it was dark, with the piste bashers driving down the mountain in convoy with Père Noël perched on the back of the lead machine. This would be followed by all of the ski instructors performing a synchronised torch lit descent and then finally the fireworks. Their seats meant that they had the perfect vantage point to see the crowds beginning to assemble. People streamed past the window. Families with children were gambolling over to the centrally cited pergola which was the base for a DJ and huge sound system which blasted out familiar pop and Christmas hits. Amongst the crowds, Michael glimpsed a face that he thought he recognised and seemed, briefly, to be staring at them. He looked again but the figure had melted into the crowd. He tried to place the face and his brow furrowed with thought, but the cocktail of warm red wine, brandy orange juice and a beautiful woman had fogged his mind. He was not able to dwell long on the man in the crowd because Francesca was soon urging him to get up as it was time to go outside and join the excited throng.

"This is very kind of you Francesca," Michael said as they left the bar and walked over the crisp evening snow, their breath forming nubilous tendrils in the crackling cold night air.

"No, it is important for us to welcome people to Pra Loup properly. I cannot have you being lonely at Christmas. What will you do tomorrow? Would you like to ski in the morning? I am free if you would like to."

Michael hesitated, momentarily dumbstruck by the offer to spend even more time with this lovely woman. Francesca appeared to think the hesitation hinted at a lack of willingness on Michael's part to spend time with her and she looked rather crest fallen as she hurriedly continued,

"Of course if you are busy or want to be alone that is fine, no problem, I just thought…."

Michael interrupted her, feeling foolish at his unintended slight.

"No, no, I can't think of anything I would rather do. It is just that I'm not sure I can keep up with an international skier. You'll have to be very patient, but if you don't mind skiing like a snail I would love to," Michael replied. Francesca laughed and smiled.

"We French love snails so shall we say ten o'clock at the Clappe lift?"

Francesca manoeuvred them towards the front of the crowd as the piste bashers began their descent.

The crowd cheered as Père Noël came into view waving vigorously from the back of the leading piste basher. He had a large bulging hessian sack by his feet hinting at gifts to come. Incongruously, for a French resort, Michael Bubble's *Santa Claus is Coming to Town* was piping out over the slopes. Moments later the ski instructors appeared at the top of the pistes, flaming torches in their hands, and they seemed to float down the mountain in huge, interlinked arcs. They finally stopped in a line in front of the cordon that restrained the crowd. They were met by rapturous applause which they stood and enjoyed for some moments before skating to the left in front of Francesca and Michael and through a gap in the cordon back to the ski schools' bases.

At the top of the slope five more figures appeared. They were bedecked with bright blue L.E.D lighting that ran in continuous strands from the end of one ski pole, up the arm, down one leg, up the other leg and across to the other arm ending at the tip of the other pole. The lights were so bright that their bodies became invisible. They dived down towards the crowd below like great prehistoric skeletal birds; quite mesmerising as they criss-crossed each other's paths. Finally, they landed in front of the cordon, their bodies revealed and their faces full of smiles and laughter.

Francesca called across to one,

"Jean Paul. Jean Paul."

A face, clearly older than the other instructors, turned towards them, the deep weather-beaten creases around the eyes and across the forehead still visible even against the ultramarine blue light that bathed them. Francesca introduced Jean Paul to Michael.

"Jean Paul is the best ski instructor on the mountain. He was my coach when I was in the team for the region. There is nothing he doesn't know about skiing... or génépi. If you want a lesson it must be with Jean Paul... and his English is perfect."

Jean Paul turned to Michael with a smile.

"She is, as always, too kind. It is nice to meet you Michael. Ah I must go. Bientôt Michael. I will see you on the mountain perhaps?."

He turned to follow the rest of the instructors through the

72

gap in the cordon. Michael watched him go. When he reached the back of the crowds, turning off the light strands as he skied, Jean Paul scooted past the figure that Michael had noticed earlier outside Le Loup Blanc.

This time there was no doubt that he was staring at them, his jaw was jutting towards them and his fists were clenched by his sides. He did not avert his gaze as his eyes met Michael's. It was Michael who looked away first as the flash of the fireworks exploded overhead. The slopes were momentarily bathed in an iridescent purple. When he looked behind him again, the man was gone. The next explosion was not that of a firework but one of realisation in Michael's brain as he remembered where he had seen the man before. He was the man who had been with Francesca in Le Tandem bar back in October.

The fireworks were spectacular, and incredibly loud, the sound of the detonations resounded around the mountains. Michael was taken by how long the display lasted. Soon enough though the DJ was thanking everyone for coming and wishing them "Joyeux Noël". Michael and Francesca walked companionably back towards the resort surrounded by a joyous laughing bevy of folk, all of whom seemed to have smiling faces. Michael toyed with mentioning the man from Le Tandem but was unsure how to start such a conversation and so left the questions he would like to ask about the man's aggressively morose staring unspoken. As they reached the road, Francesca turned to him and explained that she had to go and see her parents now. With three quick pecks on his cheek and a scintillating smile she was gone. Michael returned to his apartment, popped a pizza in the oven and opened a bottle of red wine. He sat tranquilly on the large sofa, its cushions nuzzling him into their grasp, feeling an inner calmness as he listened to his Christmas favourites playing through his Bluetooth speaker from his Spotify account on his phone. He ate the pizza and supped his wine, ensconced in a comfortable exhaustion from his day of hard physical activity. He decided to shower before going to bed and he wandered over to his picture window to draw the curtains. Above Pra Loup the stars piercing the firmament were brighter and more numerous than Michael had ever seen. The velvety night sky was pin pricked by thousands of shimmering points of light. It was a display far more awe-inspiring than the fireworks. Perhaps Georgie's spirit was out there an eternal light shining down on him. Christmas Eve was always such a special time for them. They weren't really religious but always went to midnight mass at their local church and enjoyed being at the heart of their community and belting out the carols with friends and neighbours. Then they would head home and open just one present from under the tree - it was always Christmas Pyjamas. They would wear the pyjamas that night and in the morning they opened presents, drank Bucks Fizz and ate warmed croissants smeared with deep yellow Devon churned butter. He sighed as Bing Crosby and David Bowie sang out in their mellifluous tones over the speaker and with The Little Drummer Boy in his ears and Georgie in his thoughts Michael headed to the bedroom and his shower.

Chapter Twelve

The next morning Michael drank a small cafétière of strong coffee, enjoying the caffeine buzz that coursed through his veins, and ate a croissant he had heated from frozen whilst sending and reading seasonal messages on his phone. Looking out onto the snow on Christmas morning was certainly a rather special experience and he gleefully WhatsApped images of the view to James and Tim. He also sent a message to Miriam, with a photo attached. He wrote it in French and composed it on a piece of paper, *Joyeux Noël, merci pour toute vôtre aide, c'est ce que vous m'avez aidé à acheter.* Being well aware of his own linguistic shortcomings he then checked it on the google translator and was rather pleased to see that it agreed with his own translation of *Happy Christmas, thank you for all your help, this is what you helped me to buy.* He dressed quickly as he didn't want to be late for his ten o'clock rendezvous with Francesca - although the thought of skiing with a French international skier was more than a little intimidating.

He arrived at the Clappe ski lift five minutes early but did not have to wait long as Francesca soon appeared, effortlessly elegant she slid to a halt beside him. She was not wearing a helmet but a red, white and blue headband with the French cockerel emblem resting in the centre of her forehead. Vuarnet wraparound sunglasses adorned her face and tight fitting white salopettes and jacket completed her ensemble. She took his breath away. The moment she arrived the lift operators began calling salutations and wishing her a '*Joyeuse Noël.*' Michael felt he was out skiing with a celebrity, but then he realised that of course he was. Skiing for France is like playing football for England in terms of fame and this was Francesca's home village too. They skied forward onto the carpet and mounted the lift. A couple of other skiers joined them on the lift and it immediately became apparent that they were locals as they struck up an animated conversation with Francesca. The speed at which they spoke left Michael only able to grasp the occasional word.

The effervescent torrent of words continued until they reached the top of the mountain and disembarked from the lift. Francesca's friends peeled off to the left with a cheery "A bientôt." And then they were gone. Francesca turned to Michael,

"So, shall I lead?"

"I think you'd better," he replied, "But don't lose me, I don't know the mountains as well as you."

Francesca pushed off down the Honore Bonnet piste and accelerated down the gentle incline to the Pegueiou Restaurant where she paused and waited for Michael before turning right down the steep pitch of the red Bretelle piste. Michael had never seen skiing of such pace and dynamism other than on Ski Sunday and the television struggled to accurately convey the steepness of the slopes or the awesome pace of the skiers. Francesca's body rose and fell in the long carving turns; with the edges of her skis cutting sharply into the snow. He followed as fast as he could but realised that, even though he was travelling faster than he had ever done on skis before, she was rapidly disappearing into the distance. He was fighting to stay on his skis. He was petrified of falling at this pace but equally scared of appearing to Francesca like an ancient slug meandering down the mountain. His thighs screamed for him to stop or slow down, but he dug deep and gritted his teeth and kept going. Just ahead, he could see the white figure waiting at the edge of the piste. As he approached, he skidded to a halt in a huge flurry of snow. He was aiming to look suave but realised that he was in danger of knocking her over he was so out of control. Francesca smiled at him as he attempted to gather himself.

"Ahh, not bad for an old man, but perhaps I must slow down a little."

"Thank you, that would be greatly appreciated before my thighs burst and my lungs explode!" He gasped.

They swept down the slopes and up the lifts until one o'clock when Francesca said she had to return to Barcelonnette to spend time with her family. Michael skied back to the bottom of the resort with her and thanked her for her company. She unclipped her skis and bundled them under her arm. She removed her sunglasses and her eyes and lips lit up with a smile. She stepped towards Michael, her head slightly inclined, and kissed him lightly on the lips. It was the gossamer touch of an angel.

"A bientôt, happy Christmas Michael. Next time perhaps we ski off-piste?"

Then she turned, giggling as she walked back to the car park. Michael stood gazing after her, not sure, if he was breathless from the exertions of skiing with Francesca or the butterfly kiss on the lips. After a few seconds, he sighed and skated off towards the La Clappe lift to return to the slopes.

He stopped briefly for some lunch at *Le Petit Chaperon Rouge*, the translation was Little Red Riding Hood, and it was quite apt as it was situated in amongst the trees. Lunch consisted of a wonderful salad and a beer which he ate looking across to the peak of Le Pain de Sucre angling up into the clear blue sky. Michael's legs and thighs were beginning to recover from the morning's exertions, he had never skied so hard and so fast in his life. If he were to ski with Francesca again, he would need to be a lot fitter and to markedly improve his technique. In addition, he was very much out of his comfort zone skiing off-piste, maybe he should invest in Jean Paul's teaching sooner rather than later.

He spent the rest of the afternoon gently cruising the red and blue runs above Pra Loup before ending the day skiing to the *Le Loup* Blanc bar at the front of the slopes. Here he practised his language skills on the owner, who spoke fluent English but was willing to indulge Michael's dislocated French as he sat at the bar and purchased three malt whiskies in quick succession. The owner's mother was English, but he had been brought up and was educated in France. He was younger than Michael, in his mid-thirties but had adopted the huge bushy beard that had become fashionable. He regularly stroked his hand down through the dark mass of hair, seemingly trying to mould the beard into a point, which it steadfastly refused to do, as he talked – this gave him an air of great wisdom which Michael felt was fitting for anybody who had chosen to live and work in such a wonderful part of the world. The bar gradually filled and a good-natured hubbub pervaded the room. By the time Michael stirred himself to walk the short distance back to his apartment it was dark. He didn't really want to leave the carnival atmosphere of *Le Loup Blanc* but he had brought a Christmas pudding and some brandy butter with him from England and it seemed a shame not to eat them on Christmas day. It would not be the most balanced meal, but it was his favourite dessert and he had been looking forward to microwaving it and indulging himself by eating the whole pudding in one sitting. With all the exercise of the day, he felt that he deserved this treat.

Chapter Thirteen

Michael's Christmas pudding reveries were brought to a sudden end as he emerged from the doorway of the bar into the frosty night air. Standing twenty yards away under the light illuminating the path, with his arms folded and his legs astride, was the man from Le Tandem. He was staring unwaveringly at Michael. His broad shoulders and glowering visage bristling with antipathy. Michael hesitated, he was unsure whether to return to the bar and wait for the stranger to go or to calmly walk on. What could this man want with him? He didn't know him, and apart from a brief brushing of the lips, which was more than likely just friendship, nothing had happened between Michael and Francesca. However, she was the only link he could make between himself and the stranger. As if frozen by the winter's grasp, they both stood motionless for what seemed like an age but was probably only a couple of seconds. Then a cacophony of noise burst out of the bar as a group of six revellers erupted laughing into the still evening air and weaved their way past Michael and down the path. Michael tacked himself onto the group which moved like a rolling maul and swept past the stranger in a haze of energy, good humour and alcohol. It only took a few moments for him to get clear of the man and then Michael dodged behind his apartment block and in through his front door, which he closed firmly behind him.

This was not just his imagination; this guy clearly had a problem with him. He felt uneasy about addressing the subject with Francesca as he was not totally sure about where he stood with her, but he determined that the next time he saw the stranger, in daylight and somewhere populated, he would speak to him. Now he wanted nothing more than to complete his excellent day with the long-awaited Christmas pudding, followed by a quiet hour flicking through the photos of Christmas's past on his phone and enjoying the memories of happy times spent with his beautiful wife.

During the lull between Christmas and New Year Michael took a trip to the offices of the Ecole de Ski Internationale and booked two two-hour sessions with Jean Paul which were to focus on both on-piste and off-piste techniques. The lessons would span a whole day with only an hour off for lunch. It would not be a cheap day at two hundred euros, but Michael concluded that it was a necessary expense.

On New Year's Eve, Michael got up early to ensure that he was on the piste to meet Jean Paul by the tree near the Costebelle bubble lift at nine a.m. He had spent some hours the preceding evening scrolling his iPad for articles on ski technique to attempt to ensure that his style was not too awful. He had soon come to the conclusion that it was a complete waste of time. So many of the online gurus seemed to disagree with each other and talked about sensations while on skis so alien to Michael that he ended up being more confused than when he had started. Reading the articles had been a complete waste of time for him.

Jean Paul arrived at the tree on the stroke of nine greeting Michael in his loquacious Gaelic drawl. "Bonjour Michael, 'ello. 'ow are you today, you are ready, the mountain is ready, the snow is ready, and I am ready?"

He ushered Michael into the Costebelle bubble lift station where they clambered into an empty cabin and proceeded up the mountain. Jean Paul gently quizzed Michael about his skiing and what he wanted from the day's lesson. He listened to the replies and then laid out his proposed format for the day.

"This morning we will ski on the piste and understand your level. We will do some things you may find interesting and then we will break. You will have your food and I will teach another lesson and then we will join again to enjoy skiing off the track. Is it okay?"

It seemed a good plan to Michael. The morning was spent with Jean Paul encouraging Michael to ski with his legs and feet further apart and to be more 'dynamic' in his turns. Michael had always thought that he bent his knees when he turned but he now realised that he really needed to accentuate the movement. Then Jean Paul moved on to focus upon getting him to push both skis further onto their edges to accentuate the carve they made into the crisp cold snow, whilst still keeping his third eye, 'his tummy button', facing down the slope. The lesson was useful and thought provoking, Jean Paul imparted more than technical knowledge, he talked about an approach to skiing that smacked more of a philosophy for life than just how to execute a good turn.

"Michael don't be like the other skiers, they go up, they come down. Up on the lift and down as fast as they can, that is all they do -up and down- you should do more. Every run we should try to be our best self, to ski our very best and on every run we try to learn something…to try something different and perhaps something good happens and wow, we have a 'bon moment', and we remember and we improve. Not just up and down Michael, if we are just going up and down we are not living. We must be the pilot of our skis, we must be in charge, we must strive to be better, to have a good experience." The sincerity of the man when he shared these words was clear, "Michael you must read the book 'The Centered Skier', it is old but it is a very important book, read it and you will understand much more than skiing Michael."

Jean Paul had looked intensely and deeply into Michael's eyes as he had spoken and Michael felt he had shared with him a heartfelt belief. Michael found the conversations on the lift equally fascinating. Jean Paul truly was a man of the mountains, deeply concerned about the impact of global warming on his beloved Haute Provence, he spoke passionately about the changes he had seen in his lifetime and the portents of what was to come. He spoke with similar feeling, and a great deal of enthusiasm, about his hobby of making génépi liquor. Michael often enjoyed a glass of génépi after a meal in the mountains but clearly this wasn't an occasional tipple for Jean Paul; more a staple of his diet and the making of it a fixture of his summers in the mountains. Harvesting the génépi plant from some of the highest slopes in the area around Le Chapeau du Gendarme sounded fairly risky. The plant grew amongst rocky outcrops that Jean Paul would have to seek; places where, putting a foot wrong could mean a dreadful, even fatal, accident. If the terrain was not challenging enough Jean Paul explained that the mountains were policed to limit the amount of génépi any individual could collect. With a wry smile, he described how he dodged the 'gendarme' to bring his crop back to his home each year.

The ingredients were simple: génépi plants, sugar and alcohol – forty grammes of génépi and forty grammes of sugar to forty centilitres of alcohol. The sugar would be dissolved in the alcohol, the plants added and then the bottled product stored in a cool place for six weeks. The taste and colour very much depended upon the variety of the plant and how it had grown that year.

"Michael, you must come and try my génépi one evening. You say you have tasted it in the restaurants but now you must taste the best!"

Jean Paul clearly enjoyed having someone who listened so attentively to his tales and they laughed companionably together.

As Michael ate his lunch at the Costebelle restaurant during the break, the realisation began to dawn that having lessons all day was, perhaps, not the best idea as he was already feeling very tired. The thought of laying back in one of the deck chairs on the restaurants sunny veranda for the afternoon was very beguiling. However, he had paid for Jean Paul's time and he would not let him down. There had been a heavy snowfall the previous evening and looking across the resort there were hosts of tracks cut in virgin snow away from the pistes. Part of Michael wished they had gone off-piste in the morning and taken full advantage of the fresh, fluffy white eiderdown of untouched snow. He paid for his lunch and walked over to the racks to retrieve his skis. As he clipped them on, he saw Jean Paul emerging from the top of the bubble lift.

"Ah, Michael. Did you have a good lunch? We go to the button lift and over towards Foux where I shall show you fresh powder. But first we must take the Bergerie chair."

Jean Paul skied off down the steep red slope next to the lift and Michael followed. The two sat on the six-man chair and the off-piste lesson began.

"Michael," began Jean Paul seriously, "The most important thing about skiing off the piste is to know when it is secure, when it is safe. Even the best skier in the world cannot outpace an avalanche. An avalanche can travel at well over one hundred and fifty kilometres an hour and over eighty-five percent of them are triggered by people. There are one hundred and fifty deaths a year in European ski resorts from avalanches. It is important we ski on safe slopes, so it is best not to ski off-piste for twenty-four hours after a storm to give the snow layers time to stick together. We say *'frittage'*, I think you say sintering. Weak links between different layers of snow are dangerous and the cause of most avalanches. Sintering is weak when the snow is very cold and like sugar or if it is very wet. North facing slopes are most dangerous in the winter but south facing are more dangerous in the Spring when the snow is melting and wet or it rains. Slopes that are steeper than thirty degrees are dangerous and slopes that are like an upturned bowl are more stressed and ready to avalanche. You see Michael the mountains are like me – a grumpy old man – they do not like change; too hot, too cold, too windy and they are dangerous. Last night there was heavy snow but not too much wind and it was not too cold so we can ski safely off-piste this afternoon."

Michael listened intently to all the information being imparted and then, once off the lift, followed Jean Paul down Le Grand Rouge Piste to the Lac button lift. From here Jean Paul led him over towards the linked resort of Foux D'Allos but high and to the right of the piste under the lea of the Seolan peak. A few people had already skied this path and Jean Paul skied short distances ahead, stopping regularly to explain to Michael how to manage the powder, demonstrating what he meant, then watching Michael ski and feeding back to him. Jean Paul seemed to float through the gossamer snow, downy plumes puffing upward in his wake. Michael felt less balletic as he tried to action the advice he had been given, a repeating soundtrack playing in his head *don't lean back, equal pressure on both skis, sit in the middle, bounce, steer with feet and legs, keep the upper body for balance...* He realised his upper body was letting him down somewhat as he plunged yet again headlong into the powder. He emerged laughing and looked towards Jean Paul who was also laughing.

"Michael, the most important thing is to know when it is safe to ski," he said through his laughter.

"The second most important thing is not to give up – keep trying my friend, you are getting better."

Eventually the two emerged at the bottom of the 'Quartier' lift which would take them back over to Pra Loup. The lift was old and slow but a critical link between the two ski areas of Espace Lumière. The piste towards the Foux D'Allos ran past the lift and as they came to a halt by the lift a figure skied past shouting a greeting to Jean Paul, which Jean Paul returned. Michael glanced over to see the profile of the man from Le Tandem accelerating down the piste. He had not been seen, which was a relief, but clearly Jean Paul knew who he was. Michael waited until they were perched on the old slotted-seat and the bar was securely down before he broached the subject.

"That man you spoke to at the bottom of the lift, Jean Paul, who is he?" asked Michael.

The instructor looked at him quizzically,

"That is Marc, he lives in the village. Why do you ask?"

"Ah, well," Michael hesitated, not sure quite how to proceed. "I have seen him several times in the resort, a couple of times when I was with Francesca, and he always looks, shall we say, 'unhappy' with me."

"Mmmm," It was Jean Paul's turn to hesitate, he was obviously wrestling with exactly what to tell his student and his furrowed brow betrayed his concerns. Finally, he seemed to come to a conclusion and turned to look Michael fully in the face. "He has been with Francesca since they were at school in Barcelonnette, it is a, how do you say, love and hate relationship? Parfois, sometimes, they are together and sometimes not. She does not play by the rules, sometimes she may find someone new and exciting, but she has Marc on a string and she always has him back. At the moment they are apart and the break seems more serious than usual. Marc has learnt that if you go near the bright blue flame sometimes you melt and… sometimes you get burnt." He shrugged, then turned towards his student. "Michael, stay away from him. Where Francesca is concerned, he can be a difficult man. He is, how do you say *charpentier*, working with wood."

"Carpenter," interjected Michael.

"Yes! So, don't hire him to work in your apartment, eh!" Jean Paul smiled.

"That's easy enough but avoiding him in the street will be more difficult!" replied Michael.

Jean Paul laughed. "Stay in the light Michael, stay in the light."

As they rode the lift to the top of Le Lac, the conversation returned to matters skiing as Jean Paul pointed out the cracks in the snow below the chair and the baseball sized snowballs that had rolled down the slope.

"Not a good place to ski, the cracks could turn into an avalanche if you ski over them, and snowballs on a sunny slope can show the surface is getting warm so there could be a wet snow slide."

Chapter Fourteen

Michael had learnt a good deal from his lessons, all of it interesting and much of it could really help him to keep safe both on and off the slopes! As he returned to his apartment, he mused that he really did need to plan for the first of his guests who would be arriving the following week. Breakfasts and lunches were easy enough to provide as fresh croissants were on tap only one hundred and fifty metres from his front door and there were a variety of restaurants and snack bars spread across the slopes of Pra Loup and Foux D'Allos. The evening meals would provide more of a challenge as he felt he could not really avoid cooking the odd meal for his guests. This would need some serious thought as, whilst he had always been able to follow a recipe, he needed to be sure he wouldn't be caught out by a lack of basic ingredients. He sat in his armchair facing the window which looked onto the slopes, poured himself a large glass of white wine (a rather fine Pouilly Fuissé) and started to work out a programme for the coming days. He began by sending a text to Charlotte and Harry, his first guests, to check if there was anything, they didn't eat and what time their flight landed in Marseille. He felt he could get away with catering in the apartment for the first three nights, and one of those could be a takeaway pizza, so he needed to organise two meals. He decided on spaghetti bolognaise and cheese fondue, both of which should be fairly straight forward, more so once he had purchased a fondue set and gel burners. He searched the internet on his phone for recipes and made a list.

Charlotte had been at university with Georgie and Michael but after a failed marriage, she had recently begun a new relationship with Harry, who was an accountant and apparently a very competent skier. Charlotte and Georgie had been close at university and had remained so ever since. Charlotte was a pretty girl, long legged and athletic and seemed to have boundless energy. When most people might fancy a quiet sit down, she was always up for a long walk, she crackled with her enthusiasm for life. Charlotte's first husband, Rupert, her sweetheart at school, had been a county level squash playing banker but even he had struggled with her perpetual motion. In-fact he had struggled with many things; morality, sensitivity and modesty featuring fairly highly. That he had managed to win Charlotte's heart in the first place had always amazed Georgie, but she always reflected that 'love is incomprehensible'. Michael wondered how Harry coped and would cope in the future with such an apparently inexhaustible woman. He had clearly been something of a sportsman in his day, but his girth indicated that those days were some time-ago.

Charlotte had gone into education but had worked her entire career in private schools and Michael felt her experiences had been very different to those of himself and Georgie. Teaching on a Saturday morning was certainly a negative but the fact that Charlotte was not back at school until the 12th of January was an illustration of a major positive –longer holidays. This one was enabling her to ski for a week when the resort would be very quiet. Charlotte was a patient individual and generous of spirit. Michael was happy to try out his catering on her and also the general shape of the week. If it was successful, he could then repeat the pattern with other friends later in the season. He was looking forward to having company and to showing off Pra Loup which he felt, now more than ever, was a very special place. He also had to admit to himself to wanting to show off his apartment too with its stunning mountain views.

He picked up his shopping list and walked across to the gallery of shops. There were apartments above the shops but the gallery itself was undercover and had a wooden boardwalk running along its length. The gallery was bustling with people. They seemed to fall into two general categories; those who were not dressed in ski gear and were shopping at the Spar mini-market, or the bakers and the butchers, and those who were still dressed in ski gear entering bars, leaving bars, or moving between bars. Whilst the atmosphere was bubbly and good natured one had to be wary of the second category as they were often carrying their skis on their shoulders and the more that they imbibed the less aware they seemed to become of the havoc they were causing as they turned to their right or left to look into shop windows or to talk to friends. Michael's first port of call was a shop that was a cross between souvenirs and homeware. Shelves stacked with Pra Loup wolves, novelty toys, heart shaped decorations, key fobs, postcards and a selection of kitchenware stretched back down the narrow store. He espied a limited range of fondue sets alongside a stock of the gel alcohol burners. Michael chose quickly, picking out a cast iron set that appeared to be styled on Georgie's favourite 'Le Creuset' cookware. It wasn't the cheapest, but the deep red of the pot would fit with his décor. Next, he entered the Spar which, whilst small, carried all of what he considered to be the essentials. It was more expensive than the supermarkets in the valley, but he didn't feel the savings on such a few items would warrant the drive down the mountain and back. He popped the herbs, mince, ice cream and tinned tomatoes into his basket and proceeded to the checkout.

As Michael emerged from the mini market, now carrying bags in each hand, he waited a moment so as not to disrupt the flow of shoppers and après-skiers along the boardwalk. When a suitable break came in the flow of people, he stepped out and walked back towards the road encircling the centre of Pra Loup and the shopping gallery. Progress along the busy walkway was not smooth as he tried to navigate a path which avoided swiping anyone with his purchases or being swiped by some skis. He slowly became aware of someone walking close to his left shoulder. To his right he had the shop fronts and he felt slightly boxed in as a large grey-haired woman wrapped in a voluminous fur coat with a deep collar that entirely ensconced her neck headed directly towards him. She seemed totally unaware of his proximity as she gazed fixedly into the shop window. A hand closed gently but firmly around his biceps and steered him to his left around the greying puffball in front of him. He turned to look at his saviour and found himself gazing into a familiar pair of deep blue eyes and a mouth with a bewitching smile.

"Francesca, salut," he gasped.

"Salut Michael. How are you?" She returned with a smile.

"Good. I am good. I have had a wonderful day with Jean Paul. You are right he is a great teacher."

"Ah, excellent Michael. I would like to hear all about it. You can buy me a drink?"

The question was formed by the rising intonation of her sentence.

"I would like to, but I have ice cream I need to take home first. I do have a bottle of prosecco in the fridge back at the apartment if that would do?"

"Prosecco sounds lovely but I will have to leave to have dinner with my family in Barcelonnette so I cannot be long."

Chapter Fifteen

They walked out onto the road and out of the crowds in the gallery. Francesca reached out and grasped the handles of the carrier bag in Michael's right hand.

"Let me help you with your bags."

As she pulled the bag from him, their hands touched and he felt a tingle of excitement surge through his body. She put the bag in her left hand and without any hesitation reached back to hold his now free hand with hers. In that movement, the world stood still. His whole body seemed electrified and he squeezed her hand not quite sure what message he was trying to communicate.

"It has been a long time since I have held the hand of a beautiful woman, and I have to say it is rather nice," Michael intoned quietly, worrying he was sounding rather obsequious.

"Well, I have never held an Englishman's hand before," Francesca replied, "and I too think it is rather nice, particularly when the Englishman is quite so handsome."

Michael summoned all of his courage and ventured,

"I have certainly never cuddled a French woman and I wonder if it would be nice too?"

Francesca smiled and pushed his hand backwards to turn him towards her and moved her lips to his. He felt like a drowning man, unable to breathe. He pulled her to him and kissed her again, the bags of shopping bumping against her legs. Eventually she pulled away from him smiling wryly and whispered,

"So, Michael was it nice, and do you think we might try that prosecco now?"

"It was wonderful actually, and yes the prosecco awaits us!"

They turned and walked the few yards to his front door, every step he had to fight the urge to pull her to him again and kiss her just to make sure this was really happening. Pra Loup was shrouded by the night sky uninterrupted by clouds and a lustrous moon hung over the mountains. A bone chilling cold had enveloped the town, but Michael knew that the goosebumps that covered his skin were not caused by the freezing air. He pushed open his door and almost floated into the apartment, struggling to force himself to release Francesca's hand as he did so.

They moved into the apartment and Michael took the shopping bags and breathlessly put the ice cream in the freezer and took the prosecco out of the fridge. His heart was racing, neither of them spoke. Francesca just stood and watched him put away the shopping and pop the cork on the prosecco. He poured two champagne flutes of the sparkling wine and handed one to Francesca, the bubbles tripping up through the citrus liquid. She paused and did not put the glass to her lips. The atmosphere in the room was charged. Michael was in turmoil, not knowing how pecks on the cheek had so quickly accelerated to this, but Francesca seemed serene and relaxed.

"Come on," she said holding out a hand towards him, "we will drink this when we have something to celebrate."

And with that she guided him gently towards the bedroom. He realised that he was not in control of what was happening, but it didn't feel as if that mattered as the Cranberry's song flitted through his mind *'electric blue eyes, I need you...'*.

Michael was propped upon one elbow sipping his prosecco and allowing his eyes to play over the beautiful woman who lay beside him. What had just happened? How had it happened?

Francesca turned towards him and grinned.

"Not bad for an old man."

"Thank you," he replied, "you are so kind."

He leant forward and kissed her. Her scent was intoxicating and her skin smooth and warm.

"Michael I must shower now; I need to leave to go to my parents for dinner."

"Of course, if you must. I'll get you a clean towel."

Francesca stood up from the bed, her lithe body sliding almost cat like across the room. Michael brought the towel and as she showered, he watched the hot water cascading over her toned figure.

He handed her the towel as she emerged from the steamy water and she quickly rubbed herself dry, reaching down her long legs to mop up the splashes of water. The next moment she was back in the bedroom pulling on her black lacy underwear. She stood for a moment wearing just her bra and knickers and appeared to become aware of him watching her for the first time. She seemed to enjoy the mesmeric affect her body had on him. She finished dressing, took a swig of her prosecco, and kissed him on the lips.

"Sorry Michael, I really do have to go but I will see you next year," she giggled as she walked to the door and left.

Once she had gone Michael sat on the sofa, his emotions in complete confusion. What had just happened? It was so unlike him. He had so many conflicting feelings the overriding one of the moment, was that of guilt. He presumed he felt like any married man who had committed adultery; the thrill of the moment subsumed by the all-devouring feeling of betrayal. In all the time he had been married to Georgie he had never cheated, and he knew that she would not want him to lead a monk like existence after her death. Indeed, it had been the topic of one of those conversations she had insisted on having in her last few days, one of the conversations he had really shied away from. She had been emphatic that he should live his life and she knew that would not mean that she had been forgotten or replaced, their love had been too deep and too strong for that. He sat grasping a photo of her and as the New Year arrived, he tried to make peace with his grief for the death of his wife, his contrition for the ecstasy being with Francesca had brought him and the need to move forward.

He woke during the night and lay awake revisiting his moments with Francesca. The aroma of her perfume still lingered on the bedding, stirring his memories of the evening. It was a strange thing to make love with somebody new. Her body was different to Georgie's. He and Georgie knew each other so well, knew each other's bodies so well. Sleeping with her was always joyful, he was never on trial, never had anything to prove; it had been comfortable, reassuring and yet still exhilarating. He wondered whether Francesca would want to repeat the experience. Was 'not bad' good enough? Time would tell. Perhaps he might have some sort of future with her. He was older than her, significantly so, but then his father was older than his mother and their relationship had always appeared utopian.

Not much time elapsed before Michael received confirmation that 'not bad' was indeed okay as Francesca phoned on New Year's Day morning and told him that she was free that afternoon if he wanted to see her. He tried not to sound too desperate but was exultant when they spent the afternoon together in the apartment and the early evening drinking cocktails in Grey's bar before Francesca returned home to Barcelonnette. Suddenly Michael found that he was not so keen to be hosting guests for a lot of the winter as he had found someone else with whom to spend his time, someone who seemed rather special, someone he was sure he didn't deserve to be with, but then again it would have to be somebody very special to follow Georgie.

Chapter Sixteen

James also phoned on New Year's Day. He didn't ring until late morning as he had seen the New Year in with Tim in a rather intoxicated state. That 'state' had now converted to a rather fragile one. He wished Michael a Happy New Year and the two friends chatted amicably for over an hour. Michael updated James on almost everything that had been happening in Pra Loup; from his interior design to his lesson with Jean Paul, but he kept his friendship with Francesca to himself for now. James was full of the end of term news but also confided that he might have to permanently exclude the youngest Vine boy. There was an investigation still ongoing, but it appeared that he had brought drugs into school on the last day before the school broke up for the Christmas holidays and sold them to a variety of students. James, like Michael, did not really believe in permanent exclusion but the governors were very clear that they had zero tolerance for drug pushers and would not allow any student who sold drugs to remain in the school. Ultimately, James was bound by the governors' policy.

"I can't think of a way round it Michael. I know if I permanently exclude him for selling drugs no other school locally will take him, he will end up in a behaviour unit. Although his father has said, apparently, that he won't let him attend a unit and he will be educated at home. What chance will he have then?"

"It's a tough one," Michael had replied, "But I am not sure you have any choice."

The issue had clearly weighed on James' mind all over Christmas, which was a measure of the man Michael mused. They said their farewells without Michael having even hinted about the events of the previous evening.

On Saturday morning, he rose early and drove to Marseille airport, stopping briefly at the beautiful town of Tallard to buy a fresh pain au chocolat and coffee for his breakfast. He did not know the town, but an imposing château presided over its narrow streets and squares. The pastry was warm and light, and it flaked as he bit into it. The coffee was strong and black, and he felt it percolating down his throat.

The autoroute was only a few kilometres beyond Tallard. The A51 ended or began here, depending on your point of view. Michael was of the view that it probably ended here as it came face to face with the Alps and he fantasised that the road had given up on further progress seeing the enormity of the obstacles it now faced.

It took under two and a half hours to reach the airport. It was a place Michael was fond of purely because it appeared fleetingly in his favourite film; Love Actually. Whenever he was here, he tried to work out exactly where it was that Jamie emerged from the airport to catch the taxi to find his love Aurelia. As he looked up at the terminal he smiled as his silent game continued.

Charlotte and Harry soon emerged from the arrivals gate, their flight had actually landed ten minutes early, and Michael whisked them away to the car and the journey back to Pra Loup. He chatted about the resort and the area as they drove and waited patiently for the inevitable question that all of his friends (except for James) always asked since the death of Georgie. It was always asked with the same intonations and pauses and had always drawn the same response from him.

97

Charlotte, who sat in the front passenger seat, eventually turned to him. He felt her eyes looking unwaveringly on his face.

"So, Michael... how are you?"

As ever the emphasis was on the how, the pause just before it trying to make it clear that this was a very deep question and required a very honest, thoughtful answer. Michael had mostly answered by saying he was 'Okay... no, really I'm fine.' which was of course a complete lie but seemed to put people at ease and meant they had fulfilled their duty to be sympathetic and caring towards the grieving widower. Today, being asked the same question, he wanted to say, 'I am still devastated by Georgie's death, but I am having great sex with a gorgeous French woman and skiing every day, so actually I am good,' but he hesitated thinking better of it and trotted out his usual line,

'Okay... No, really I'm fine.'

Charlotte patted his arm in some sort of show of solidarity and understanding and then shifted the conversation to ask if there was a good shop for ski hire in the resort and whether they would go and hire their skis straight away on arrival in Pra Loup.

Michael was unsure how he felt about introducing Francesca to such an old friend of Georgie's so early in their relationship, if that was what it was. He was also still feeling pangs of guilt about being with Francesca no matter how hard he tried to intellectualise and rationalise the situation. He would need to ring her when he had a moment alone or pop into the Immobilier and see her.

Francesca had shared Michael's unease at meeting his friends when he got the chance to ring her.

"I want to see you, but we need time together Michael before we are with others. I think we will have to be apart until next Saturday after you have taken them back to the airport. It is a long time, but we can do it."

Michael was not sure he wanted to do it, but there appeared to be little choice.

Charlotte and Harry seemed to enjoy their week. Conversations about Georgie were negotiated and they survived Michael's cooking. Michael got the opportunity to get to know Harry rather better than before. Harry could not be accused of being a good-looking man but cuddly certainly. His face had the look of a Chinese shar-pei puppy, the flesh below his eyes hung down in loose pockets forming great pouches that dragged towards the voluminous folds of his cheeks. These, in turn, slouched, towed down by gravity, to numerous chins that sat in layers upon the collar of his shirt like the folded edges of a pile of freshly pressed towels. Michael suspected similar rolls covered his trunk which, whilst it was not vast and certainly didn't hamper his skiing, gave him the look of a well-loved and worn teddy bear. Harry was everything his predecessor had not been, softly spoken, kind, sensitive and unbendingly loyal to Charlotte. He did not have the chiselled chin of Rupert but what he lacked in definition he made up for in volume. Michael soon discovered exactly how Harry managed Charlotte's eternal exertions. They had been sitting having lunch at Costebelle on their first day and had just finished eating when Charlotte bounced from her seat ready to return to the slopes. Harry had smiled up at her and gently but definitively stated that he was going to sit quietly, enjoy the sunshine and have one more beer with Michael before skiing again but that she must feel free to carry on and meet them back here when she was done. Charlotte seemed entirely content with this arrangement and having checked her phone was switched on disappeared down the gentle blue slope. Harry had smiled at her receding back and then turned to Michael,

"I am a very lucky man, I lost my first wife like you and I thought I would never love again, but I was wrong. I always believed that everyone had a soulmate and if you were really fortunate you would find them and spend your life with them. It turns out that my presumptions were entire nonsense. I didn't get to spend my life with my soulmate and then discovered in my depths of depression that actually she wasn't my sole-mate. So now, whilst I will never forget Michelle, I am utterly besotted with Charlotte. I just can't really believe that she loves me".

Michael realised he really liked this gentle-man and could certainly relate to his feelings of inadequacy but didn't feel now was the moment to reveal Francesca's existence,

"Of-course she loves you Harry, you are kind, considerate loving and a really good skier. You're the full package, what more could she want? You're just what she needs."

"Ah." Harry smiled "Perhaps a package where the wrapping isn't quite so loose would be preferable?"

Michael loved showing them around his beloved Pra Loup. The skiing was superb, with blue skies and plenty of snow on the well-groomed pistes. Harry particularly enjoyed the two outstanding mountain restaurants, Costebelle and Le Petit Chaperon Rouge, both of which provided wonderful food at very competitive prices and where the staff were incredibly attentive and welcoming. They were interested in his explanations of the local geography and were suitably wowed by his favourite view from the top of Le Lac looking towards Les Agneliers and beyond to the Mercantour National Park. The park, one of the largest in France, covered six hundred and eighty-five square kilometres and stretched for ninety kilometres down the Italian border from Barcelonnette to the Cote d'Azure. From Le Lac the edge of the park wrapped its wooded arms around the lower slopes of the mountains. His guests found the views awe inspiring, but Michael was also pleased to discover that Harry shared his interest in history. Whilst he was an accountant by trade Harry had become an avid member of his local history group back in the UK and was particularly fascinated by vernacular architecture. Michael's home in Devon was the focus of a long conversation as was Harry's recent efforts to detail his own family tree. It was very enjoyable for Michael to have a guest where there was never a shortage of topics for interesting and engaging conversations.

An absolute highlight of the week had been dinner at Jean Paul's 'table d'hôte' which he ran in the evenings with his wife Dominique. The term translating as 'the host's table' and it felt to Michael like an authentic French mountain experience. There was no choice of menu and the meal was eaten in Jean Paul's farmhouse living room, which was dominated by a roaring fire and huge oak dining table that could easily seat twelve. Their host had been at his best, gently preaching about climate change and even more impassioned about the making of génépi than during Michael's lesson. His avalanche talk was more morbid.

"If you survive the impact of the snow, which you will feel like being hit by surf of concrete, you need to be found in five minutes if you are likely to survive. Ninety percent of people survive if they are found in five minutes, twenty to thirty percent if they are found in the first forty-five minutes… and after two hours your chances are virtually zero."

The evening had concluded with a number of glasses of Jean Paul's génépi which was, as he claimed, far better than in any restaurant. It ran down the throat in smooth molten sips – floral but not too sweet.

Despite the week having been such a success, and Michael enjoying spending time with his good friends, he was impatient to reach Saturday afternoon when he could be with Francesca. His feelings see-sawed from guilt about Georgie to disbelief that Francesca was interested in him. Despite his desire to spend more time with Francesca Michael could not help but to feel a tinge of sadness that he would be waving off a couple with whom his friendship had grown and blossomed during the week and whose company he had really enjoyed. He had also discovered that he and Harry had a shared passion for cricket although they supported different counties. Harry seemed to be as passionate about Kent as Michael was about Somerset. Harry's heroes were different, and he had tried hard, but without success, to convince Michael that Richard Ellison had made Viv Richards look like a mere mortal, at times, with his pacy outswingers. This was a subject that they would always find plenty to disagree upon but as they bade each other farewell at the airport they both committed to meeting up to watch some cricket in the summer and for Harry to come and 'inspect' Michael's ancient Long House in Devon. Having driven Charlotte and Harry to Marseille he had rushed back to Pra Loup, remembering too late the speed cameras on the descent down the mountain before Barcelonnette, but not even the speed camera's flash of light in his wing mirror could dull his anticipation and excitement at seeing Francesca again.

Chapter Seventeen

He had hoped that the afternoon might be spent in bed, but she had other ideas and delivered those dreaded words that caused his heart to sink.

"I want to go shopping. I need a new ski jacket, mine is worn out."

Clothes shopping was one of those activities that Michael saw as an unfortunate necessity and something he only did when he knew exactly what he wanted and it couldn't be avoided. His ideal experience, if he had to shop for clothes, was to walk into the shop pick up the article he wanted in the size that he needed, pay for it and leave. The claustrophobia of walking up and down aisles of clothing, picking out the occasional item, trying it on and then discarding it was an anathema to him. Online shopping may not support local business or the high street, but he could certainly feel its attraction.

He stifled a sigh and walked with her around the shopping gallery and up to the steps towards Godille Sports. She clearly had a particular jacket in mind, which came as a huge relief to Michael who had foreseen the remains of the entire afternoon disappearing in a cloud of Gore Tex and down.

Francesca pulled a beautiful blue Toni Sailer jacket from the rack. Faux fur skirted the hood and despite its thick lining its tailoring ensured that it accentuated her slim waist and muscular shoulders. The label described the jacket as being 'light pacific' in colour, which was helpful for Michael as he now knew how to describe the colour of Francesca's eyes! The assistant came over, she obviously knew Francesca, but she turned and spoke to Michael, the assumption that he would be funding this purchase was communicated very clearly from the look in her eyes and studious focus upon him.

"The Clara Splendid Fur is a beautiful jacket; the wide jet board creates a cool blouson look; Madam looks beautiful in it."

Michael wondered for a moment how she knew he was English but presumed she had heard him talking.

"It is very beautiful, and she looks very beautiful in it," he said turning to gaze at Francesca. Francesca smiled back and plucked at the tag on the sleeve.

"It is lovely Michael but look at the price."

He glanced down to inspect the figures and took a gulp as he read nine hundred and eighty euros.

"It is too much for an estate agent to pay I think."

Francesca looked at Michael as she said this, he sensed the expectation and anticipation in her face. He didn't want to see that look become one of disappointment or contempt, he knew what was expected of him and after all he could afford it. Michael took another gulp and then committed himself.

"You look stunning in it; you must have it. Let it be my treat, a thank you for finding me such a wonderful apartment."

Francesca beamed, immediately his gesture felt worthwhile,

"No Michael, no it is too much, oh but thank you! I want to take a photo of us and this moment, do you have your phone Michael?"

"Yes," Michael replied handing it to her.

"What is your pass number?" she demanded as her fingers hovered over the screen.

"Nineteen sixty-six."

104

"Why 1966 Michael, you were not born then?" she enquired

"No," he replied with a smile, "I am a little older than that! I was a history and geography teacher and I always taught the children the three most important dates in English history, 1066 the Battle of Hastings, which by the way happened at Battle and not Hastings, 1666 the Great Fire of London and the big one, 1966, when England won the world cup!"

"Oh, I see," giggled Francesca happily indulging his quirky sense of humour, "So my pass numbers should be 1998, 2018 and should I add in European Champions as well 1984 and 2000? You could do the same… But your pass number won't change!"

"Oh yes it would, 2022, or doesn't women's sport count? I'm surprised at you Francesca!"

"Ah yes, of course the Lionesses, I forgot them-I am sorry!"

The photo was taken, the jacket quickly bagged and Michael's bank balance severely lightened. He made his way to his apartment with an effervescent Francesca by his side, her whole being seemed to crackle with the intoxication of the purchase. He had never seen her quite so bubbly and excited. He very much liked her like this he thought, clearly presents were a good idea.

The following weeks fell into something of a pattern. When Michael didn't have guests, he skied most days - at least one of those with Francesca - and they would spend three or four evenings a week together either at restaurants or in his apartment. Usually, once a week, she would stay over, and he would also have the joy of waking up next to her and the delight of breakfasting together. When Michael had guests, Francesca acquiesced to eat with them at least once during their stay and to ski with them for a day. Michael was thrilled to show off his girlfriend, as he supposed she now was, and to bask in the reflected glory of her awesome skills on and off the pistes. It was always a joy to watch her cutting down the slopes, or through the powder, with perfectly symmetrical interlinked turns, power and speed blurring into an almost artistic aesthetic.

Michael was becoming besotted with Francesca; the way she moved, the way she smelt, her smile, he was transfixed by her gaze. When her blue eyes looked deep into his he felt intoxicated and powerless, like a fly in a web. He tried to rationalise what he was feeling; it was not the deep unquestioning love that he had felt for Georgie but it was certainly much more than just lust. They were not spending every minute of every day together by any means. In fact, the sporadic nature of when they could see each other meant that, certainly for Michael, with every meeting there was a tinge of excitement and expectation. He was looking forward to James' visit and when he phoned to check everything was okay, he was thrilled to hear that Tim was coming for the first weekend and that the pair would hire a car so that Michael wasn't travelling to and from the airport twice. Michael had told James about Francesca's existence but resisted saying too much. He certainly didn't want to sound like a lovesick teenager, but he did want to see James' reaction when he first saw her ski.

Michael had discovered that La Petite Cave de L'Ubaye, the wine shop in Barcelonnette, sold a variety of very good wines at reasonable prices. He was sure that, with James and Tim's imminent arrival, he should buy in some decent wine in honour of their visit; so, after skiing on the Thursday afternoon he drove down the mountain road to the town. The light was failing by the time he had parked his car in the market square and walked through the narrow streets to the Rue Manuel, the main shopping thoroughfare. The street was bathed in lights from the shop windows. La Petite Cave had a large vat of strong vin chaud sitting outside, the smell from which invaded his nostrils and clawed at the back of his throat with its red wine, orange and cinnamon scent. They seemed to be doing a brisk trade selling their concoction at four euros a beaker. Michael stopped and peered into the vat and inhaled the orangey alcohol laden aroma deeply as he walked into the store. The smell was reminiscent of the bouquet of Christmas. He focussed on the shelves stacked with red wine, which was the preferred tipple of both James and Tim, and after a few minutes perusal he made his choice. He turned to the shop owner a tall brown-haired gentleman who was sitting at the counter gently sipping at a beaker of the vin chaud, obviously quality control was an important part of his job and one he took seriously. Michael didn't want to disturb the man's reverie, but after a slight hesitation, asked for, "Six bouteilles de Châteauneuf-du-Pape deux mille dix huit, s'il vous plaît."

The owner was obviously pleased to be making such a large sale, the six bottles costing two hundred and thirty-four euros. He happily left his vin chaud to retrieve a case of the wine from his storeroom, at the rear of the shop.

Michael mused, "These buggers better be grateful for this, I am spoiling them." He smiled to himself and walked back to his car. The lighting in the car park was rather dim but Michael's Volvo's indicators flashed as he squeezed the central locking button on his fob. He opened the back door and slid the wine onto the back seat. As he stood to close the door, he heard the scrape of a boot on the ground behind him. A strong hand grasped his shoulder and spun him roughly around so that his back was forced up against the car and he was looking into three faces full of enmity.

The shock quickly flicked to realisation as Michael recognised the tallest of the three men; the one who held his shoulder and now stepped closer thrusting his face within an inch of Michael's. It was Marc, Francesca's ex! His beery breath washed hotly over Michael, who was struggling to break the grip on his shoulder and push away the forearm that was being shoved hard under his chin.

Marc's two wing men stepped in closer so that Michael was completely unable to move. His eyes met the angry stare of his attacker. This was not a common experience for a retired headteacher who was feeling scared, but also deeply indignant. How dare these bastards even touch him? The words he managed to splutter out did not seem to calm the situation, "Fuck off, Marc."

He could see from the look on his assailant's face that he was surprised to have been recognised, but the flicker of hesitation quickly dissipated and was replaced by snarling aggression; his chin jutting towards Michael and a vein in his neck standing out and pulsing.

"English man, you stay away from Francesca, or it will be bad for you," he growled.

It sounded as though Marc had learnt the phrase specially to deliver this threat to Michael. He continued to stare furiously at Michael's face and then suddenly pushed away with his left forearm. Michael was still penned in by the other two men, who he was only really aware of in his peripheral vision, which meant that he had no space to move and no time to react as Marc swung a brutal punch into his stomach. He was unprepared for the punch which crushed the air from his lungs, and as the three men stepped back almost as if choreographed he collapsed onto his knees in the snowy car park retching and gasping. The three men looked at him briefly and he heard Marc say,

"Pathetique." Then they strode off with their barking laughter ringing in Michael's ears.

Michael squatted on all fours trying to breathe, spittle dribbling from his mouth. He gradually became aware that his hands were freezing and his trousers sodden around the knees. He scrambled up using the side of the car, closed the back door and, feeling his way around, he reached for the driver's door. He opened it, clambered in and sat, his head resting on the steering wheel, before retching again.

Jean Paul had been right, he should have stayed in the light, but he hadn't expected such an extreme reaction from Marc. Actually, he had been so swept along by the excitement of being with Francesca that he had not given Marc a second thought; that, he now realised, was an error of judgement. Eventually Michael recovered sufficiently to be able to drive out of Barcelonnette and back up to Pra Loup. The question that played through his thoughts was what he should do about Marc and his thug friends. Following his instructions of keeping away from Francesca was a non-starter and going to the police didn't seem a great option.

It would be his word against theirs and they were three locals and there was absolutely no evidence to support any accusation he made, that didn't seem like a winning hand. So, what alternatives did he have? He felt reticent about raising the matter with Francesca but, he supposed, he probably had little choice. He was due to see her on the following evening, the Friday before James and Tim were expected to arrive at around eight p.m. - if the flight was on time and there were no hiccups with the hired car. He was not looking forward to it, but he knew he needed to discuss it with her then.

He parked outside his flat and carried the box of wine inside, at least they had not damaged it which was a slight silver lining to the evening. Michael found sleep difficult that night. As he tossed and turned images of Marc's puce features growled at him. He got out of bed on one occasion and fetched a glass of water. He sat on the edge of the bed and tried to rationalise his thoughts, which were a tumult of fear and an all-consuming desire to beat the living daylights out of Marc. Eventually, in the early hours, he dozed off until the sounds of the beginning of the ski day filtered into his bedroom and his consciousness. He clambered out of bed and plunged himself into his lava hot shower. As he stood there in the steaming stream of water, he tried to let the tension in his limbs and the tightness in his chest evaporate. He had not experienced this sense of stress and anxiety since he had retired and he felt a deep resentment that this bastard could affect him like this. Michael made a cup of coffee and sat at his dining table looking out onto the slopes, but he felt so shaken by the previous evening's events that he could not stir himself to go out and join the growing throng of skiers peopling the slopes. He sat there with a deep malaise soaking through him and poured another coffee – another couple of hours in bed seemed preferable to leaving the apartment.

Sleep actually came quite easily and Michael did not stir again until late morning. He mooched around the flat doing some cleaning and tidying in preparation for his guests that evening and then sat morosely eating some cheese from the fridge and watching the TV highlights of the night slalom from Schladming, on Eurosport. After his lunch, he continued to wallow in front of the television but flicked to Sky Sport's cricket channel and watched Botham's Ashes. Having spent an hour back in 1981 watching the great man bludgeon the Australians; making the impossible possible and at the same time dragging the whole nation from its knees and giving it hope Michael felt a little uplifted. He wasn't dealing with a terrifying fast bowler like Dennis Lillee, but a jobbing carpenter – Marc. He physically shook himself as he stood up and clicked off the television. He glanced at the clock. Blimey, he was meeting Francesca in an hour and he wasn't even dressed yet!

Chapter Eighteen

Michael was meeting Francesca at Gray's bar for a cocktail at five p.m. He showered, shaved and dressed in record time and then walked around to the Gallery and along to Grey's. Francesca was already there, standing by the bar talking to one of the bartenders.

"Hello Michael, bon soir," she cried.

Michael felt his spirits lift as he returned her greeting. "Salut Francesca," he said as he kissed her gently on the lips.

They ordered their drinks and went to sit at a table by the window with two White Russians in their hands.

"So, Michael, what is wrong? You look sad today," Francesca enquired sympathetically.

Michael had no idea how his face was such an open book to her while he, on the other hand, had no idea what she was thinking. Her blue eyes twinkled and he felt somewhat on the back-foot. He had intended to tell her about Marc but had thought that he would be able to slide it gently into the conversation later on. However, it seemed that now was the moment. He stroked his chin for a moment and then took a deep breath and girded his loins.

"Francesca, I have a problem, or maybe we have a problem. Yesterday your friend Marc and two of his friends ambushed me in Barcelonnette. They punched me and told me in no uncertain terms to stay away from you."

Francesca looked surprised "You didn't go to the Police, did you?" she demanded, rather frostily in Michael's opinion.

"No, I thought it was best to talk to you."

"Good. It is nothing. Michael he is just fooling around with you. I will speak to him," she continued tartly.

"Well it didn't feel like 'fooling around'. It was really nasty," Michael replied, not feeling he was getting the sort of response, or indeed sympathy, he had expected.

"Michael, stop. I have told you I will speak to him. I am sure you are exaggerating."

The pair sat in barren silence, the tender greetings of ten minutes ago having evaporated in the bar's warm fug. After what seemed like an age, Francesca looked up from her drink into Michael's eyes.

"Michael, you need to have confidence, trust in me. Our relationship is young and my friendship with Marc is old, I will speak to him, but trust is very important for us. You are older than me and in Pra Loup I am well known, perhaps even a little famous and popular but I have chosen to be with you because I like you. You are handsome and funny and I trust you, I trust you with other women, I trust that you care about me, and I trust that we have a future together and that beyond that future you will make sure I am well looked after. Do you trust me Michael?"

"Of course, I do, I was just shocked. People just don't behave like that in my world!"

She smiled at him,

"Well Michael that is because you come from England where passion is unusual, it is lucky for me that you are an unusual Englishman and Michael… this is your world now."

He smiled back and they held hands across the table and Francesca asked him,

"So, what are you feeding your friends tonight?"

The question seemed to close the door on any further discussion of Marc for now and probably forever.

Michael felt a sense of relief at the assurances he had now received and also that the conversation had moved on to a far less emotive topic.

"I am getting them a take-away pizza when they arrive, and I hope to buy some nice cakes from the Boulangerie, Pain des Pistes, at the top of the resort after we have finished our drink."

"Ah yes, they do sell delicious cakes. I will walk with you and buy some cakes for my family too and then I will drive back to Barcelonnette. Tomorrow evening I will meet your friends and on Sunday and next Friday I will ski with you, OK?"

"That sounds great," Michael replied feeling that an awkward moment had passed, not a moment he understood, but perhaps she was just embarrassed at having been in a long-term relationship with such an unpleasant and indeed violent individual. Hopefully, Marc would disappear from their lives after Francesca had 'had a word' with him.

They rose from their table and walked arm in arm along the Gallery boardwalk, looking in the shop windows and talking amicably. They climbed the steps on the boardwalk past the Godille clothing store where he had bought Francesca's jacket and walked around to the Godille ski shop where Michael had bought his skis and boots. He could see Gerard inside kneeling in front of a woman for whom he was fitting new ski boots.

"This is where I bought my skis and boots," he said to Francesca.

"Ah yes, the best ski shop in Pra Loup, they always service my skis here," she replied.

The pair paused and looked into the brightly lit interior.

"Oh, look Michael, those skis are the same colour as my

lovely new jacket!" Francesca exclaimed with excitement.

Michael glanced to his right where a rack of new Stockli skis were displayed in the window. She was right they were the same blue as her jacket.

"You don't need new skis, though do you? Yours go like they are rocket fuelled," he commented.

She giggled back at him, "Michael you know it is me who is rocket fuelled, my skis are very nearly finished, the edges have been sharpened so many times there is nearly no ski left."

"Really?" he said shocked.

"Really Michael and look at these skis. They are Stockli Lasers, women's slalom skis; their FSI edition. A great ski for a great skier."

Michael felt a slight pain in his chest, but he knew it wasn't his heart that was protesting but his wallet. Before he had really appreciated what was happening, he was inside the shop and Gerard was showing them the skis and fetching the bindings he would recommend with them.

"So, Gerard," Michael found himself asking, very much aware of an excited Francesca at his side, "how much, 'combien', is this package?"

Gerard told them the price. "Pour Francesca Monsieur, our, how do you say, World Cup skier un bon prix une mille, deux cent euros."

"One thousand two hundred euros," Francesca repeated back to clarify the price to Michael giving the impression that it was a snip of a bargain. Michael turned, looked into her eyes and felt like a helpless drowning man, *'electric blue eyes I need you, always be near me.'* She smiled at him, leant forwards and their lips met for a lingering kiss. Gerard obviously realised that this signified that the deal was done and fetched the card machine for

Michael. Michael input his pin number as Gerard and Francesca discussed the logistics of bringing her boots in for the bindings to be fitted and the settings adjusted. Once this was all done Francesca marched Michael around to the Boulangerie, her arm tightly around his waist pulling him in towards her.

Michael chose three religieuses au café - a concoction of choux pastry, coffee cream filling and coffee icing. Francesca chose a large raspberry tart. They emerged from the shop and, carefully cradling their purchases, kissed passionately before Francesca pulled away smiling broadly at Michael,

"A demain, see you tomorrow." She turned on her heel and was gone. Michael bounced back over the road to the apartment and realised he was actually whistling as he went.

Chapter Nineteen

James and Tim made good time and actually arrived in Pra Loup at half past seven. Michael let them in and within seconds they were all sitting in the lounge slurping the beautifully smooth Châteauneuf-du-Pape which he had opened half an hour before to allow it to breathe. The three friends chatted animatedly. James was disappointed that he would not be meeting Francesca until the following evening, but Michael just grinned and told him she would be worth the wait. He wasn't certain that he had intended to, but he had also found himself telling James and Tim about his encounters with Marc.

Tim winked as he said, "Three to one, perhaps this Marc isn't that brave. I expect a word from your young lady should sort it all out."

"I do hope so," Michael sighed. "I don't want to be spending all my time looking over my shoulder. Anyway, guys, you should unpack and I'll go and get the pizza from the Crêperie de Patinoire. I shouldn't be too long."

Michael pulled on his jacket, walked out of the apartment and down the road towards the ice rink and the adjacent restaurant that sat in front of the gallery. It served delicious takeaway pizzas bubbling with local cheeses as well as having an excellent sit-down menu. The ice rink was busy with what looked like a school group screeching their way around the rink. Michael patted his pockets for his wallet as he approached the take-away window and immediately realised that he had left it behind. He could see it in his mind's eye lying on the kitchen counter. He spun round and began scurrying back towards the apartment. The snow had become icy and slippery underfoot and Michael knew he would have to pay attention or he might end up on his rear end. There was a sudden movement to his right and three familiar, but unwelcome figures exploded from between two parked vans to his right. They grabbed him and despite his attempts to pull free bundled him down the side of the cabin that housed the local bins and out of the glare of the streetlights. He was shoved hard against the wooden cladding of the building, he felt it rough against the back of his head. The two thugs pinned him by the biceps and Marc pulled back his fist and buried it in Michael's stomach. This time Michael had been prepared and he had tensed his stomach muscles so whilst he was winded, he did not collapse completely. Marc slid his hand into his jacket pocket and pulled out a thin wooden object that he pressed. Michael realised with horror that it was a flick knife. This was getting too serious, and he pulled against his captors and screamed for help. He didn't expect anyone to hear him, he was sure his cries would be masked by the shouts and music from the ice rink. Marc leant into his face and pressed the point of the blade against his throat.

"Putain de merde, t'es tellement con," he spat through gritted teeth.

Michael's French was not anywhere near proficient enough to understand what Marc had said but he did recognise the word 'merde' – 'shit' – and presumed the rest would be of the same ilk. Marc's eyes bored into him, his stare dripping with malevolence, his eyelids narrowed with hate. He pushed the blade harder and the point felt as though it was about to break through the soft flesh and thrust towards his jugular. Suddenly Marc's eyes widened in surprise and he screamed as a large muscular figure appeared behind him, pulled his knife arm down and twisted his fingers into an unnatural angle. One moment Michael was fearing for his life and the next he was looking down at his attacker writhing in agony at his feet. The huge, muscular, figure of Tim stepped over the body and swung a huge right fist into the face of the man holding his right arm. It impacted with a sickening squelch of collapsing sinew and erupting blood. The second assailant joined the first on the ground. The third had had a moment to see what was happening and stepped back from the carnage but he was far too slow if he was thinking of fleeing. Tim seized him by the left hand and twisted viciously; he let out a howl and fell to his knees as his wrist snapped. Tim then turned to Michael.

"You forgot your wallet." He grinned. "Is this the ex-boyfriend?" he asked nodding downwards towards Marc. Michael nodded his confirmation.

Tim knelt down beside Marc and whispered in his ear "Si vous le derangez encore, je vous tuerais." He stood up and smiled at Michael. "Come on, let's get that pizza I am starving."

Michael gazed at him in awe. Tim had just beaten three thugs to a pulp in seconds and he clearly didn't give it a second thought.

"What did you say to Marc?" he asked Tim.

"I told him that if he bothers you again I will kill him. Come on let's go."

"Looking at him, I think he might just believe you." Michael smirked, a huge wave of relief washing over him as he turned away from the three prostrate bodies.

"He should do, don't you?"

Michael was not at all sure that Tim was joking or how to respond to his guardian angel.

They walked back into the light and around to the take-away

window and placed their order.

Later that evening, as they polished off the pizza and moved to the second bottle of Châteauneuf-du-Pape, Michael regaled James with a moment by moment account of his brother's assault upon the three attackers. James was concerned that they should go to the police, particularly since Marc had had a knife, but Tim seemed confident that there would be no further problems with the group and was quite clear that he had no desire to spend his holiday speaking to officers of the law, particularly when it was Marc and his comrades who were the ones carrying some rather brutal wear and tear from the evening. Michael tended to agree with him, bullies often backed off when they got a taste of their own medicine.

"Well," said James, "this Francesca better be pretty special if she is worth putting life and limb on the line for!"

"You can make your own mind up on that question tomorrow," Michael replied.

James turned to his brother and continued,

"So, Tim, you've ridden in on your white charger and dealt with Michael's problems, what about sorting Mr Vines out for me?" He laughed as he made the suggestion. "Or do Facebook assaults get a different response to those made in dark alleys with knives?"

Tim chuckled, "I think your governors might have a problem with a response to complaints that included actual bodily harm".

"Hmm, pity really. Are we having those cakes Michael or are they just for show?"

Chapter Twenty

The morning brought a perfect Pra Loup day; crystal clear skies and manicured pistes awaited them. Even after picking up hire skis for James and Tim they still made the first lift at nine a.m., Michael took them straight up La Clappe and then Pegieou lifts to gain height before heading across to the Lac drag lift and up to the top of the mountain. Here he allowed his guests a moment to drink in the views before they careened down the red Quartier run towards Agnelier and the links into the Foux D'Allos valley. They rocketed down the slopes into the heart of Foux D'Allos and then rose up on the other side of the resort on the Champ chair lift followed immediately by the Observatoire chair lift which took them to two thousand six hundred metres above sea level. Perched at the top of the lift was a small building Michael had always presumed was the observatory. They stood on the high ridge scanning the horizon in silence. Michael interrupted their reverie.

"I've been told that it is possible to see the Mediterranean Sea from here on a clear day. I have been here on many clear days, just like today but I have never seen it."

"Aw well," Tim replied, "you didn't see Marc coming either, so it could just be your eyesight! However, to be fair, I can't see the sea either."

They peeled away to skim back down into the bowl of the resort. Having skied all morning, they eventually stopped for lunch at the foot of the 'Vascal' chair. The restaurant was strangely at odds with the rest of the beautiful area. It looked like the remains of a World War II concrete military installation – a single storey, rectangular building that had nothing to recommend it aesthetically, but which fortunately served excellent food at very reasonable prices for a mountain restaurant. They only ordered omelettes, as they were aware they were meeting Francesca for dinner at La Marmite restaurant that evening, but they were delicious.

All thoughts of Marc, and indeed Mr Vines, disappeared as the friends raced, flew and fell down the pistes. Michael was the only one of the three who didn't take a tumble and enjoyed shouting out to James and Tim; "If you are not falling, you're not trying," to which their standard response was,

"Well, you aren't trying very hard then!"

They skied until just before four thirty when they stopped for a round of génépis at the Pegieou restaurant, where they sat staring over the mountain peaks until the pisteurs arrived to say it was time to go as they were shutting the runs.

They returned to the apartment tired but exhilarated and very ready for a hot shower and a cold beer. James and Tim agreed with Michael's assessment of the local beer, both coming back for second and third bottles. It was a very mellow group of men who finally left the flat to walk the short distance to La Marmite restaurant which sat two thirds of the way along the gallery. Their tales of the day's skiing exploits became more extreme as the alcohol disappeared. The slopes had become steeper, their falls more spectacular and their speeds bordering on supersonic. They arrived laughing at the restaurant and were shown to their table where they sat down and wasted no time in asking the waiter for a round of beers. As their drinks were served Michael looked with mock seriousness at the brothers and said,

"Well gents, however fast you think you skied today you will need to double your speed if you're going to keep up with Francesca. I fear you may crash and burn tomorrow!"

Chapter Twenty-One

As if that were the cue for her entrance Francesca appeared at the door of La Marmite, eyes twinkling and a smile playing on her lips. Her impact was instant as James and Tim were promptly silenced by this svelte vision, dressed in tight fitting black trousers, ankle length boots, a black turtleneck sweater with a black gilet over the top and a holdall strapped over her right shoulder. Her blue eyes held the brothers entranced. Michael sprung to his feet and with an arm outstretched in Francesca's direction he introduced her.

"James and Tim meet Francesca. Francesca meet James and Tim."

Francesca stepped towards the group and inclined her head slightly.

"Bonsoir, James and Tim."

Finally, the brothers seemed to regain some control and they both stumbled to their feet welcoming Francesca as Michael pulled out a chair for her to sit on. She sat down and turned to Michael.

"Am I having something to drink or is it just you boys drinking tonight?" she cast all of them an appraising look, "because I think I have quite a lot of catching up to do looking at the state of my musketeers."

They all laughed and immediately a heated debate began as to which of them was Porthos, the portly comic musketeer.

Tim cut through their debate, "I will play Porthos, but I am

Porthos from the 2014 film – trim, sexy and played by Howard Charles. You guys are quite trim… but sexy? Francesca, I don't know what you see in him." He nodded his head towards Michael.

Francesca leapt to Michael's defence, "Oh no, he is my D'Artagnan."

"D'Artagnan's grandad more like," Tim chortled.

"Thanks Tim," replied Michael, "but when I leave you behind on the slopes again tomorrow, you'll realise that there's a lot of life left in the old dog yet."

Their amiable interchange was interrupted by the arrival of the waiter at the table. Michael turned to Francesca,

"What would you like, a beer, a cocktail or…" he looked at the brothers enquiringly, "shall we all just move on to some wine?"

Francesca paused briefly before looking to the waiter and saying

"Un Kir Royale et une bouteille du Sauvignon Blanc Videl, s'il vous plaît."

"Right," said Michael somewhat surprised at the sudden decision without any consensus being sought, "Is that all for you or are we allowed some wine too?"

Francesca smiled, completely unphased, "If you are good boys you may share my wine."

"We'd better be good then," interjected James. "It's my favourite and I like it with any meal."

The waiter quickly returned with the Kir Royale and the white wine which, after having offered a taste to Francesca, he put in an ice bucket on the table. He then brought four menus to the table. After much discussion, the group decided on sharing a cheese fondue for two and a meat fondue for two between the four of them. Tim insisted that anyone who lost the contents of their fork in either of the heated liquids should pay a penalty and have to empty their wine glass. A competitive element crept in with the meal and a high level of sabotaging of each other's forks ensued, some quite subtle and others rather more blatant. The pile of cubed bread, vegetables and meat had not decreased a great deal before it became necessary to order a second bottle of Sauvignon Blanc. Unfortunately, for Francesca the three men seemed intent on ensuring that barely a morsel passed her lips without it being followed by a deluge of white wine. She did complain but all three protested their innocence.

"Do you sell property all year round Francesca?", James asked looking into the hypnotic eyes.

"Most of the year. I have a month off in June and head to the coast for the sunshine, but I am busy the rest of the time," she replied, "Pra Loup is beautiful in the summer; but I love the sea too, so I rent an apartment in Cap d'Agde and lay in the sunshine."

James smiled, clearly savouring the image that Francesca had created in his mind.

"So, you won't be spending the summer watching Michael playing cricket then?" He suggested wryly.

"I cannot think of anything worse," she chortled, "From what I have heard of cricket it is the most boring game in the world. If Michael wants to see me in the summer, he will have to come to Cap d'Agde, if he is too busy playing cricket you can come instead James", she smiled coquettishly.

"Strangely, I think I will be able to squeeze you in in June Francesca and unfortunately James is at school then," Michael interrupted with a laugh.

"Good," beamed Francesca holding Michael's gaze in her dazzling eyes, "You are much more handsome even if you're so very old!"

"But Michael, she is right, watching cricket is like watching paint dry! The best thing I have ever seen at the County ground in Taunton was Rod Stewart in concert, now that was awesome," James continued, even though Michael knew he was a big cricket fan.

"Ah James you are showing your age. Rod Stewart! We younger men prefer more contemporary stars like Tim Minchin and Jack Savoretti," Michael responded, but regretted taking the bait almost as soon as the words were out of his mouth as the smiling assassin delivered the coup de grâce,

"Really, so why do you always listen to Matt Monroe and Nat King Cole?" the drowning man struck out for shore with one last effort,

"James, I thought you knew class never ages, they are just like me, ripening like fine wines!"

Eventually the fondues were finished, and the debris was cleared from the table – oily patches left to mark the fact that they had been there. The menus returned and strangely all four of them chose to have profiteroles followed by a cappuccino. Tim did not propose any drinking games with the deserts or coffees and a modicum of restraint returned to the meal. Tim and James insisted on paying the bill which had arrived with four complimentary glasses of génépi – which were summarily dispatched. They rose from the table, bidding the waiter goodnight, and opened the door to step out into the cold night air. The shock of the plummeting temperature came almost like a physical blow; the naked skin on their necks and faces felt as though it was being scoured with frozen wire wool. The group hurried down the boardwalk and turned left up the road to Michael's flat. No one spoke as they all concentrated on expending the maximum energy, moving as quickly as possible to the warmth of the apartment. As they burst through the door they were enveloped by the welcoming warmth.

Michael made four hot chocolates and they sat comfortably in the apartment cradling the warm mugs in their hands as the impact of the icy night air dissipated. James turned to Francesca and asked her,

"So, were you brought up here or elsewhere in France?"

"Ah, no I am as local as you get, this is and always has been my home, my parents and my grandparents were all born here. My parents live in Barcelonnette, one day Michael I may let you meet them, but I am worried because you are older than my father!" Francesca replied mischievously.

"Well, he must be a very remarkable biological specimen to have become a parent at, what, eight years old," Michael responded, laughing, "I would be happy to meet them, they can't be as scary as James' and Tim's parents. Their father is a retired army Colonel, only I don't think he knows he is retired. He is truly terrifying. After you have experienced Colonel Piper any other sets of parents have to be pussycats!".

"And you're lucky Michael you have only met him a couple of times, we both grew up with him and still have to see him. He hates me because I became a teacher and didn't follow the family tradition of joining the Royal Artillery and he just about tolerates Tim because at least he went into the armed forces even if, in his eyes, it was a second-rate arm!" James continued before being interrupted by his brother,

"James, he loves us in his own way, it's just not a way that a normal human would recognise, and you've turned out okay so relax!"

"I have to admit I was very fortunate, my father was thrilled that I became a history teacher, I think, secretly he wished that was what he had become given his love of history, anyway, night cap anyone, I think a little drink might calm James down?" Michael offered.

"Not for me," Francesca replied. "I am going to bed; I have a long day tomorrow looking after beginners on the slopes." She kissed Michael on the cheek and walked through to the bedroom.

"A little Amaretto?" He asked of his two remaining guests, both of whom nodded enthusiastically.

Michael poured the drinks and proffered them to Tim and James who were comfortably ensconced on the sofa. As Michael sat down in the armchair James looked at him conspiratorially and said in a hushed voice, "She is absolutely bewitching, how on earth has she fallen for you? I'm not surprised her ex has come after you with a knife, I would. She's worth fighting for, although I don't think I could afford to keep her on my salary."

Michael looked at him and smiled ruefully. "Honestly James, I have no idea. It could be my boyish good looks, my charismatic personality or my bedroom performance but I suspect the most likely answer is that she likes antiques with large bank accounts!"

Chapter Twenty-Two

At breakfast the next morning two large cafétières of coffee were consumed in an attempt to lessen the impact of the previous evening's drinking. Michael, James and Tim were a little disconsolate that their fragility did not seem to be shared by Francesca who was particularly effervescent and clearly excited to collect her new skis from Godille Sports. She and Michael walked around to the shop whilst James and Tim finished getting ready and gulped down a final cup of coffee. Francesca clung tightly to Michael's upper arm and her head was tucked into his shoulder. She was in a buoyant mood and he wondered if she knew about Marc getting his comeuppance on Friday evening. He toyed with mentioning the incident, but he didn't want anything to cast a shadow over the day. Gerard smiled at them as they entered the shop and came forward to greet them with the new skis and poles in one hand and Francesca's boots in the other. The blue of the skis, her jacket and her eyes all sung out in a beautiful harmony. It would be a shame when she put on her sunglasses to ski, Michael thought. Francesca sat down and pulled on her ski boots, leaving her ankle boots in Gerard's care, and then they were off to rendezvous with James and Tim at La Clappe lift. They could see James and Tim waiting for them as they approached, and they got on the lift together and were whisked off up the mountain. At the top, they swung left onto the wide blue Clappe piste and skied down to the Pegieou chair lift. Francesca allowed the three men to ski ahead down the run as she fiddled with her boot fittings and then took a few exploratory turns to become familiar with the capabilities of her new skis. She followed a couple of yards of short turns with some longer, faster and wider carving turns. She accelerated, tiny crystals of snow flew up in her wake as she flew past the rest of the group and then waited patiently at the bottom of the lift carrying out a range of gentle stretches.

"So," Michael gasped as he came to a stop next to her, "How are the skis?"

"Oh Michael, they are fantastic. I think I will need to see just how fast they go in a minute. You boys may get left behind," she giggled.

"Just remember that if you lose us, you'll have to pay for your own lunch," Michael quipped.

"Well then, perhaps I will wait for you," she laughed again.

The morning was spent travelling at break-neck speeds, or so it felt to Michael. He knew Francesca was taking it easy and yet he, James and Tim were skiing right at their limits. He could not conceive of how they would keep up if she actually let off the handbrake! Michael had promised James and Tim that they would lunch at the Costebelle restaurant at the top of the Costebelle lift. The restaurant had been run by the same two brothers for over forty years and the food was superb. With the beautiful blue skies overhead, they decided to sit outside and resist the allure of the enchanting interior. Francesca was still as fresh as a daisy whilst the companions were all extremely grateful for the opportunity to sit down and relax. Tim surveyed the group.

"Well, I was feeling jealous that James has the rest of the week here and you two have the whole season, but after the exertions of this morning I'm looking forward to getting back to the UK tomorrow for a rest!"

"To be fair," Michael responded, "I've organised to attend an education conference in Paris for a few days next week. I'll probably get some new thighs fitted whilst I am there!"

Tim looked puzzled, "I thought you were retired?"

"I am, essentially, but I plan to do a bit of consultancy in the summer and autumn to make sure I don't go stir crazy or become a complete cricket bore. The conference is presenting new research on teaching and learning so I thought it would be good for me to keep up to date... And a couple of meals in nice restaurants doesn't seem like a bad idea." replied Michael.

"Is your French up to a conference?" enquired James.

"Probably not, but it is an international conference held in Paris and, as always with these things, conducted in English. So, I think my English will suffice," grinned Michael.

"Sounds great to me," chimed in Francesca, "It will mean I can have my day off to ski properly next week without having to wait for the old man."

"Oh Michael," teased James, "That sounds so tough, poor you, you have to go to Paris. Whereas I have an appeal hearing at County Hall in Exeter next Wednesday morning. Mr Vines has appealed the permanent exclusion of his son, even though it is absolutely clear he was selling drugs. He says I am picking on his son. I hate these appeals. The panel seem to go out of their way to find any possible loopholes in the process or procedure to beat the school with. The Chair of Governors has to come with me and, as you know Michael, he's a great guy but he never reads any paperwork at all... let alone thoroughly. It could be a real nightmare and I'll have to sit in the same room as the vile Vines and listen to his vitriolic nonsense."

"What do you earn James?" Tim snorted, "Because I reckon,

I probably earn half of what you do and when I go to work, I could get shot at or blown up. So, I don't think listening to some alcoholic arsehole is too much of an ask."

"You don't know the half of it." James prickled, "The evening after the lad's exclusion every window in the front of the English block was smashed and when I looked at the CCTV the person who did it had a cap and mask, but I swear it was Vines, he's a psycho."

"I swear you're paranoid," Tim said grinning.

They all laughed, and their focus moved to their drinks order and the menus. All four of them ordered the dish of the day, which was Boudin Noir, a French black pudding. The dishes soon appeared and were beautifully presented but extensive and they required a great deal of their focus. As the meal progressed, with three of the group being English, the conversation inevitably moved on to the weather. Michael had looked at the weather app. on his phone. Forecasts were notoriously unreliable in the mountains as the weather changed so rapidly, but he had found that the Bergfex app did a pretty good job, and it was showing snowstorms coming in for the next day as well as Monday and Thursday.

"James, snow is forecast tomorrow. You do have snow chains with your hire car don't you? If you don't, I'm happy to drive Tim to the airport." said Michael.

"No, it's fine, it has chains, and I am okay about driving in the snow. I also quite like my brother's company, which I know may seem strange given the kind of guy he is, but hey, he is my brother!" laughed James. Tim blew him a kiss.

"Okay, just remember the offer is there. Given that you are driving yourself to the airport on Friday afternoon and it's probably going to snow on Thursday do you mind if I book an off-piste lesson for after lunch on Friday?"

"No," replied James, "that's fine, we'll ski in the morning, eat and then I'll head off. Will the lesson be with the legendary Jean Paul that you keep talking about?"

"It will if he can squeeze me in."

Finally, all four of them sat back from their assaults upon the black pudding feeling more than a little bloated but with their plates clean.

"Wow," said James, "That was absolutely superb, but I cannot eat another thing, or I'll burst."

Tim chuckled, "Are you sure I can't tempt you with one wafer thin mint, sir?"

"No, no mint but perhaps a little génépi to help my digestion."

As their plates were cleared Michael ordered coffee and génépi and they all sat back in their chairs soaking up the winter sun. The conversation skipped from Tim's exploits to Francesca's ski career, but eventually further exercise could not be avoided. Michael and Tim paid the bill and they plodded back to their skis, put them on and meandered down the piste to the Bergerie lift. The three men were hugely relieved to see that Francesca was feeling the effects of the Boudin Noir, even if last night's alcohol had had no impact.

All too soon, the afternoon was coming to a close and they were twisting their way down their final piste and heading back to the apartment. Francesca went with Tim and James to Godille. Tim returned his hire gear and she picked up her shoes. She then waved them off as she returned to her car to drive back down to Barcelonnette.

Chapter Twenty-Three

In Pra Loup the three musketeers decided a quiet evening was in order, and an early night given that James would have an early start and a long drive to the airport and back. They sat on the sofas quietly supping on Michael's stock of the local beer and watched the outline of the mountains transform from sparkling white to looming black and their blue backdrop metamorphosise into a starry firmament. The three men chatted amiably about their day and both brothers spoke at length about Francesca's skiing and her beauty. They observed that Michael was a fortunate man and that either of them would be happy to swap places with him if the relationship ever came to an end! Michael smiled smugly at their comments and enjoyed the peaceful evening feeling as relaxed as he had been for several years.

They woke to heavy grey skies and light flutters of snow which had covered the resort with a thin translucent sheet. James was keen to set off as quickly as possible, hoping that he might avoid heavier snowfalls on the way to the airport which would necessitate putting on the snow chains. They left the flat as light first broke. Tim hugged Michael, thanking him for his hospitality and telling him to look after himself. Michael went back into the kitchen and sat down with another cup of coffee. Looking out of the window at the low cloud and poor light he decided that today would be an 'admin' day. There was no pressure for him to ski in poor conditions given that two months of skiing still stretched ahead of him. He moved to his armchair and settled down to read his emails. He spent some time reading about the seminar choices at the upcoming conference and perusing the excerpts from the papers the speakers had submitted. By the end of the morning he had chosen the sessions he would attend alongside the major keynote speeches, and he sent his choices to the event organisers. He kept in regular contact with James, monitoring the progress of his journey, and he sent a text to Francesca telling her how much all three of them had enjoyed the previous day's skiing. She replied with a smiling face emoji. After a snack-lunch of local cheeses Michael prepared a cottage pie for himself and James to eat that evening and popped to the patisserie to purchase a tarte tatin. All his chores complete he opened another bottle of Châteauneuf-du-Pape and slurping on its oaky notes watched the evening news on Sky. James texted to say he would be back shortly, but the increasingly heavy snowfall had held him up and he had been forced to battle with putting on the chains.

They sat down to supper together, nearly an hour later than planned, large glasses of red wine in hand.

"That was a fair old drive. Tim was probably back in the UK before you were back here," Michael commented.

"Yes," James concurred, "And he sent his thanks again. He had a great weekend and he wants to come back out with me at Easter. You'll never be rid of him now!"

"You're both welcome any time. You ought to come out in the summer too, it is fantastic then as well."

"I suppose there's mountain biking and white water rafting and plenty of walking," mused James.

"Yes, and apparently there's a huge amount of road cycling. It is a big thing around here. The Tour de France has had stages that ended in Pra Loup, one of which was pretty legendary. That yellow arch with the black and white checks on it at fifteen hundred was constructed in its honour. It commemorates the 1975 stage when the Belgian cyclist Eddy Merckx, the greatest road cyclist of all time who was known as 'The Cannibal', was defeated by the French cyclist Thevenet. Merckx was on course to win the Tour for the sixth time when he was attacked by a French spectator who punched him, bruising his kidneys, in an attempt to bring his reign to an end. He managed to carry on though and still wore the yellow jersey when it came to stage fifteen. Merckx still led by nearly a minute at the foot of the climb to Pra Loup. Thevernet had been battling to catch him throughout the stage and, although exhausted, decided to try one more move on the ascent. He passed Merckx where the arch is at fifteen hundred. Merckx lost the stage and never wore the yellow jersey again. Thevernet won the tour, having defeated the 'Cannibal'."

"Very interesting," replied James, "So are you going to buy a bike in the Summer and ride up and down the mountains?

"There are a couple of bike shops in Barcelonnette, and it is a beautiful countryside to cycle in, but whilst I would be happy cycling down into the valley, I have no idea how I would get back up to sixteen hundred. I can't see me ever being fit enough for that climb unless I get an electric bike!"

Tuesday and Wednesday saw the return of the beautiful blue skies and, with the addition of a layer of fluffy new snow, the conditions were perfect. James and Michael skied from the first lift to the last, only breaking briefly for drinks and snack-lunches at the on piste snack bars – one at the foot of the Agneliers lift and one on the forest run above Foux D' Allos. Both snack bars had outside seating areas flooded with sunshine. Thursday brought the expected snow which fell all day. The clouds sat low on the mountain wrapping it in a grey silence. Large snowflakes drifted down continuously, resting in the branches of the forest trees that reached well up the mountain and lined the pistes. The thick layers of snow clung to the larch limbs which would emerge from the gloom as the two men picked their way down the pistes, which were themselves hidden under a covering of deep fresh snow. Not many skiers were braving the conditions and at times, with the cloud limiting what they could see and the eerie silence of the insulated snow scape, they felt isolated and alone on the mountainside. Michael found the conditions difficult. With such poor visibility he often could not see the contours of the snow and began to feel the effects of motion sickness. James was not affected in the same way but was finding staying upright in the deep snow challenging. There was a shared determination to stay out on the mountain since it was James' last full day – he would be driving back to the airport after lunch on Friday. However, they decided on a long morning coffee break, an even more extended lunch sitting by the huge log fire at the Costebelle and a lengthy stop for vin chaud in the afternoon to round off their skiing. They felt a good deal of pride in the fact that they were amongst the hardy few who had spent the day on the slopes, even if the majority of it had been spent in restaurants and most of the time on the piste had been spent trying to get James back to a vertical position from a horizontal one.

Chapter Twenty-Four

Michael and James opted to go for an early evening drink before meeting Francesca for dinner. After changing out of their ski gear they walked through the falling snow towards Gray's Bar. The roads had been cleared continually throughout the day by a small team of snow ploughs and a digger with a large front bucket. This work had left great mounds of snow on the roadside which was tricky to navigate on foot as the pavements were lost under these man-made mountains and pedestrians were forced out onto the road. Michael was impressed that the ski shuttle buses were still running, even though there was little demand for their service. However, despite all the hard work that had gone on during the day, the relentless snow continued to fall and pitch on the road. It didn't look like the work of the snow ploughs would be finished any time soon. The lights of the gallery shone through the drifting flakes as they picked their way towards the boardwalk. On the other side of the road Michael caught sight of a figure in his peripheral vision. He grasped James' arm and nodded to the man standing outside the Immobilier. Michael could just make out Francesca at her desk through the window of the office. Both men stopped.

"That," hissed Michael under his breath, "Is the delightful Marc."

Marc stood and stared back at them briefly. His arm was in a sling across his chest and his fingers were splinted. After a few moments he turned, shoulders down, and slouched away.

"I guess the splint is for his broken fingers," James laughed. "You don't want to cross my brother!"

"No, you don't," agreed Michael. "I just hope he hasn't been bothering Francesca."

"She's a big girl Michael, I doubt she'd have any truck with him. Come on. I'm looking forward to a White Russian so I'm hoping they serve them at Gray's."

The two of them sat in Gray's Bar supping cocktails before heading to La Marmite at six thirty to meet Francesca. They were a little early, but Francesca soon appeared, lighting up the restaurant with her smile and scintillating eyes. James seemed to Michael to be as much under her spell as he was, and he smiled to himself as only one of them would be spending the night with her and it would not be James! James began recounting the tales of their day's skiing. He managed to make them both sound as out of their depth in powder as each other. Michael protested his superior technique and ability to Francesca who smiled back,

"Well, you can prove it tomorrow when we ski."

"No, no," interjected James. "Tomorrow morning is my last morning and I am skiing strictly on the piste. You will have to go off-piste after lunch for your demonstration."

"That is no good for me," said Francesca. "I am only skiing in the morning, my colleague is unwell and I have to cover her tomorrow afternoon, sorry."

"And I have a lesson with Jean Paul anyway," chipped in Michael.

"So that is the answer for you Michael, get Jean Paul to video you skiing off-piste tomorrow afternoon. Do it on your phone and then you can show me the evidence and send it to James. We will see if these lessons have been worth it!"

"Indeed," replied Michael. "But the problem is that I feel

seasick when the visibility is bad."

"Michael there are no waves," laughed Francesca.

"I know but not being able to see the snow makes me feel awful, just the same as being seasick, and that is the worst feeling. I remember in a Dick Francis novel his hero said about seasickness, one moment you are frightened you are dying, the next moment you are frightened you are not and he wasn't wrong!" Michael grimaced.

"I didn't know you were a Dick Francis fan I thought you were an Agatha Christie devotee," said James.

"Oh yes I am, but I have read all her books and now Dick Francis is my guilty pleasure. I have all his books too back in Devon. He was prolific and since his death his son Felix has continued writing similar novels, all with some link to horse racing, just like his father's stories. I've just finished his most recent book."

"I'm not a big horse racing fan but I love the stories and they have *spurred* an interest in the equine world. Can I borrow it?" asked James.

"Ha ha! Of course, you can as long as we have no more dreadful puns."

They finished their meal and wandered back to the apartment, the three of them walking in a line with their arms linked, laughter rippling all around them. The snow was resting on their heads and shoulders like confetti at a wedding.

They were up early to ensure they made the most of James' last morning. The snow had stopped, and the clouds had cleared to reveal an iridescent blue sky. The pisteurs had been working hard and the pistes were flattened to a regular corduroy. They hurried to the Clappe lift where, as all over the mountain, the lift workers reverently greeted Francesca and they were whisked up the mountain, high above the still empty pistes. They skied straight to the Pegieou lift, which James had nick-named Peggy Sue and on which he insisted on singing the Buddy Holly classic very loudly... and very badly. Michael gave a contented sigh – it was a great morning to be alive. Once at the top they skied straight down the blue and red pistes to the Le Lac button lift. Snow crystals arced in granulated showers from their skis as they carved beautiful sweeping turns down the pistes. James let out a whoop of joy as they crossed the drag lift and swept down before being thrown back up the mountain and speeding on to the lift. The morning rushed by in a whirl of thrilling descents and ecstatic shouts, until suddenly it was lunchtime and the Petit Chaperon Rouge restaurant was calling. They descended to the restaurant and sat down basking in the sunshine and the glory of the morning's skiing. The food was, as usual, delicious and the service attentive but it couldn't be topped off with the customary génépi as James was driving and Francesca working. Just before two o'clock, with Michael's lesson beckoning and James' drive to Marseille imminent they stood to leave the restaurant and say their farewells.

"I need to get on," James reflected, "I have to take my skis back, change and pack the car."

"I will come with you," Francesca said. "I will leave my skis at the apartment and change before I see my client this afternoon."

Michael moved forward and embraced his friend.

"Travel safely. You *have* got the spare keys to the apartment, haven't you?" James nodded in affirmation. "And I've left the Felix Francis novel out on the breakfast bar for you to borrow. Don't forget it."

"I won't," replied James returning the embrace. "Thanks for an amazing week. I'll give you a buzz when I get home and I'll see you at Easter my friend."

Michael shook James' hand and gave Francesca a peck on the cheek.

"You can have my keys in case you leave before James, if you're not back before me I'll pick them up from your office".

He slipped the bunch of keys into her jacket pocket and zipped it up.

Chapter Twenty-Five

He watched as the pair skied off down the slope towards Pra Loup. He made his way to the moving carpet that carried him up from the restaurant to the foot of the Peguieou lift, which he rode to the summit. He sat alone on the six person chair and enjoyed the quiet of the mountain which enveloped him. At the top he slid from his seat, turned right, and cruised down the Honore Bonnet red and focussed on trying to execute every turn perfectly. He bore left to take the Courtil button lift. The button lift required skiers to insert a 'button' between their legs, which was attached by a long pole to an over-head cable, and then be dragged, hence the interchangeable name for this kind of tow – 'drag lift', up the slope with their skis tracking along beneath the cable in the snow. The Courtil lift would drag him up to a point where it would be a short ski to his rendezvous with Jean Paul at the top of the Costebelle lift. Courtil presented a daily challenge for Michael because there was a blackboard at the foot of the drag upon which was written a different philosophical message every day. His French was improving but these 'bon mots' were often a real test. Today was no exception, 'aimer tout le monde, faire confiance a quelques-uns ne faire de mal a personne', Shakespeare. Michael admitted defeat and as he was towed up the lift pulled his phone out of his pocket and opened google translate-'love all, trust a few, do wrong to none'. As ever he thought wise words. He tugged the button lift from between his thighs and scooted off down the piste to the top of the Costebelle gondola. The lift had recently been refurbished in a multi-million euro overhaul and the new bubbles were pristine, each one emblazoned with the Pra Loup double headed wolf logo. He did not have to wait many minutes before Jean Paul appeared carrying two rucksacks. He spotted Michael and walked over.

"Ah Michael, ça va bien? Today I am going to teach you about the safety equipment for off-piste skiing. I hope you never have to use it. Then we will head up the Gimette drag lift and enjoy some fresh powder. So, let us go over here." He indicated a spot to the side of the lift arrival area out of the way of the decanting skiers. Having walked across the piste together he put the two rucksacks on the floor and opened one of them. He pulled two rectangular plastic boxes from it, both about the size of a mobile phone but a couple of centimetres thicker. They were identical and had coiled leashes attached to one corner and a screen and controls on the other.

These, Michael, are transceivers and you should carry one when you go off-piste. They are called this because they send out a signal and receive a signal but are useless if they are not switched on! We wear them in a safe place on the body where they cannot be ripped off by an avalanche, not in the bag but in the inside pocket and we clip the leash to our jacket. We must keep them away from our portable phones as they will affect them and can reduce their range and cause a false signal. The battery will last, trois cent, three hundred, hours if it is full. We always make sure we have, quarante, forty percent when we start to be safe. Before we ski, we check that they are working. We set them to send. Then one to receive and check it hears the other." He did this and the receiving unit began to beep. Then he did it the other way around.

"If I am in the avalanche and you are not you switch yours

to receive and run to where you last saw me. The numbers on the screen show how close you are. The little man shows when to go left and when to go right. When you reach ten metres you stop running and walk. The signal from the transceiver comes out in the shape of an onion so as you get close you will follow the curve. When you are two to three metres away you get on your knees. So, you run, then walk, then on your knees with the transceiver above the snow but level with the snow. You sweep it left and right to find the closest number on the screen. When you reach the number sweep beyond the point to check. When you have that place you need the sonde, I think it is probe in English."

Jean Paul took out what looked like a cluster of short ski poles and flicked them outwards. The cluster de-concertinaed into one solid length well over two metres.

"This you push in the snow at ninety degrees." He demonstrated on the slope and then pulled the probe out of the snow. "You push in a spiral around thirty centimetres as you move out. When you feel the person stop. Leave the probe and get your bêche."

Jean Paul pulled out a telescopic shovel from the rucksack.

"Spade," interjected Michael.

"Ah thank you, your spade. If the pole is one metre or less in the ground you dig just below it, throwing the snow behind you. If it is more than one metre you dig one and a half times down the hill."

Michael looked puzzled. Jean Paul tried to explain again.

"Ummm. So, if the pole goes in two metres you dig three metres down the hill but level and throw the snow behind. It is hard work to dig but you must do it quickly. Get to the person's airway and clear it as soon as you can. Then clear all round them and dig them out. Do you have any questions?"

"What happens if we are both buried and the people trying to dig us out have different transceivers?" asked Michael.

"Ah but that is not a problem since, mille neuf cent quatre vingt seize, 1996, all transceivers have to have the same frequency, four hundred and fifty-seven kilohertz. They will all hear each other, Okay?"

"Great!" said Michael, "But you are not going to take me where we will need them are you?"

Jean Paul smiled. "Michael, the mountain will decide where there will be an avalanche. We will avoid the obvious places, but the mountain is not predictable, she is fickle."

The two men attached the transceivers to their jackets, switched them on and slipped them into their inside jacket pockets. They slung the rucksacks containing the probes and shovels on their backs and skied down to the Gimmet button lift ready to do battle with Jean Paul's capricious mountain. The path under the drag lift had only just been cleared and the lift opened, so the two men would be amongst the first few skiers to enjoy the fresh powder at the top. When they reached the top of the lift, they peeled off right and surveyed the deep snow.

"Jean Paul," Michael began, "Can you film me sometime this afternoon? Francesca wants to see how I am progressing."

Jean Paul raised an eyebrow and looked enquiringly at him.

"Michael, are you another moth flying too close to the flame? I will film you, but I have spent my whole life watching the mountain and watching people and all I will say to you is, my friend, to be careful with that woman."

Michael grinned back. "I was born careful Jean Paul; you must have seen that from my skiing!" Michael handed over his phone to the instructor, showing him quickly how to take a video on the appliance. As he did so, he noticed a couple of missed calls from James. The snow was deep, enveloping both skiers up to their thighs, but it was light, fluffy and forgiving. After a couple of descents Michael found that he was able to follow Jean Paul's line and when he looked back up the mountain his interlinked S shaped track was not very different to that of his teacher. Jean Paul congratulated him.

"Well done Michael. You are improving. I think now is the time to film the powder hound of Pra Loup. I will go first. Wait until I stop and wave, then begin your descent. I want you to dance down the mountain. Think of a tune with a great beat and sing it in your head, or out loud to the mountain, and turn to the rhythm. Dance Michael; or count to three and turn each time the mountain won't mind if you sing to her or not, but I will film!"

Jean Paul snaked down the mountain for a couple of hundred metres before stopping on top of a slight ridge. Michael watched as Jean Paul stood still, with his skis across the mountain, planting his poles in the snow. He saw him remove his gloves, fitting one onto the end of each pole with their fingers pointing towards the sky. He watched as Jean Paul took the phone from the thin pocket of his salopettes and took a moment or two to select the correct function. Then he saw Jean Paul wave and he was off. Michael thought of singing 'Peggy Sue' but immediately stumbled over the words so reverted to a simpler challenge and launched himself forward.

"One two three (turn),
One two three (turn)
One two three (turn),
One two three (turn).
One two three (turn),
One two three (turn).
One two three (turn)

One two three (turn),
One two three (turn).
One two three (turn)
One two three (turn) Four five!"

Michael came to a breathless halt next to Jean Paul.

"Bravo Michael, bravo, well done. A good film I think."

They watched the video back and Michael allowed himself a little smile. He was no expert, but he did think he looked pretty damned good. Although he berated himself for his childlike behaviour, he could not help but want to rush off and show Francesca the video and receive her praise just as he had received his doting father's praise fifty years ago when he had shared his achievements with him. He knew it was silly, he was nearly sixty and acting like a ten-year-old, but he could not curb his excitement. Jean Paul clapped him on the shoulder, "Now we go back." He pointed his skis downhill and swooped towards the blue piste below. Michael followed and they were soon carving their way back to Pra Loup. They came to a halt near the ski school and Michael handed his rucksack and transceiver back to Jean Paul.

"Thank you so much, I have had a great afternoon the snow was fantastic."

"Yes it was Michael but we have to ski the snow however it is and that is something to remember, do not have expectations of the snow-it is what it is. Our challenge is to ski it wet, soft, hard, icy and however it is we learn! Good job today Michael". The instructor took the ruck sack, "Au revoir Michael, Have a good evening."

"A bientôt Jean Paul", Michael responded as he left his mountain guru.

Chapter Twenty-Six

Michael removed his skis, clipped them together and slung them over his left shoulder with the poles hooked over the ski tips and dangling behind him. He headed back to the apartment, which was closer than Francesca's office. He hoped that Francesca would have seen her clients and would be back so that he could show her the video and not have to go in search of the keys! As he approached his home, he pulled the phone from his pocket and clicked on the video. As he opened the door Michael reflected that it was not very long-ago when he could not have conceived of feeling so happy, again. He missed his Georgie, she was in his thoughts every day, but now he was looking back with joy at their life together rather than being overwhelmed by her desperately premature death.

He pushed through the door with a clatter of skis and boots calling out Francesca's name. He leant his skis against the wall and ploughed forward, his phone held high as if it were as trophy.

The sight that met his eyes stopped him dead in his tracks. In that moment, his whole world changed. Francesca was sitting semi naked on the sofa. Her sweater was draped around her shoulders. Her eyes were red rimmed. She had a large red weal on her cheek and dribbles of what appeared to be semen scarred her inner thighs. She looked imploringly at Michael but could not speak. Her mouth was trying to form words but only sobs gasped forth. Michael too was dumbfounded. He could not comprehend what he was seeing. He stepped forward, putting his phone down on the kitchen counter next to the Felix Francis novel which, abstractly in the midst of his confusion, he noticed James had forgotten. His arms reached out to Francesca.

"What's happened?" he stammered.

Her eyes were cast down, her shoulders hunched in defeat, as she whispered one word.

"James."

As Michael reached her, he knelt down, pulling her towards him in a strong embrace. He buried his face in her hair and breathed in her intoxicating scent. Michael could see she was shivering. Tiny goosebumps sprinkled her flesh. He pulled the throw from the back of the sofa and wrapped it around her. He asked again, his voice muffled against the nape of her neck. "What on earth happened my darling?"

"James m' a violée," she whispered.

Michael heard the words and understood the translation but couldn't believe what he was hearing.

"James what?"

"James raped me," she replied a kind of anger rising-up in her voice.

"James raped you?" Michael echoed incredulously.

"You heard me," Francesca spat out with a venomous edge to her voice. "Your bastard friend raped me."

Michael was struggling to think clearly or to respond appropriately. He was at a loss to know what to say or do and stumbled clumsily into saying entirely the wrong thing.

"Why?"

"Why?" Francesca's growing anger erupted into incandescent rage. "Why? Because I am so fucking ugly you idiot. I trusted that man. You brought him here. He sees me in my towel after my shower and can't keep his dick in his trousers.

149

Your friend raped me. This is your fault, and you ask me why!"
Her eruption finally ran out of steam and she sat with her
shoulders heaving up and down as she tried to drag some air into
her lungs, fresh tears cutting rivulets down her cheeks.

"Oh God I am so sorry. I never thought he would do anything
like that. For Christ's sake he's a headteacher," spluttered
Michael.

"Oh, so teachers are all saints in England are they Michael?"
retorted Francesca pulling angrily away from his embrace. "I
want a shower to wash him all off me."

"But we must contact the police, and they will want to
examine you," said Michael realising the heavy handedness of
his words as soon as he had uttered them.

"No Michael, there will be no police. I don't want to be
examined, prodded and questioned by some gendarme. Anyway,
it is one word against another, and I have been embarrassed
enough. I never want to see, or hear of, that bastard again."

"Okay, okay, of course it is up to you. How long ago did he
leave?"

"I don't know, half an hour ago perhaps."

"Right. I'll go and see if I can catch him and deal with him
if he hasn't gone far," Michael suggested.

"Do not bring him back here, don't you dare bring him back
here," Francesca muttered as she gathered the throw about her
violated body as if it could provide some sort of protection from
what had happened and disappeared into the bathroom.

Michael looked after her, his mind was in a whirl of
confusion and bewilderment but feeling he had to do something
no matter how hopeless he dashed out of the door and down to
the car park where James had left his car. The shock and disbelief
that he had felt at first were quickly being replaced by an all-

consuming fury and indignation, his own breaths were coming in short gasps punctuating his anger. "Who did James think he was? How dare he treat a woman like that? How could he treat his best friend's partner like that?" His whole body was fulminating with rage. His knuckles whitened as his fists bunched by his side. He found the car parking space, it was empty. He screamed in frustration, his head thrown back, his eyes turned to the sky. His tumult of emotions drew querying looks from several passers-by, but Michael was inured to their raised eyebrows. He wasn't sure what he would have done if James had still been there but right now beating him to a bloody pulp seemed like a good option. James was not going to get away with this. He couldn't to do this to Francesca and not pay a heavy price for his actions. His best friend had raped his girlfriend and he had let it happen, he had invited him into his apartment, and he had done this. Michael's apoplexy was, however, underpinned by absolute incredulity – this just wasn't James. He stood motionless on the road overlooking the car park and moments from the last week played through his mind as if on a video recording. He knew that James was under Francesca's spell, but he had never thought that his admiration of her could possibly lead to something like this. Michael had felt rather smug at James' reaction to her, now he felt deep pangs of guilt. The three of them had walked up this very road arm in arm laughing together. How could James abuse Francesca and abuse their friendship so? Michael sighed and turned on his heel to walk back to the apartment. He had to look after Francesca, although he wasn't really sure what to do. How do you support your girlfriend who has just been raped by the man you always considered to be your best and most trusted friend? He opened the door to the apartment and was conscious how different his mood was now to how he had felt when he had walked in half an hour ago. He went into the lounge and could hear Francesca in the bedroom. He went through to see her standing by the bed fully dressed and packing things into her bag. She turned to him as he entered, a bleak greyness seeming to sit behind blue eyes.

"I have decided to go to my parent's house for a few days," she said firmly. "I need some time alone to think."

"Is there anything I can do? I won't go to the conference. I'll stay here with you," Michael said downcast.

"No Michael," she replied, "It is better if you go to the conference and I see you when you get back. I will be better alone for a few days; I need space to work out how I feel and what I need to do to heal. You must go, the conference is important, and we will sort this out when you get back, your keys are here, he seems to have taken the other set. Michael, trust me, I don't want to see that man ever again and I don't want you to see him either. I don't want you to speak to him or to email or text him. I hate him and what he has done to me... To us. I have to go"

Michael responded, he was distraught but wanted to understand what had possessed James to do this,

"I need to speak to him; I need to understand."

Francesca's whispered her reply, her voice one of barely contained fury,

"No Michael, no, I thought you trusted me, I thought you loved me or am I wrong? Is he more important, do you want to give him the chance to lie and make excuses, to hurt us even more, no Michael if you speak to him, we are done?"

Michael could feel their relationship slipping between his fingers and desperately wanted to hold on to it, he didn't want to be alone again so soon, he had lost his wife and he had lost his friend, he couldn't lose Francesca.

"Okay, of course, I won't speak to him, I am so, so sorry".

"Do you promise Michael, do you promise to trust me?" she asked softly emphasising each word.

"Yes, I promise, I won't talk to him, I give you my word".

She picked up her bag with a sigh, slung it on her shoulder, pecked him on the cheek and left.

Electric blue eyes ran through Michael's head...

Electric blue eyes always be near me,
Electric blue eyes I need you,
If you should go, you should know
I love you.
If you should go you should know I am here.

Chapter Twenty-Seven

Michael felt as if he was in a complete vacuum. He did not know what to do. He did not know who he could talk to. He was not sure what he felt, and he was not even sure if he and Francesca were still an item. If they were not an item was that his fault? His one glimmer of hope was that she had left her ski clothes and her skis, and boots were still by the front door next to his. He hoped that this meant she was intending to return. Michael opened a bottle of the Châteauneuf-du-Pape and poured himself a large glass: he gave it no time to breathe and took three large gulps. He sat down on the sofa and took three more large mouthfuls. He looked wistfully at his glass and was surprised to see that it was already empty. He got up, fetched the bottle, and poured himself another large glass. He rested the bottle on the floor by his feet. He leant back, into the sofa, and took another long slurp of the wine as he sought solace in its silky berried flavours. Already he was feeling a slight muzziness as the alcohol took effect. He felt like screaming. He felt like crying. He was so angry, and yet also so swamped with sadness. He was in complete turmoil and whilst he fought to think logically, his emotions and the red wine swept him into very dark places. All too soon he found himself pouring another glass of wine and it was not long before he was stumbling across the lounge to get the corkscrew to open the last bottle of the case. He switched on the television and selected the Sky Greats channel. He was vaguely aware of a young Kirk Douglas playing a slave leader in Spartacus but with the aid of further wine refills he soon slipped into a comatose state.

He didn't wake until deep into Saturday. Even the extraneous sounds of the ski resort moving into full swing had failed to wrestle him from his stupor, and when he did finally wake, he wished that he hadn't. The remains of the second bottle of wine lay in a large pool on the lounge floor. An empty glass lay next to the capsized bottle but the thumping in his head assured him that the vast majority of the wine had been poured down his throat and not onto the floor. He had not drunk like that since his university days and his beating temples, the pain behind his eyes and his growing nausea reminded him why. He groaned in a deep rumble of self-pity. Why on earth, he lamented, had he thought that nearly two bottles of wine would help the situation? And what a waste of a fantastic red as he couldn't remember tasting it after the first couple of glasses. He felt the bile rising in the back of his throat and scrabbled a weaving path to the kitchen sink. He retched once and then was violently sick. A sea of bile and wine spewed from his mouth and nose, its acidity marking its path. He reached for the tap and flicked it on. The water washed the evidence of his stupidity down the drain. He poured a large glass of water and took it back to the sofa. He took a few sips before collapsing prostrate and seeking refuge from his splitting headache in sleep. He woke intermittently from his fitful slumber and sipped at his water, but it was late evening before he rose from the sofa, suddenly aware that he had not rung Francesca to see how she was. Waves of guilt washed over him and, if that was possible, made him feel worse. His self-indulgent binge had meant that he had let Francesca down again. He stood unsteadily and surveyed the apartment, looking for his mobile phone. He could not see it and patted down his pockets, but to no avail. He slowly and methodically searched the apartment, checking jacket pockets, bedside tables and under cushions, but it seemed to have disappeared from the face of the earth. He had a sickening feeling that he might have dropped it in the snow when he had rushed out to the car park the evening before. He pulled on his shoes and ski jacket and made his way gingerly out of the apartment to retrace his steps. Although it was a dark night the streetlights bathed the road in a yellow glow, but there was no sign of his lost phone. Michael had known that it was a fool's errand. If he had dropped it, it would either have been found or obliterated by a passing vehicle. There was no evidence of the latter, so his only hope was that some kind soul had handed it in to the police or the tourist office. If that was the case, he would visit both in the morning when he didn't reek of vomit and stale alcohol. He trudged back home, drank another glass of water and made himself a hot Bovril which he sipped at as he composed an email to send to Francesca.

Chère Francesca,

I have lost my phone so I cannot ring you. I hope you are feeling better. I am so sorry about what happened. I know that I cannot make it right but if there is anything I can do just let me know. I will check if the police or the tourist office have my phone tomorrow as I would really like to hear your voice.

Amour et bisous

Michael

The Bovril trickled down his throat and the strong beefy taste filled his mouth and nostrils. It reminded him of his childhood when his mother had made it for him when he had come in, freezing and wet, having played football with his friends at the local park. That was a long time ago, a time when life was simple and he felt safe and loved.

Michael sent the email and then went into the bathroom

where he peeled off the stinking clothes that clung to his malodorous skin. He stood under the jet of water in the shower and twisted the control dial until he could only just bear the scorching flow. As the scorching water seared across his flesh and through his hair to his scalp, he allowed his mind to explore the idea that had evolved somewhere in his drunken stupor – how he was going to deal with James' betrayal . Such was his anger with the man that he struggled to even bring himself to think his name let alone speak it. As the scalding water trickled down his skin Michael made a huge admission to himself. He had always been a fairly measured man; he did have a temper, but Georgie had always cuddled him when he had been angry about something and somehow that had made the feelings drain away. Since he had retired there had been little to make him angry, just Marc and now this. This time he needed to do something, perhaps something unimaginable. He needed revenge, revenge for Francesca and revenge for himself, revenge for an indescribable betrayal. He needed to put things right, to assuage the deep wound that James had inflicted. A plan had formed in those dark hours, a dark plan, a plan that it was difficult to believe was actually his own... but the bastard had to pay. His actions had truly been a Judas kiss and his treachery was going to be dealt with through the ultimate punishment.

Michael realised that he had not had anything to eat for well over twenty-four hours and with his headache finally receding he slipped on some clean clothes, mopped up the spilt wine and headed to Le Crêperie Sophie for a quick supper. Michael sat in the small restaurant looking out at the Gallery boardwalk. He was not prepared to give up his reputation, his future with Francesca, his winters in Pra Loup or his long house in Devon in order to gain his pound of flesh; however, the plan he was formulating might just mean he didn't have to if everything went smoothly. He knew he would need to be diligent in his preparations, attention to detail was everything, well almost everything, attention to detail and a little bit of luck and he might just get away with it. Was it really possible, he mused, to get away with murder? As he voiced the words in his head it shocked him. Was he really going to do this, was he even considering this? Could he do this? Then he thought of Francesca, demeaned and bruised and fury swept through every sinew in his body. The bastard would pay.

Chapter Twenty-Eight

Michael finished his supper, swallowed the last mouthful of his coffee and headed home. He needed to sleep and prepare and, if possible, to find his mobile phone. He really wanted to hear Francesca's voice... and see her face. He knew Georgie would not condone what he planned to do but James' vicious act could not go unpunished. If the same thing had happened to Georgie James would have suffered the same consequences whether Georgie approved or not. Michael's father flitted across his consciousness, he almost felt relieved that William was not there to offer counsel or advice because it would not be supportive of Michael's plan. He could hear William's voice in his head talking to him about the sanctity of life and found himself responding under his breath,

"If it had been Mum you wouldn't have sat back, you would have acted Dad," but even as he muttered to himself, he knew it was not true. William believed in doing things right and that meant following the strictures of the law, but in this situation, Michael mused, doing things right was different to doing the right thing and the right thing sat outside of the law. His father was not there, and the responsibility for dealing with what had happened was entirely his own and he could not, would not, let James go unpunished.

When Michael reached the apartment, he opened up his emails and found a reply to his earlier message to Francesca.

Cher Michael,

I am in a difficult place, but my Mother is looking after me. I hope you can find your mobile, but if not, I have put my number below so that you can ring me from another phone. I have left all my ski kit at your apartment and if I feel better, I might want to ski whilst you are away. Can you leave a key for me? You ask what you can do to help. I am not sure there is anything you can do. I need to heal and that will take time. Maybe you could pick me up something expensive and pretty from Paris?

The email finished with a kiss and a winking emoji. Michael read and re-read the email. It certainly didn't read like a technological substitute for a 'Dear John' letter, and he felt slightly encouraged that perhaps all was not lost. He typed a brief reply to Francesca telling her that he would drop the key off at her office and that he would, of course, scour Paris for something that might bring a little smile to her lips. He closed his emails. Now he had to focus on vengeance, on justice.

In the morning, Michael walked down to the gallery and treated himself to a croissant and a coffee for breakfast. He felt vaguely human now and the fact that he knew what he was going to do about James helped him to direct his thoughts and emotions purposefully. He finished eating and walked directly to the tourist office to enquire about his lost phone. He had talked to the receptionist there before; she was a French Canadian and spoke perfect English. She had a soft voice and features to match with wrinkles that rolled into each other smoothed to a velvety sheen by the mountain weather. Her tone and demeanour were calming and reassuring but she did not have any good news for Michael. She advised him to try the police and the office of the resort Director. She explained that that was where the management of the pistes was coordinated and where a pisteur would take the phone if they found it. Michael took her advice but drew a blank at both destinations. He left his details just in case the phone reappeared, but he realised that the chances of being reunited with his phone were pretty much zero. He returned home cursing his carelessness and starting to formulate ideas on implementing his project. The rest of the day was spent planning. The key issue was how he could get over the Channel and back without being detected. He was unlikely to be a suspect if he was not in the country and no one would suspect him of having a motive since Francesca had refused to go to the police. He decided he needed to check that she remained implacable on that issue. No matter how carefully he planned he had no doubt that his guilt would be laid bare if close scrutiny followed, the revelation that such a strong motive existed. He did not want to spend the rest of his days locked up with his reputation in tatters. He wanted to exact his revenge, their revenge, but it had to be the perfect murder, one that left him with a life to lead, a woman to love and mountains to ski. He poured over maps and train schedules and made lists of what he needed to do and to acquire.

He decided to grasp the bull by the horns and emailed Francesca again knowing he was likely to get a frosty response.

Chère Francesca,
I have had no luck finding the phone. I don't know how to deal with James, are you sure you don't want to report him to the police?
Amour et Bisous, Michael x.

The reply was short and to the point,
No Michael and I don't want you to,
Francesca x

Chapter Twenty-Nine

So, there was no alternative, James would pay a heavy price for treachery, for rape and it was down to Michael to exact that price.

It would be an early start given that the conference registration was on Monday afternoon, followed by the opening sessions. Michael had been looking forward to hearing about the most recent research into learning and teaching, but he knew he would be attending very few of the sessions. He began to pack for the trip; passport, trainers, chinos, business shirts, tie, plain black hoody, spare sweatshirt, cap, underwear, black bin bags, medication and an empty rucksack all went into the holdall. He laid out his clothes for the morning, a sports jacket, business shirt, tie, grey flannels and shoes. Then he popped a couple of facemasks in his jacket pocket for use on public transport and elsewhere. These were interesting times, ever since Covid had swept the globe wearing face masks in public had become 'de rigeur' in large cities and on public transport although it was no longer statutory. In 2010, the French government had passed a law aimed at the Muslim community prohibiting people from wearing clothing that covered the face. Later, in the light of Covid-19, they then had had to make face masks mandatory in public places and large towns and cities. They saw no conflict between that decision and the 'burqa ban'. One decision was to promote gender equality and the other to promote public health. The irony was not lost on Michael. Wearing facemasks was now down to personal choice but many still chose to wear them, particularly on public transport.

He had not worn, a jacket, shirt and tie since he retired and getting them out now seemed strange. He had decided to catch the train from Grenoble to Paris – also known as the Train à Grande Vitesse or T.G.V. It would make short work of the journey given that it travelled at three hundred and twenty kilometres – one hundred and ninety-nine miles – per hour. He had considered getting the train from Gap to Grenoble to link up with the T.G.V. but the services were too intermittent and anyway he loved the drive through the mountains. The journey by car from Pra Loup to Grenoble station took a good three hours. Whilst the carpark was linked to the station Michael still felt he should allow forty minutes for parking, buying a ticket and any other contingencies that might occur. The train was due to depart at seventeen minutes past eight in the morning, so Michael set his alarm for four a.m. With the prospect of such an early start, he flopped down on his bed, not expecting to find it easy to sleep given all the plans and emotions that were whirring in his head. In-fact sleep came quickly, perhaps because he was exhausted by the whirling vortex of his feelings, and it was with a start that he awoke from a deep slumber to the sound of his alarm trilling through the darkness. He sat on the edge of the bed for a moment, gathering his thoughts and his resolve, before feeling his way to the bathroom his right-hand fumbling against the wall for the light switch as he went. The harsh fluorescent glow swamped the room and he found himself staring at his reflection in the mirror. The face that stared back was mostly bronzed and only interrupted by a jaw wrapped in grey stubble. Dark rings framed the dull and lifeless eyes. Was this the face of a killer he wondered? He felt absolutely justified in the course of action he was embarking upon but, he considered, was that the same with every murderer? Did they all feel they could justify their actions, some in the most contorted and irrational ways perhaps, but to the individual was it always an act that they could exculpate? What was it Agatha Christie had written in the voice of her famous detective Poirot, "Everyone is a potential murderer-in everyone there arises… the wish to kill – though not the will to kill"? Well he felt that resolve bubbling in his chest.

He splashed his face with cold water, cleaned his teeth and then took his razor to the contours of his chin, after which he packed his wash bag and returned to the bedroom to dress. Michael made himself a cup of coffee which he drowned in milk so that he could drink it quickly. He pulled his ski jacket over his sports jacket, picked up his holdall and double checked that he had everything he would need; iPad, wallet, passport, clothes, trainers, wash-kit, rucksack, conference papers, black hoody, sweatshirt, black plastic bin bags and a cap.

He walked out of the apartment, put his bag in the Volvo, turned on the engine and set the heater to full blast. He left the car with the engine running as he walked down to the Loup Immobilier and popped an envelope with Francesca's name on the front and his keys inside through the letterbox. The resort was silent and the mountains dark. He returned to his car and climbed in. He shrugged off his ski jacket and put it on the passenger seat before reversing out of his parking space and manoeuvring out onto the road. The route down the mountain was deserted and he soon found himself crossing the river at Barcelonnette and turning towards Gap. He put his Spotify playlist on, and the car was filled with the sounds of eighties hits as he twisted his way through the mountains and travelled through the villages along the valley floor. Michael skirted Gap and drove on towards Grenoble, dropping down to his destination just as a beautiful sunrise sprung from behind the mountains. The light of the new day contrasted sharply with the darkness he felt in his soul. A darkness he hoped would dissipate once he had extracted his revenge on James.

Grenoble station was only a short distance from the A480 and Michael drove directly to the 'Parking Grenoble Alpes', passing the front of the station. It was an imposing sight. A wide pedestrian precinct sat in front of an extensive glass facade which was only interrupted by a block of pale stonework at one end that carried a huge clock face. The pedestrian area was only punctuated by a huge cast iron installation; three intertwining triangles which melded together and rested with one point from each triangle on the ground. The French seemed to have a great love of such abstract statues. On his journeys to the mountains, Michael was always struck by the huge paperclip structure that reached skyward next to the auto-route. He had no idea as to the significance of the triangular sculpture and shifted his focus to the carpark. He swung into the entrance and took a ticket at the barrier. He scanned the tariff board and realised that the parking was going to cost him in excess of one hundred and thirty euros – not much less than the return ticket to Paris he reflected ruefully. He parked his car, pulled on his ski jacket and scooped up his holdall before walking through the concourse and into the station. He spotted a ticket machine, inserted his credit card and paid the eighty-five euros for the journey to Paris. The machine chuntered his ticket from the slot, Michael took it and walked to read the board detailing the departures and their platforms. He walked towards Platform E to wait. He headed for an empty bench on the platform, only making a short detour enroute to make use of a coffee machine. With a double espresso in his hand, he sat on the bench and sipped at his coffee. In broad daylight, he was riven with doubt about what he was planning to undertake. If he was unlucky there was a real chance that he would spend the rest of his life in prison. Even the best-laid plans could be driven off course by circumstances. Events that could not be predicted, even with the most diligent planning and careful consideration, could sweep away his tenuous control of the situation and destroy the remnants of a life that he was struggling to hold together. Then Francesca's tear-stained face and red rimmed eyes would resurface in his brain and a wave of anger would galvanise him and strengthen his resolve.

Chapter Thirty

He was jolted from his cheerless reverie by the voice on the public address system announcing the arrival of his train. The sleek silver serpent of the T.G.V swept into the station. Michael slipped on a facemask and climbed aboard storing his bag and ski jacket in the overhead luggage compartment. He was relieved to find that all the seats faced forwards in pairs and that the seat next to his was empty. He had always found it deeply irritating when travelling on the train from Devon to London that so many people tried to keep two seats to themselves by putting their bags on the spare seat or sprawling across both seats. It wasn't so bad if the train was empty but unfortunately even when the train was packed the Great British public pulled the same tricks. He remembered a time when the train had been bursting at the seams and he had completely lost his temper with an older woman who had spread herself across two seats. As if to underline the permanency of her position, she had removed her shoes so that her knobbly sweating feet sat on the armrest and protruded into the aisle. He had decided to challenge her, rather than be the typical 'Brit' and do anything to avoid confrontation and had asked her politely to move. She had refused and the polite request had soon turned into a shouting match. It was not one of Michael's proudest moments, or memories, and it had ended with the guard showing him to a seat in another carriage.

He slumped into his seat and the movement of the train and his early start soon overcame the turbulence in his mind, and he fell fast asleep. He was vaguely aware of the train pulling into Lyon St. Exupery, but only awoke fully at Maçon when the guard asked for his ticket. At this point, he decided to take the opportunity to have some breakfast in the buffet coach which was two carriages along from his. He bought a cappuccino and a ham and cheese baguette. He ate his breakfast standing at one of the kidney shaped islands in the middle of the coach, next to a couple of French businessmen who poured over a laptop whilst they drank their coffee. Michael admired their tailored suits and noted that their shirts were open at the collar. They certainly cut dashing figures and he became rather self-conscious about the tie at his neck which he felt clearly marked him out as an English man. Michael felt a little lost without his mobile, he couldn't look at news articles or text Francesca, but he decided he would not replace it just yet. He had watched too many American crime series where the perpetrator was caught because the FBI or CIA or NYPD located their whereabouts through pinging their mobile phones. He had no idea whether it was really possible to do that, but it did not seem worth the risk. He could survive without a mobile for a few days. After the breakfast, and some sleep, Michael was ready for the day ahead. He looked at his watch and noted that it was just past eleven o'clock. He made his way back to his seat and pulled down his holdall and coat from the overhead storage in preparation for exiting the train. The voice on the public address system announced that the train would soon be arriving at Le Gare de Lyon. As the train slowed and pulled into the station Michael's eyes flicked down to his watch again. It was eleven sixteen. He wondered how was it that trains on the continent could travel hundreds of miles and arrive on schedule and yet in the UK the trains couldn't get from Newton Abbot to Exeter on time. The train shuddered slightly as it came to a standstill. Michael walked to the door, which had opened automatically and stepped out onto the platform. He was immediately faced with hundreds of people moving purposefully along the platforms. He followed the flow down to the main concourse. The sound of music reverberated around the cavernous space, playing as a backing track to the general hubbub. He walked through the station to the Metro and saw the source of the music – a jazz quartet playing on a temporary stage in front of the Montreux Jazz Café. The café announced its existence in an iridescent pink and was framed by the intricate wrought iron work of two staircases that led from each side up to a balcony and the entrance to the famous Le Train Bleu restaurant on the first floor. Michael stood and gazed up at the restaurant, glimpsing its ornate interior. He had completely forgotten that it was here. The restaurant had been built in 1900, at the same time as the station, for the World's Fair and had been opened by the President; Emile Loufet. However, for Michael its interest was that the restaurant had been named Le Train Bleu in 1963 in honour of the Paris Vintimille line and the legendary train that served towns on the French Riviera. It was the train that had been the setting for Agatha Christie's book 'The Mystery of the Blue Train'. The Belgian detective Poirot solved what appeared to be the unfathomable murder of an heiress on the train. Michael hoped that this was not a bad omen and that no such detective would be hunting him down! Mr Bean's holiday had been filmed here and he certainly would prefer the competence of a Mr Bean to a Monsieur Poirot. He continued his path to the Metro entrance, stopping only briefly to withdraw one thousand five hundred euros in three separate transactions from a cash machine. He descended to the underground station and purchased a ticket from the machine. He then followed the signs to line fourteen and trains travelling in the direction of Saint Lazare. The station was vast with great orange beams above supported by round fluted metal columns that were painted a glossy yellow. The platform was incredibly wide compared to any underground station Michael had ever experienced and he wondered why that was. He did not have to wait long for a train to arrive and he noted that, just like the Docklands Light Railway in London, there was no driver and the system was automated. The turquoise and white carriages were separated from the passengers by a transparent screen of glass. Sections of the screen in line with the train doors slid back when the train was stationary. Michael stepped through and boarded the light, bright, clean train enjoying his anonymity in this metropolis. Surely, no fellow passenger could see beyond his bland exterior to the tortured soul beneath or read in his eyes his dark intentions. He sat down only briefly, as he had to change at the next station; Châtelet, Châtelet was less sophisticated and more reminiscent of a London tube station than the Gare de Lyon. No glass screens were in evidence. Michael walked through to line fourteen and caught the next train to Château d'Eau. He emerged from the metro and walked the few metres to the Hôtel Liège Strasbourg where he had booked to stay.

Chapter Thirty-One

All the rooms at the hotel hosting the conference had been taken so Michael had used Booking.com to find himself a decent hotel nearby. The hotel appeared to his left. From the kerbside it looked very impressive with its seven storeys delineated by intricate black railings that ran around the balconies and across the lower portions of the windows. The stone frontage was decorated with geometric designs and neo-classical pillars built into the walls. Michael entered the lobby and was struck by the contrast between the elegant plasterwork on the ceilings and walls, belying the building's history, and the very modern plastic and veneered functional furnishings. A very pleasant young woman checked him in, taking a photograph of his passport before handing him his key. She explained where to go for breakfast, how to find the gymnasium, where to find the lift or the stairs depending on his preference. Despite his room being on the fourth floor Michael decided to take the stairs. He had a definite aversion to small spaces, especially lifts. He stood at the bottom of the stairs and looked up through the void that revealed their full elongated, spiralling height. He smiled; Georgie would be impressed at all of the steps he would be doing! By the time he reached his room he was a little breathless *but not too bad for an old man* he thought sardonically. In his room he shed his ski jacket and unpacked his holdall transferring the conference papers, his black hoody, sweatshirt, cap, trainers, bin bags and face masks into the rucksack. He perched on the side of the bed and turned on the iPad. He flicked through to his emails and found Francesca's mobile number. He pressed three for an outside line on the bedside phone and then punched in her number. He listened as her phone rang several times, but she did not answer. The phone clicked to voicemail and he heard Francesca's voice

"C'est Francesca, laissez un message."

Michael had not expected that and stumbled out a few words. "Hi, it's me. I've arrived at the conference. Hope you are okay. Email me if you need anything." He put the phone down, then he stood up from the bed, slung the bag over his shoulder and headed back downstairs. The conference was being held a few hundred metres up the road at the Hotel Rocroy which boasted extensive meeting and lecture facilities. Registration was from mid-day onwards and the opening address would be at two in the afternoon. Michael was keen to register as early as possible. He wanted to network and be seen by people who would remember he was there. The opening lecture was being given by an English Professor from Bristol University who Michael knew quite well and who had quoted some of Michael's observations on educational leadership in a recently published book. Michael wanted to be sure to speak to him and ensure his presence was noted. He reached the conference hotel at just after one and walked into the beautiful Parisian building to register. Luck was on his side; Professor Ed Powell was standing with a group of colleagues just to the side of the registration desk and saw Michael immediately.

"Michael," he called across the foyer, "How are you? I saw your name on the delegate list. It is great to see you."

"Hi Ed. I'm good. Fresh from skiing in the Alps and looking forward to you stirring my little grey cells."

Michael signed in and Ed ushered him over to join the group

of English academics he had been talking to and introduced Michael to each one in turn.

"Are you here for the whole conference Ed?" Michael asked.

"No unfortunately not. I am just here this afternoon and then I'm back in Bristol. I have to attend a big funding meeting, which will be a complete bore." Ed responded.

"That's a shame," Michael lied. He was relieved that Ed was going as he would have been bound to want to dine with Michael at some point and that would have been tricky. "I had hoped we would have been able to have supper together one evening. Never mind, maybe another time."

The conference coordinator moved to Ed's side and told him it was time for him to go through for the last-minute checks before his lecture. Ed shook Michael's hand and disappeared into the conference room. Michael continued chatting with the group, a couple of whom were due to be presenting papers later in the week. Just before two o'clock the double door to the conference rooms were opened and the assembled throng were ushered through to take their seats.

Professor Powell was introduced by the coordinator and he launched into his talk which focussed on how school leaders should lead and embed 'learning powered' approaches to teaching amongst their governors and staff. Michael tried to listen as Ed always had something interesting to say, but his mind kept wandering to the next step of his plan. His attention returned to the room as the session was thrown open to questions from the floor. Ed answered the final question, rounding off his answer with a sound bite Michael was sure was pre-planned to be the final words of the lecture.

"So, leaders who fail to embed the pedagogy that they believe in will leave no lasting legacy in their schools."

Chapter Thirty-Two

As the applause subsided and the room began to empty Michael picked up his rucksack, slipped out into the foyer and left through the front doors of the hotel. He stopped at the side of the doors under the red awning adorning the front of the hotel. He slid off his jacket, retrieved his black hoody from his rucksack and pulled it over his head. Then he took out his trainers and put them on, stuffing his shoes back into the rucksack. He took a facemask from his jacket pocket and put it on before folding his jacket and pushing it to the bottom of the rucksack. After flicking his hood up over his head, he dragged the rucksack onto his shoulder and set off for the Rue de Chabrol.

When he had first booked the conference, Michael had hoped to spend time wandering around some of the local sightseeing spots. The Sacré Coeur and Montmartre were both nearby. They were a far cry from his current destination as he scurried towards Bricolex; a hardware and do it yourself store. He knew exactly what he needed but felt the pressure of time as his next train journey was at four fifty-nine and it was already four twenty-five. He dashed into the shop keeping his hood up and face mask in place, hoping that in the current situation this would not draw attention to him but rather enable him to maintain anonymity. With a basket in his hand, he scurried round the shop. He wasn't sure whether it was the shortness of time or the nerves and ensuing adrenaline that was driving him to rush so manically. He took a deep breath and slowed his pace. He moved to the tool shelves and picked up; a multi pack of screw drivers, two flat headed and two pozidriv, a pair of short bolt cutters and a short black jemmy. Then he moved on to the decorating section and selected a box of latex decorating gloves. It contained twenty pairs which would be far more than Michael could conceive of needing, but it was better to be safe than sorry. Finally, he moved to the automotive section and selected two twenty litre black plastic fuel cans and a chunky black rubber covered torch. He took his basket to the checkout and paid a disinterested youth forty-six euros. He was grateful that the young man was not unlike many youngsters Michael had taught in the UK – he asked no questions about the purchases and barely managed a grunt at any point during the transaction. He took no interest in his customer and Michael could not imagine he would ever be able to describe him to an interested police officer. Michael put the four euros change in his pocket and the tools and gloves into his rucksack. He took two black bin bags out of the rucksack and put a fuel can in each one. He put the rucksack on his back and carried a bin bag in each hand as he headed for the Gare du Nord Metro Station. He strode quickly along the busy streets noticing little on his way. He knew that if everything worked out, and he wasn't caught, he would have to find a 'high-end jewellers', to pick up something 'pretty and expensive' for Francesca. Now was not the time for such distractions.

He approached the huge edifice of the Gare du Nord. He admired the honeyed stone surrounding the huge arched window above the entrance with its six statues looking down on the travellers below. The graffitied entrance to the Metro sat to the front right of the station. Michael descended the stairs, looking more like a graffiti artist than a conference attendee, and purchased a ticket before heading to the platform of line four which headed towards Mont Rouge town hall and waited for the train. Abstractedly he noticed the small white rectangular tiles that covered the walls arching over the platform and lines. They reminded him of the tiles Georgie had chosen for their kitchen, she had called them 'Metro Tiles'. He boarded the train with his packages and got off after four stops at Revar Sevastapol. He made his way across to line three and took the train for six stops to Saint Lazare. He emerged from this subterranean journey under the futuristic glass dome in front of the west entrance to the station. It looked more like a very grand French château than somewhere to catch a train. He walked through onto the platform and was pleased to see that he had made his destination with fifteen minutes to spare. He approached one of the ticket machines, relieved to see it took cash, and inserted a twenty euro note. He pulled the ticket that popped out, took the change that clattered into the metal well and headed to the waiting train. He found a forward-facing seat near the end of a carriage and stored his rucksack and fuel cans in the overhead rack. His face mask was certainly not out of place and he felt fairly relaxed as he made his way up the train to the buffet bar where he bought himself a beer and a hot dog, or as it was labelled 'un hot dog'. He ate the food and returned to his seat. Now his mind began whirring. The next part of the plan was the tricky bit for so many reasons; firstly he was not an experienced seaman, and yet he intended to cross the busiest stretch of water in the world – mostly at night; secondly he needed to steal a boat without getting caught; thirdly it had to be a boat up to the crossing with a tender so he could get ashore and finally he had to ensure it had sufficient fuel for the job at hand. He was not sure which was the greatest hurdle. Oh, and he needed a bike as well. The train charged on through the darkness. Michael was not keen for the journey to end and he realised it was because he was scared. He was scared of getting caught, he was scared of the sea crossing and more than anything he was scared of killing another human being.

Chapter Thirty-Three

The train arrived one minute late – so much for continental efficiency! Cherbourg station was a squat square modern building which Michael walked through with trepidation. He pulled the iPad out of his rucksack and looked at the route to Port Chantereyne on the map. He had chosen this marina because it was large and busy so it seemed fairly likely that the Harbour Master and his team would not know many of the boat owners personally or know when they were or weren't sailing. Cherbourg also gave him a relatively straight run across the Channel. End to end it would be about one hundred and seventy-five kilometres. Michael put the iPad away and began to walk in the direction of the marina, keeping his eyes peeled for his next potential acquisition. As he came to cross the road in front of the station, he looked back up the road to see if there was any oncoming traffic. There wasn't, but what he did notice was a rack of bicycles against the side wall of the station. He stood and studied the area. There were CCTV cameras at the front of the station entrance, but he could not see any to the side of the building. He turned and walked in a wide arc along the pavement edge and round to the bike rack. He walked the length of the rack. He needed something in good order but with straight handlebars in order to give him some hope of being able to ride whilst grasping the two bin bags. He suddenly realised that someone was approaching the rack from the station entrance. Michael dropped to his knees and pretended to be tying his shoelaces. The stranger stopped, pulled out a key and unlocked a bike to Michael's left. He pulled it out of the rack, bid Michael "Bonsoir" and rode off. Michael let out a long sigh. He put down the bin bags and pulled his rucksack from his back. He pushed his hand inside and rummaged amongst the contents. His fingers located the bolt cutters and he pulled them from the bag. Slowly and nonchalantly, hoping he looked like anyone undoing their bike lock, he moved to the rack. He cut through the cable on a high-end blue and red Peugeot. The seat seemed to be designed to act more like a razor blade than a comfy ride and Michael did not look forward to spending long on the saddle. He gathered his belongings and clumsily pushed off. He hadn't ridden a bike for some time, but even clutching the bin bags he managed to make his way steadily down the road to the marina.

The marina was packed chock full with rows of pleasure craft. Sailing boats were in the majority but there were plenty of motor cruisers, many of them sea-going. Michael propped his bike amongst a small clump of trees and bushes that sat across the road from the row of parking that flanked the marina. He took out his iPad and then stuffed his bags into a gap in the bushes, surveying the marina in front of him. He was relieved to note that the access to the pontoons was straightforward with only a waist high gate in the way – in contrast to the Mayflower Marina, where James moored his boat, in Plymouth where he would have had to scale a security gate that was well above head height and was under the constant scrutiny of its own surveillance camera. It appeared the French were a little more relaxed about security. Armed with his iPad to research the boats that he thought might meet his criteria Michael walked slowly around the marina. He wanted to avoid any boat that was not French as he felt that visiting boats with foreign owners were more likely to have people on board, or be about to be used, so their theft may be more quickly discovered and the authorities alerted. Michael needed a French owned boat that wasn't used too often. It had to be something that was not too high end or ostentatious – he needed to be inconspicuous. Something French owned, perhaps French made, with a decent sized fuel tank. He looked at several boat types moored up and punched their models and names into his iPad. There was a beautiful Princess Five at the end of one of the pontoons. However, whilst that would have made short work of the trip, the Plymouth built boat's specification was far too high end for Michael. He needed something easy to steal and he suspected that, given their reputation, these criteria would rule out a Princess. Michael presumed that the Harbour Master and his team would operate like English marinas and undertake a midnight inspection. He wanted to have located his target by then and have established if it needed more fuel.

He walked down the pontoon furthest from the Harbour Master's offices, it was labelled D dock. At berth thirty-four sat a Beneteau Antares Eight. It displayed a French registration; CH666007. It was a tidy boat, but clearly not new. It had an inflatable tender with oars strapped to the stern. This was a distinct possibility. He typed Beneteau Antares Eight into the iPad and read the specifications and reviews of the boat. The only downside was that with a three hundred litre tank, even if it was full, he would need another sixty litres of fuel to be sure of covering the distance. He turned on his heel and walked back to his bike and bags. He picked up the rucksack and walked back up dock D. He had not wanted to be found mooching around the marina with a crowbar and bolt cutters, but now he had found his boat he needed them. He walked purposefully up to the French built boat which was named 'L'Amour Vrai', pulled a pair of latex gloves from his bag and put them on. Then he climbed up over the bow rail. He made his way around the wheelhouse and the saloon and stood on the rear deck.

"Right," he thought to himself, "This is it. There's no going back now. Stealing a bike is one thing, but a motorboat is quite another."

He pulled the tools and torch out of the rucksack, rested the screwdrivers and bolt cutters quietly on the deck, picked up the crowbar and moved towards the saloon door. It was a sliding door in a plastic frame and opened from the right-hand side of the cabin housing. It would slide to the left behind a built-in seat and storage unit and in front of a similarly formed full-length window. Michael prised the jemmy in between the door and the frame and pulled heavily back. The door cracked open with a splintering sound He picked up his torch, turned it on and stepped forward to slide the door back.

That was much too easy, he thought.

Chapter Thirty-Four

The saloon was quite large and doubled as the wheelhouse. His torch played over an open doorway that led down below. He shielded the torch beam with his hand and examined the cabin more carefully. To the left of the galley entrance were two bench seats, which each converted into a double bed, with a table in between. He eased himself through the door opening and down the two steps where he discovered a large king-sized bed in the bow with an adjoining bathroom. He turned back and began looking for hatches set into the floor. He found one set into the steps in the fore berth. It contained the boat's batteries. The panel of switches to turn on the electrics sat above the bench seat on Michael's left. Once he had ensured all of the switches were in the off position, he flicked the one-marked instruments and then turned the master isolator knob. Other than the yellow beam of his torch, the boat remained in complete darkness. Michael climbed back up into the wheelhouse and played the torch beam over the helmsman's controls. He was interested in one particular gauge. It sat on the left-hand side of the console and Michael let out a sigh of relief as he saw that the arrow on the fuel gauge pointed to full. He returned to the electric panel and turned the switches off again. Then he went back into the wheelhouse and pulled up a further hatch set into the floor. He hoped it would be the engine access, and it was. Michael shone his torch down into the void and immediately spotted what he was looking for - a large red plastic knob sticking out from a black mounting. The 'engine isolator' was within easy reach from his kneeling position on the deck. He didn't turn the knob but left the hatch open for easy access later. Michael walked out onto the rear deck and searched for storage areas. There was an area under the bench seat, but it only contained some spare ropes and cleaning materials. The large hatch in the centre of the deck pulled up on two small hydraulic pistons and revealed what he had been hoping to find – a spare fuel can and a large funnel. He lifted it up onto the deck and realised at once that it was only part full.

"Hmmm," he mused, "That will add to my night's work."

Michael put his rucksack and tools into the wheelhouse, slid the door shut, picked up the fuel can and moved back around to the front of the boat. With one hand on the bow rail, he sprung back onto the dock. Keeping a watch out for prying eyes he walked back down the dock. The marina was very quiet, and he only noticed a couple of boats with lights on, and therefore, presumably inhabited. The next part of his plan was going to be a bit of a slog, but if his research had been worthwhile, it shouldn't present any major problems. Fuel can in hand Michael retraced his steps from earlier and headed towards the station, leaving the dock to his left. He came up to a bridge that spanned the dock, and he broke from the route to the station and crossed the expanse of water. He continued straight along the road opposite the end of the bridge and after about half a mile, he saw the glowing red lights of the Total petrol station.

As he expected the kiosk was closed but the pumps were open twenty-four seven, as advertised, and just as crucially, took cash. He found it odd to pay first, fill up, and then receive your change but it certainly avoided thefts from the garage. He opened the can from the boat and filled it. He managed to squeeze in twelve litres. He took the four euros change from the twenty euro note he had put into the machine, picked up the fuel can and set off back to the marina. The filled can was heavy. He had been right to fill one can at a time because carrying two full cans this sort of distance would have been a real battle and trying to manage one on the bicycle would have been impossible. He took the full can back to his hiding place in the bushes and left it there. He swapped it for one of the empty cans and repeated his journey. It was certainly easier carrying a completely empty can to the petrol station, but the twenty litres of diesel were just as heavy on the way back. Having nearly completed the second-round trip with the second can Michael checked his watch and realised that it was midnight. He could see the marina laid out ahead of him but decided to stop where he was and wait amongst a group of parked cars, some two hundred yards short of the bushes, in order to see if there was a midnight inspection taking place. He put down the can and crouched in the shadow of a Range Rover, surveying the scene. He did not have to wait long for his supposition to be confirmed as accurate. Two uniformed men with long flashlights appeared from the harbour office and made their way methodically around the marina bathing the boats in sweeping swathes of light as they passed. Michael was impressed. They walked up and down every pontoon in turn. They clearly took this part of their job very seriously. The downside was that Michael didn't feel he could move from his vantage point without drawing attention to himself and now that he was no longer carrying petrol cans on a brisk walk, he was getting very cold very quickly. The sweat he had generated was now soaking his back like an icy flannel. He should have brought a coat – his sweatshirt gave him little protection – and, he hoped, he was about to sail across the channel. The midnight rounds lasted until after one a.m. Michael was freezing cold. When the officers disappeared into their warm building, he tried to stand up and nearly cried out in pain. Every area of his body felt stiff. His lower back was like concrete. He picked his way tentatively back to the bushes and swapped the full can for the remaining empty one. As he walked to the Total Station his muscles began to ease and by the time, he had filled the can and was making his way back over the bridge he was feeling more normal. This time he did not make a stop at the bushes but went straight to the boat and put the can on the aft deck. He then retrieved the second can and then the third. He walked back to the bushes for the last time to collect the bike and the two empty bin bags. He rode the bike up the dock feeling completely exhausted by the three forty-minute round trips to get the fuel. He put on a fresh pair of latex gloves and clambered back over the bow of the boat and heaved the bike after him. He gradually manoeuvred around the wheelhouse, holding the bike out in front of him, his back against the boat and the bike suspended over the water.

"Dropping you now could be a disaster," he muttered to his burden.

Finally, he swung the bike round onto the cluttered rear deck and laid it at an angle against the tender which protruded across the stern. Michael took the bin bags and split them down their seams lengthways. He slid open the cabin door and stepped inside. Closing the door behind him, he took the bags and laid them on the bed. He returned to the wheelhouse and took his jacket and iPad from the rucksack. He then went through to the forward berth, set an alarm on the iPad and using the jacket as a pillow and the bin bags to keep him off the bed's actual surface he lay down to sleep. It was very late, and he intended to leave at first light, if not just before, so he needed some rest. His sleep was fitful as he realised that lying on bin bags had major drawbacks. Early on, he woke twice with black plastic stuck to his cheek and neck and on a third occasion shivering uncontrollably. He fetched his spare sweatshirt and put it on under his hoody, then pulled the hood drawstring tightly closed. Finally, he managed a couple of hours uninterrupted sleep.

Chapter Thirty-Five

Michael woke at six am to the buzzing iPad alarm which he quickly switched off. He was parched and had had nothing to drink for hours. Foolishly, he had completely omitted to buy anything to quench his thirst now or on the upcoming crossing. He pushed his way up into the wheelhouse and searched the cupboard in the small galley unit behind the helmsman's seat. The only liquid was two cans of Stella Artois, not quite what Michael had hoped for, but he had no choice. He eased back the ring-pull on one of the cans and took a long swig. What was he coming to? Alcohol before breakfast, mind you he had not brought any food either.

Michael ducked into the forward berth and the electrics control panel. He turned the isolator knob and flicked on the bank of switches, including the running lights. Back in the wheelhouse he reached down through the engine access hatch and turned the engine isolator lever. He shut the engine access hatch and moved his attention to the control panel in front of the helmsman's seat. He pressed the start button and the inboard engine coughed twice and fired into life. He looked carefully at the AIS, the Automatic Identification System, that sat on top of the console. He knew there were essentially two systems, one that would transmit the boat's position as well as receive information to identify the position of other boats, and one that just received. Michael thought that on a boat of this size and specification it would be a receiver only. If it wasn't, he could just break the aerial so it did neither, because he certainly didn't want the boat's position to be tracked. He needed to know because breaking the aerial was a last resort. He would prefer to know if other boats were close by in the dark, hitting a ferry or a fishing boat was not part of his plan. He turned on his iPad, plugged its charger into the port on the console and uploaded the marine traffic website. He then searched his location and to his huge relief discovered there was no signal showing. He decided to leave the iPad on the website for a few minutes just to make sure there was no lag and the boat's signal didn't suddenly appear. He now moved to the bow and released the ropes tying the boat to the dock. After that he returned to the cabin and sat in the helmsman's seat and took up the VHF radio microphone. He checked that the radio was tuned to channel nine, which was the frequency used by the port authorities. Now was the real test of his French accent. He hoped the reception was not too good and would help to mask his Anglo-Saxon tones.

"Chantereyne, Chantereyne c'est L'Amour Vrai du yacht qui quitte le quai D couchette trente quatre." Michael took a deep breath and awaited a reply. The radio receiver crackled, and a French voice burst into the cabin,

"L'Amour Vrai, L'Amour Vrai, c'est Chantereyne, au revoir, bonne journée et a bientôt."

Michael set the microphone down on the console and put the boat's engine into reverse. The boat pulled gently back from the quay. Then he pushed the gears into forward and turned the wheel hard to the right, pointing the boat towards the marina exit. His was the only boat moving in the marina, but he knew that as soon as he left its confines he would be in a very busy waterway. Many of the fishing boats would be sailing now at first light and the Brittainy Ferries', Mont St. Michel, would be coming into the port just after six thirty. On top of that, there was the possibility of the French Navy, who had a base at Cherbourg, adding to the mêlée. Sailing at such a busy time was a considered choice as Michael felt he would be less noticeable amongst a throng of other boats and he could follow them out of the harbour, which would be very helpful as he had no idea about the route vessels were supposed to take!

L'Amour Vrai emerged from the marina and Michael tucked her in behind a small fishing trawler that looked like it was heading for sea. The trawler was not travelling quickly, and Michael assumed that there must be some sort of speed limit within the outer walls of the harbour. The sea here was flat and oily black. Michael hoped that the crossing would be blessed with calm seas as he really didn't have anything approaching 'sea-legs'. He checked the iPad again and was reassured that L'Amour Vrai had not appeared. He closed the website and brought up Google Maps which he intended to use to navigate his way across the channel. He suspected using his iPad as a navigation tool would mean he would have to get rid of it at a later date as he didn't want some clever tech savvy policeman tracking his movements through it after the event. As he passed through the outer wall the light of 'Fort de Chavagnac' shone out on his left. He felt a change in the motion of the sea, noting the gentle swell that was now under the boat. He intended to take a direct route across The English Channel and head for Salcombe before finally working his way round to Bantham Bay, his intended destination. He pushed the throttle forward and pulled away from the fishing vessel's wake and headed roughly north east on the boat's compass. Dawn was winning the battle for supremacy over the darkness and a sullen grey sky began to reveal itself. According to the information he had read about the

Beneteau Antares Eight online it was most fuel efficient when travelling at just over twenty knots. Michael reckoned that if he cruised at twenty-two knots, about forty kilometres per hour, he should be able to make the crossing in under five hours. The swell was slight and the wind gentle, so in terms of a Channel crossing he was lucky. He checked the AIS regularly for other craft and continually scanned the horizon. There were a number of fishing vessels out, but they seemed to be peeling away further to the east. There were a few vessels on the AIS that were travelling east to west or west to east further out in the Channel. As he pushed on, he studied his iPad, trying to work out whether he was heading in the right direction or whether he needed to adjust his trajectory. He soon became aware that taking his eyes off the horizon to look at the AIS or the iPad was having a definite effect on his digestive system. He resolved to keep his eyes on the horizon as much as possible and to only glimpse at the instruments occasionally. This was going to be a long haul and the nausea that was beginning to announce itself was not a good portent. He was still thirsty, but he worried about drinking any more lager in his current state.

Looking at the iPad, he altered his course to a slightly more westerly direction. Michael looked astern and was surprised to find that France was already out of sight, he wondered how long it would be before he could see the English shoreline. He knew he would feel much more confident when that was the case. L'Amour Vrai cut its course through the grey water, throwing out a spray from its bows and leaving a foamy turbulence in its wake.

As the boat ploughed on into the morning Michael realised that he was going to have to surrender to the growing nausea that was clawing at the back of his throat. He turned, released the wheel and dashed out onto the deck. He urged in a long rocking belch over the side of the boat, but only a splash of larger mixed with bile appeared in his mouth. He spat it out down wind and urged again. He felt as if his throat was trying to rip itself out. More lager bubbled up and he vomited over the side. He felt a little relief and knew he had to grab the moment and keep the boat on course. He returned to the wheel and checked the slight turn the boat had taken in his absence. He took a sip of lager and swilled it round his mouth and swallowed it, the taste of the alcohol replacing the acid protestations in his throat. He settled into his chair and kept his eyes fixed on the horizon... was that a smudge of land, or was he just fooling himself?

Chapter Thirty-Six

The hours passed and the closer the L'Amour Vrai came to England the flatter the seas became. The nausea gradually subsided and Michael focussed his attention on the coastline ahead and his Google Map. The AIS had served him well and he had managed to avoid any close encounters with other vessels. His next goal was to spot Salcombe and turn left, from there on in he was going to be in familiar territory, it was a stretch of the coastline he had cruised frequently with James and Tim. He was probably a mile offshore when, according to Google Maps, Salcombe should be directly ahead, and there it was the inlet to Salcombe. He closed to within eight hundred yards of the coastline and turned east. He was soon cruising past Hope Cove, South Milton and Thurlestone, beaches that had all been favourite stomping grounds for him and Georgie. As he passed Thurlestone he could see the golf course on the cliff tops and ahead Burgh Island came into view as Bantham Bay opened up to his right. Michael brought the boat in under the lee of Burgh Island and dropped the anchor. When it hit the bottom, he let out another three metres of cable to allow for the rise of the water level with the tide. Without looking at any charts, he could see that it was low tide as the sandy causeway between Bigbury on Sea and the island was completely revealed. The 'Sea Tractor', which took visitors across to the Hotel at Burgh Island when the tide was in and the island entirely cut off by the sea, was parked on the sand at the bottom of the slipway leading up onto the island.

The tractor had four huge wheels several feet above which sat a large platform with open fenced sides. The engine was caged in the middle of the platform and there was room around the cage for the passengers. It had been built in 1969, having been designed by Robert Jackson in exchange for a case of champagne. Michael had always found the story quite charming. The hotel stood out, chalky white against the grey day, its art deco lines contrasting with the rugged contours of the island on which it sat. It had been refurbished in the last few years and its art deco exterior was in tune with its beautifully preserved interior. Michael and Georgie had celebrated their twenty fifth wedding anniversary here, enjoying cocktails before dinner amid the nineteen thirties glamour, wonderful food and an afternoon swimming in the secluded lagoon. It was a special place. It had been one of Georgie's final wishes to walk to the top of the island and look at the breath-taking views. She had been very weak when they had last come here. They had travelled across to the island on the tractor and begun walking up to the peak in the island's centre. It had soon become clear that Georgie wasn't strong enough to complete the walk and Michael had lifted her wasted body and carried her up the final hundred yards. Standing on the L'Amour Vrai he could still see her face as he held her in his arms, her skin almost translucent in the sunshine and stretched tight across her cheek bones. They had stood and looked out at the bay, the sea undulating in its eternal motion. Georgie had seemed to take some comfort from the thought that the sea would still sweep back and forth long after she was gone and by being there she was part of a timeless landscape.

Michael looked up to the top of the island where he and Georgie had stood; he missed her so much. He smiled wryly as he remembered that this was also the setting for two of Agatha

Christie's novels and that 'Evil Under the Sun' had been filmed here with David Suchet playing Poirot. Poirot was becoming a constant feature of this trip, but that was hardly surprising given that so many of Christie's stories were set in South Devon; Galmpton, Dittisham, Torquay, Dartmoor, Dartmouth and of course her summer house was Greenway. Michael hoped that he was not leaving any clues for a modern-day Poirot to follow, but knew that in reality, and with modern science, the perfect murder was almost an impossibility.

Chapter Thirty-Seven

He checked the fuel gauge before turning off the engine – there were about a hundred and twenty-five litres left. He reckoned that, even with the sixty litres he had in his spare cans, it was going to be touch and go as to whether he could complete the return journey. He moved to the stern of the boat and, using two of the flat headed screw drivers, he twisted open the cap to the fuel tank. He carefully poured each of the fuel cans down through the funnel he had placed in the throat of the fuel pipe. He couldn't afford to waste a drop. Having poured all the diesel into the tank he gathered up his rucksack and belongings, he would leave his sports jacket, plastic bin bags, shoes and fuel cans on board and moved to unfasten the tender. With the tender in the water, he placed the oars in its bottom, alongside the rucksack, and then dragged the bike over the stern of the L'Amour Vrai and balanced it across the bow of the small inflatable. He clambered in, slipped on a facemask, pulled his hood up, placed the oars into the rowlocks and carefully rowed towards the shore. He kept a very close eye on the precariously stored bike the entire time.

Eventually he reached the shore and waded the final few steps through the shallows, pulling the tender onto the sand. He wheeled the bike up to the foot of the slipway that was tucked into the far corner of the beach. He left it there and returned to the inflatable. He towed it up to the base of the low cliffs. He made sure he pulled it up between the rocks, well above the high tide mark and reasonably hidden from sight. The last thing he needed was for it to be stolen, that really would complicate matters. Looking up and down the beach, he could only see a few dog walkers meandering across the sand. Michael slung his rucksack onto his back and pushed his bike up the slipway. Then, with one foot on the left-hand pedal he scooted on the other foot three times before swinging his leg out, over the rear wheel and down onto the right-hand pedal. Almost immediately, he was forced to try and work out how the gears functioned as he faced the long steep hill out of Bigbury on Sea towards the golf club.

It was nearly two o'clock as he left the village and struggled up the hill. He had hoped that skiing all winter would mean that the ride would be less challenging, but the hills of Devon soon made a mockery of that idea. He had read about the benefits of training and living at altitude and how it could improve athletic performance by one or two percent. However, those benefits were only found amongst elite athletes and not the general population. Apparently as elite athletes acclimatised to high altitude their number of red blood cells increased which meant that their blood could carry more oxygen. He did have to admit that he was a long way from being an elite athlete!

After nearly three miles of the ride, and one rather enjoyable free wheel down from the beautiful Bigbury golf course which skirted the cliffs and boasted spectacular views out to sea as well as a challenging course and manicured greens, Michael arrived at St Anne's Chapel and gave a sigh of relief to see that the village store was open. He got off his bike and leant it against the shop wall to the right of the front window. Hollywell Stores was a godsend. He walked in, keeping his head tilted down away from the shop's CCTV. He picked up a wire basket at the door and navigated the store, picking up four five hundred-millilitre bottles of water, a bar of Cadbury's dairy milk, two pasties, a sausage roll, a small white loaf and a pack of butter. He went to the till and paid cash for his purchases. His appearance stimulated a raised eyebrow but, in true British style, no comment. He stuffed all the goods into his rucksack apart from one bottle of water and the bar of chocolate. He stood outside the shop and gulped down the entire bottle with hardly a pause for breath, the cold water rehydrating his desert like mouth and swilling around his stale plaque coated teeth. With his thirst sated, he tore open the chocolate bar and devoured it ravenously. The immediate sugar hit re-energised him and he climbed back onto the bike with renewed vigour.

Chapter Thirty-Eight

The light was disappearing as Michael concluded his journey and his long house finally came into view. It was at that moment that the realisation struck him like a stone dropping through his consciousness that he had left his house keys in Pra Loup! He had been looking forward to having a hot bath since dawn and he was so tired that he sobbed in utter frustration. After a moment, he shook himself, struggling to regain control of his frayed emotions and of his current predicament. Stay calm, think logically he told himself. He wheeled the bike in through the gate and around the side of the house and out of sight of anyone walking past. He leant it up against the utility room's external wall. This was the best window to break, he thought, if he had to break one and it now seemed inevitable that he would have to. The panes here were small and there were six to a window. By breaking just one he would be able to reach in and undo the latch, lift the stay and clamber in. His neighbours were far enough away that they were very unlikely to hear the breaking glass and it was lucky that he had come equipped to break in! Michael took the jemmy from his bag and gave the window a short sharp blow in the bottom corner. With a splintering crack the glass shattered and fell inward onto the windowsill. Michael slid his hand through the gap and opened the window. He eased himself in and scrambled over the work surface and down onto the utility floor. He sighed with relief, waves of tension seeming to evaporate from his body with his exhaling breath, before turning to pull the window shut. He took the torch from the rucksack and switched it on. The one thing that would definitely give away his presence was electric light spilling through his windows. He had left the heating on the timer for an hour each evening to prevent burst pipes whilst he was away so he felt confident that turning on the hot water and heating now would not attract any attention, as the steam from the flue was a daily occurrence. He walked through to the kitchen and emptied his bag onto the table. He put the two pastries, butter and sausage roll in the fridge and the latex gloves, tools, remaining bin bags, iPad and bread he left in a heap on the table. He took off his trainers and popped them into the tumble drier. Georgie had always told him off for drying his trainers like this, but he had always found it a far more effective method than stuffing them with newspaper and putting them on a radiator. He stripped off his clothes, emptied his pockets and put them all in the washing machine. He wasn't sure that his shirt could ever be worn in company again as it had large sweat stains that betrayed his activities of the past twenty-four hours. He popped up to his bedroom and pulled on his dressing gown before lying on his bed and dozing whilst he waited for the water to heat up. He wanted to watch the television, but he was worried that the activity on his Sky account could be monitored in some way. He knew that if the television wasn't used for thirty days his Sky Go stopped working in France. That had proved to be a good way of monitoring that James was checking in on the house at least monthly. Michael supposed that it was possible that James could make a visit that evening to make sure the house was okay. That would present certain problems because Michael did not want a body found anywhere near his home. He didn't want anything to stimulate the police to look in his direction at all.

Torch in hand he walked through to the bathroom and ran

the hot water tap. It ran cold for a minute and then, finally, hot water began to splash into the bath disturbing the fine film of dust that had settled on the ceramic surface during the months of Michael's absence. Whilst the bath ran Michael shaved at the sink before plunging into the deep steaming water. He lay in the bath's embrace, allowing the strains of the past day to soak away. Eventually he washed his hair and climbed out of the bath. He enjoyed the rough texture of the towel as it excoriated his skin. Georgie had always washed their towels with conditioner but since losing her, he had discovered the joys of a rough towel on his flesh; it was refreshing but hardly a silver lining to losing her.

Michael pulled on clean pyjamas and went downstairs to heat one of the pasties in the oven and warm a tin of beans from the cupboard on the hob. He ate his meal, complimented by a glass of water and a hot Bovril, and then took his iPad and a large brandy up to his bedroom. He put the iPad on charge in the socket next to the bed. He checked his emails to see that Francesca had sent a brief reply to his earlier phone message.

Cher Michael, All I need from you is something nice from a Parisian jeweller. Enjoy the conference, see you on Saturday. Francesca xx

Michael smiled to himself, that message was clear, and then hunkered down to watch YouTube highlights of Botham's greatest matches. His mind wandered. He loved his skiing, but he could not imagine a summer without cricket. He had enjoyed hot holidays with Georgie, where they had lain by the pool sunbathing and reading during the day and eaten at local seafood restaurants in the evening for an entire week but the thought of a whole month of that just didn't seem like fun. He had been so lucky with Georgie. She had not been a huge cricket fan, but she tolerated it with a smile and, before Taunton Deane had paid caterers to provide teas and then COVID had removed them all together, she had regularly toiled to provide wonderful spreads on a Saturday afternoon. When he had been playing, and she was not there, she had been genuinely interested in how he had played, how many runs he had scored or catches he had taken. If he was to pursue this life with Francesca it would be very different. He stopped himself and wondered where the 'if' had come from. It seemed to have bubbled up from his sub-conscious without invitation at what seemed like an incredibly inopportune moment. Michael decided to park the thought. He would examine that issue once he had dealt with James. James had to pay; for what he had done to her, for the humiliation he had caused, for the betrayal of their friendship and, Michael reflected, someone like that should be nowhere near schools or children. Michael put the iPad down on the bedside table; he really needed to sleep and the following day he would need to ensure every detail of his plan was in place.

Chapter Thirty-Nine

Michael awoke in the morning with a great sense of foreboding about what the day had in store for him. He was sure that he had remembered James talking about being at the Vines' appeal hearing this morning, which should mean that he would be back in school later on in the afternoon to lead the Senior Management Team meeting which always took place on a Wednesday from 4 p.m. to 6 p.m. Michael's plan was to be in the woods by the car park where James always parked – which was helpfully a couple of hundred yards away from any buildings – well before six. The wood had a public footpath running through it which was occasionally frequented by dog walkers but after dark he expected it to be deserted. If, by some chance, James did not return for the meeting Michael would have to go to James' flat which would make things very complicated.

He washed and went downstairs to make himself several rounds of toast and butter. He made a black instant coffee to which he added two teaspoons of sugar to make it vaguely palatable. Whilst he waited for the toast to 'pop', he searched through the kitchen implement drawer and found what he was looking for, their old carving knife. It was a knife that he and Georgie had had for years but that had been superseded when they bought themselves an entire new set of kitchen knives at the Devon County Show. They had watched a demonstration by a very convincing and committed gentleman who was able to get the knives to cut almost anything, and despite their misgivings about buying form such stalls they had bought them. It had actually been a good decision which they had not had cause to regret. He took the old knife in his hand and inspected it. The maker's information was stamped on the blade 'stainless steel, twenty-five-year guarantee Taylor's Eye Witness'. The irony of the name was not lost on Michael and he sincerely hoped that the knife would be the only witness at the scene. The blade was rather blunt and one of his father's sayings came to mind, 'You could ride bare-back to Scotland on that'. He was sure it needed sharpening. He ate his toast, finished his coffee, got dressed and took the knife and his pile of tools from the rucksack out to his 'man-cave'. He wiped down the tools with white spirit to ensure that they bore no clues as to how they had been deployed and was about to put them all away on the shelf when his eye caught sight of the petrol can he used to store the fuel for the lawn mower.

"Hmmm," he muttered to himself, "I think you are coming with me on a little trip."

He put all the tools away apart from the two screwdrivers which he would need to open the fuel tank of the boat. The can only held five litres but that extra five litres might just be what was needed to ensure the successful completion of his journey and he could fit the can into his rucksack. He stepped outside with the can and poured away the remaining unleaded petrol that it contained. Then he went back into the shed and sharpened the carving knife on his grinding wheel. After running the blade up and down the spinning stone for a couple of minutes, he pulled it away and flicked his thumb over the ground edge. It was razor sharp and ideal for the task ahead. He took it back into the house and wiped it clean with a tissue to prevent fingerprints before wrapping it in a carrier bag and putting it in the rucksack. He spent the rest of the morning finishing his laundry and checking train times from Cherbourg to Saint Lazare. He ate both his sausage roll and his second pasty for lunch and yearned for some vegetables or fresh fruit. He took another look at the ride to the school. He knew every yard of the route, but he had always driven it, not cycled it. He thought he should probably leave at about three thirty. It wouldn't be a problem if he arrived a little early, but he didn't want to miss James and then have to go to his flat, that only introduced more opportunities for things to go wrong. Michael spent the remaining time in the house packing and preparing to leave. Alongside the knife, which was already packed, he put into his rucksack; a packet of kitchen surface wipes, his cap, the screw drivers, his iPad, the latex gloves, the torch and the fuel can. He dressed, putting on a running base layer rather than his ruined work shirt, his sweatshirt and finally the black hoody went on the top. He pulled on his beautifully dry trainers and took a tour of the house to make sure that, apart from the broken window, there was no sign that he had been there. He checked that the hot water was off and the heating back on the timer. He put on his facemask, pulled up his hood, slung the rucksack on his back and left the house. He wheeled the bike on to the road before mounting it and cycling off, the temperature had dropped considerably and he was immediately thankful for his hood's warmth as well as the anonymity he hoped it would provide. He could ride down the A38 for a short distance and buy the diesel and supplies he needed from the Shell garage, but he felt that any cyclist visiting a petrol station on such a busy main road would hardly go unnoticed and it was literally too close to home. He decided to take the back route via Wrangaton and South Brent. The road took him past the Glazebrook House Hotel which had been the place that he and Georgie had most liked to dine out. They would take any excuse to go to the delightful boutique hotel. The food was fantastic and the interior design of the hotel wonderful, or more accurately a 'wonderland' as the bedrooms were all designed on an Alice in Wonderland theme. Timothy Oulton, the designer, stated that the ground floor reception rooms were created to give, 'a British revival décor with sumptuous handmade furnishings in a beguiling, vintage and retro-curios style'. Michael and Georgie had loved having it almost on their doorstep and despite it being so close had still indulged themselves with overnight stays. All of the eight bedrooms were fabulous, but they preferred to stay in the 'Cheshire Cat'. As Michael cycled past the driveway, he was taken back to intimate evenings and delicious meals shared together. The hotel's owners had decided to retire and close their magical creation just after Georgie had finally lost her battle with cancer. The Glazebrook's doors had closed and one more part of Michael's life had slipped away. He had had something very special with Georgie, he had never really understood how attraction and lust turned to love. He'd had another girlfriend at University before Georgie but whilst the relationship flickered for a moment it hadn't found the oxygen to burn with any real intensity and then Jenny had quit college at the end of the first year and he had let her depart not only her studies but his life without any regrets. With Georgie it was different, the early infatuation and passion melded into a relationship where, at times, Michael felt as if they were just one person. Georgie would hold him when he needed holding, support him when he needed supporting and challenge him when he needed challenging. There were disagreements and arguments, but Georgie always managed to pull positives from any friction and turn the grit into pearls. Her self-confidence and competitiveness wrapped themselves around Michael's shoulders and helped him to achieve far more professionally than he would ever have done on his own. Georgie's love had been the elixir that soothed his very human fear of death and allowed him to relish life. Grief, he felt, was the victory of mortality over joy, its shroud blotting out light and happiness. What he also now knew was that just by thinking about his life with Georgie the warmth and the smiles returned, and the veil of misery could be pulled back. He began to realise that actually he didn't want to 'move on' from Georgie, he wanted her on his shoulder, not in his rear-view mirror. Whilst Francesca was beautiful, and at times great fun to be with, he was coming to realise that at his heart he was a one-woman man. He had a life to lead but he didn't need a partner to lead it with, he already had one and always had. Despite what he was about to do he felt a calmness descend upon him. He didn't want to hurt Francesca, she had been through enough, but this moth needed to gently flutter away from the flame. Deep down he knew too that he was too old for her and she needed someone younger and more exciting, more dynamic.

He cycled through South Brent and up the hill on the other side. This was really hard work and he decided he definitely could not have been Eddy Mercx, he needed to travel up hill in a lift. The high Devon hedges masked much of his view of the countryside and as he reached the rise above the top of Buckfastleigh the light began to fade and Michael became aware of the heavy grey clouds gradually enveloping Dartmoor, they had the glowering look of snow clouds. Snow was not forecast but he was only too aware that whilst the Meteorological Office was only based a few miles up the away at Exeter this was no guarantee of accurate forecasts in its locality. He remembered numerous occasions when parents at the school, who lived nearby, would travel to work at the weather centre, leaving torrential rain at home and yet the 'forecast' would still be reporting sunshine for the area. Perhaps they operated on a higher plane? He took his torch from his bag and held it on his handlebars, as the bike itself had no lights. The darkness made cycling along the Devon lanes much more dangerous, but Michael welcomed the greater anonymity which it gave him. He was going to have to ride through an area where he was known but could not afford to be recognised. He kept his head down and ploughed on.

Chapter Forty

As he approached the school, Michael checked his watch – it was ten minutes past five. He cycled past the front of his former place of work and could not help but take a sidelong glance as he pedalled on. The buildings were flooded with light as the cleaners did their rounds but soon everywhere, except the sports centre, which was open to the public, would be plunged into darkness. Beyond the buildings, Michael turned left away from the road, climbed off his bike and pushed it up the muddy footpath that disappeared between the trees. He walked a further fifty yards before diverting from the path into the trees that shielded the car park from the public right of way. He leant the bike against the trees, screened from the sight of anyone out walking and pushed through the lower branches of the trees to stand on the boundary. A fence of three single wire strands separated the wood from the car park. It was there to mark the division between the school grounds and the local quarry's property across which the footpath ran. It did not provide any deterrent to somebody who wanted to move between the two as you only had to crouch below the top wire and step over the middle wire to pass through. Michael turned off his torch and scanned the carpark for James' car. He was relieved to see the black 2010 Mercedes E class, even though it sat squatly under the glare of one of the six mushroom shaped streetlights that ran the length of the car park. Michael removed the rucksack from his back and pulled out a fresh pair of the latex gloves from it. He put them on, pushed his hand back into the bag and pulled out the plastic bag containing the carving knife. He unfurled the bag and looked at the sharpened knife. He placed the rucksack on the ground by the trunk of a tree some five feet back from the wire. He sat down next to the rucksack, rested his back against the gnarled wood, and placed the knife on the ground to his right-hand side. The damp leaves and woodland floor smelt musty and as he sat there, he became aware of the sound of small beasts and bugs in the undergrowth. They were the only noises to disturb the quiet of the evening. From his vantage point, he had a clear view of the car and also of the entrance to the car park. From here, he would be able to see James' arrival and any of the owners of the other three remaining parked cars, who might disrupt his plans. He stretched out as he was not really expecting James for another hour at least, maybe longer if he went back to his office to work after his meeting. The passing minutes ticked by and Michael found himself checking his watch incessantly, but the hands seemed to be moving obdurately slowly.

"Having time to kill," he mused, "was not good when you have a friend to kill."

The whole situation felt surreal, it was as though he were playing a role in a film or a play. Was he really going to go through with this? He was immersed in a Shakespearian tragedy and, like Macbeth, was riven with doubts. But even Macbeth had managed to complete the deed despite his doubts. The famous lines that he had spent so many hours learning at school tripped through his mind.

'Is this a dagger I see before me,
The handle toward my hand?
Come let me clutch thee.'

He looked down at the carving knife as it lay beside him, very real and lethally sharp. King Duncan had done nothing to deserve being stabbed, James was a different matter and Francesca was no Lady Macbeth. She did not even know his plan and certainly was not exhorting him to commit murder. She wasn't demanding that he 'screw your courage to the sticking place and we'll not fail'. Michael tried to gather himself with Macbeth's words ringing in his ears 'I do all that may become a man; who dares do more is none.'

He felt his resolve ebbing away as the cold night air gnawed at him and a quiver of snowflakes were highlighted by the lamps of the car park as they sashayed their way to the ground, silent but strikingly beautiful. Michael's mind was drawn away from the stark reality of his present situation by the eddies of snow. He remembered a childhood story that told how snowflakes were actually goose feathers plucked by the Old Grey Woman who lived in the sky, she pulled out the feathers and scattered them on the earth below, they delicately fluttered, tumbling, tossing, whirling…

He brought his thoughts abruptly back from the warmth of his childhood to the raw intentions of his adulthood, could he really stick a carving knife into James without giving him a chance to explain himself? Could he hurt him at all? Perhaps he should hold the knife to his throat and make James justify himself and then, when he was sure James had raped Francesca, he would know what to do? Michael's emotions were in turmoil, did he really doubt James' guilt? William's voice ran through Michael's head as a conversation from forty years ago re-emerged, *"and then there was the case of Timothy Evans who was executed for the murder of his wife and child, the jury were convinced, but they were wrong and an innocent man lost his life"*. Who was he to be self-appointed judge, jury and executioner and yet Francesca had been a mess, she had been utterly defiled. She was bruised and red eyed and distraught, and that could not go unpunished… but perhaps the death penalty was just too drastic a solution. Another Agatha Christie line slipped into the forefront of Michael's distressed consciousness, "Every murderer is probably somebody's old friend", but then not every murderer is actually killing their old friend he gulped into the evening gloom. His mind wandered back to the slopes of Pra Loup and the blackboard at the foot of the Courtil lift, what had it said? 'Love all, trust few, do wrong to none'.

As these thoughts were racing in a tumult through his head Michael saw a figure enter the far end of the car park. The figure made straight for the Jaguar parked next to James' car. Michael recognised the figure; the cigarette in his hand gave away his identity – Nick, one of the Assistant Heads. Michael knelt up on his haunches, Nick's presence meant that the senior management meeting must be over. Michael watched as he climbed into his car, flicking the cigarette stub out of the window and onto the ground, switched on the ignition and drove slowly out of the car park waving at another person as he swept out onto the road. The new arrival emerged and walked to the black V.W. Beetle. He thought it must be a new member of staff, as he didn't recognise the woman. Now there were just two cars left in the car park – James' and a grey Citroen parked by the trees near the entrance. Michael hoped his wait would be over soon, but the minutes turned to hours and he felt stiff and cold when, as eight thirty approached, he saw movement. Michael peered across the tarmac and felt a cold chill run down his spine, it was James.

Chapter Forty-One

Michael's grip tightened around the stainless-steel carving knife and he inched forward under the overhanging branches, which he hoped would continue to conceal his presence. James had his phone to his ear and appeared to be speaking. Michael prepared to move out from the tree just as James was approaching his car, but he froze stock still as he noticed a movement in his peripheral vision. He turned and saw another figure walking purposefully across the carpark. Michael groaned silently with frustration. James was not yet in his car but was patting his trouser and jacket pockets with his spare hand clearly, as ever, trying to locate his keys. Michael hoped that it would take him a bit longer to find his keys and perhaps by then the interloper would have left, and Michael could still make his move.

The stranger suddenly turned back, raised his arm and veered towards James. As he did so Michael saw two things in the glare of the overhead lighting and through the flicker of the snowfall – a knife blade glinting and the clearly visible profile of… Vines. What on earth was Vines doing here? Michael watched stunned as Vines' arm swept down a pile-driving stab of a blow to the bottom of James' neck. James crumpled to his knees like an accordion closing, his phone dropping to the ground. Vines stamped on it and then bent to stare into James' eyes before turning and jogging away to climb into the grey Peugeot. He drove at pace out of the car park, and slewed into the road with a screech of tyres. Vines had acted on his threats; he was truly deranged. Michael had not moved. He couldn't comprehend what he had just witnessed. In the next moment, he found himself dropping his own knife and running towards his friend. A few paces brought him to James' side. He looked down into the face of the man he had planned to kill, the man who was his closest friend on the planet, and saw the glazed and bewildered look.

"Michael?" gasped James.

Michael knelt and held James' right shoulder.

"It'll be okay. You'll be okay. I'll get an ambulance," he whispered, but as he was talking James sighed and seemed to shiver. His eyes were no longer bewildered but still and staring into eternity.

Michael stood up and took a pace back lowering James' body to the ground. He didn't know what to feel. Should he be thanking Vines for saving him a job or abhorring him for murdering his friend? What should he do? What could he do? Michael started to walk away from the body then stopped and came back to check James was really gone. The huge pool of blood on the floor and his absolute stillness told their own story. James was truly dead. Michael walked slowly back to the wood and picked up his rucksack and his knife. He put the gleaming unsullied knife back in the plastic bag and stuffed it into the rucksack. He didn't want to leave James here alone in the car park his life blood seeping into the gravel snowflakes settling on his shoulders and in in his black hair, but he had no phone and no explanation as to why he was there.

He felt horribly guilty. He hadn't committed the act, but would he have? If he were to admit to being here, what police officer wouldn't see him as the prime suspect. The evidence told the story; a knife, a stolen boat, a girlfriend who had been raped and a desperate claim that a man he had previously accused of

212

harassment was the killer. He had to leave; Vines was a problem for another day. It would just be too unjust and too cruel if Vines murdered James, but it was Michael who was locked up for the crime. He could not let that happen. Michael could not let Vines win he could not let Vines walk away free but another feeling also began to percolate into Michael's consciousness–the creeping feeling that he himself deserved to go to jail purely for what he had planned to do to his best friend. What kind of a person had he become, perhaps one as heinous as Vines.

Chapter Forty-Two

He fetched the bike and pushed it back along the muddy track and out onto the road. He put on his mask, turned on the torch, mounted the bike and cycled with his head down back towards Bigbury and the boat, the snowstorm gently abated to nothing as he headed for the coast. With every down stroke of the pedal and every yard he travelled away from James, Michael felt the tortuous twistings of grief and guilt strangling him, choking any joy or hope from his soul. He replayed the events in the car park through his mind over and over again. Could he have stopped Vines? Could he have shouted, or dashed out from his hiding place? He almost wanted the answer to be yes because he deserved to wear that knowledge as a hair shirt for the rest of his days; but actually, he had to admit that it was not the case, he was just too far away. The truth was that Vines had stabbed James before Michael had realised what was happening and there was absolutely nothing he could have done in that moment to prevent it. The only consolation was that at least his presence had meant that James's last few seconds on this earth had not been spent alone.

Michael pedalled on, but the hill out of Buckfastleigh was just too much for him so he ended up getting off the bike and walking up the long incline which ran parallel to the A38. As he climbed, he could see the busy road to his left running through the valley floor. He heard the sirens of the emergency services vehicles before he saw the blue flashing lights, but they soon raced into view. Two police cars and an ambulance tore up the dual carriageway from the direction of Plymouth heading, he was in no doubt, for the school. The image of James kneeling, motionless, in a pool of blood flashed into Michael's head. It was an image he wished he could erase but he knew it would be his constant companion and bedfellow. The words of Macbeth invaded his thoughts once more

'Had I died an hour before this chance,

I had lived a blessed time; for, from this instant,

There's nothing serious in mortality;

All is but toys; renown and grace is dead;

The wine of life is drawn'

He wished he had not been so inspired by Mr Walters, his English teacher at school, that he had felt the need to learn so much of the play by rote. He would be happy without the words as a commentary to his current desperate malaise.

As he reached the top of the rise he rode on, needing to be as far away from the murder scene as possible and as soon as possible. The ride seemed interminable and the hills even steeper than they had been earlier in the day as he retraced his route towards Wrangaton before turning left and joining the coast road. Eventually Michael swung down the hill to California Cross where there was a BP garage and shop opposite the pub. Michael planned to stop there to fill his fuel can and buy some food and drink for the journey. If they sold them, he would also buy some sea sickness tablets. The garage shut at 10 p.m. so he would be just in time. He leant his bike against the low wall by the two empty parking bays of the garage, adjusted his facemask (which had slipped down beneath his nose as he was cycling to allow him to breathe more easily) and walked over to the pumps. He pulled the old can from his rucksack and squirted five litres of diesel into it. He secured the screw cap tightly and slid it back into his bag. He entered the shop, picked up a basket and walked around the aisles. It was well stocked, and Michael picked up; a packet of three granny smith apples, three 500ml bottles of diet coke, an egg and cress sandwich, a 200g bar of dairy milk and a large bag of soft liquorice. He also moved across to the vending machine and pressed the button for hot chocolate. The hot chocolate was a welcome bonus and made up for failing to find any sea sickness tablets. The man at the till was grey haired and balding and rested his eyes rather speculatively on Michael's gloved hands. Michael hoped that 'Covid' would save him from anything more than the enquiring look and the curt "good evening". He paid for his shopping and fuel and popped all his goods, except the hot chocolate, into his rucksack. He slung the bag over his left shoulder and carried the hot chocolate in his right hand as he made his way back out onto the forecourt. He stood by the bike and sipped at the hot sweet liquid, enjoying the feeling of its velvety passage down his throat whilst making sure he faced away from the forecourt CCTV. James would never enjoy a drink again, he mulled, and he would never enjoy sitting in The Ship supping a Doom Bar with his friend again. Michael was engulfed by a black cloud whose damp fingers plucked at his very soul. He pulled his mask up, threw the empty cup in the nearby waste bin, remounted his bike and headed on towards Bigbury.

He was sodden with sweat when he finally topped the hill by the golf course and could see the sea below. He freewheeled down the hill and the cold air that rushed past him seemed to freeze his damp clothes to his body. The slope bottomed out and the entrance to the slipway appeared from the gloom, he broke left and rolled gently down it, only stopping as it disappeared into the sand. He laid the bike down and turned his torch towards the base of the cliff. Thankfully, the inflatable was still there. He pulled the tender from its rocky retreat, stuffed the extinguished torch in his pocket and towed the boat down to the water's edge. Although the tide had not fully receded it was well on its way out, certainly it was quite far enough out when one had to drag a boat along the sand to meet the water. Michael then went back for the bike and laid it across the bow. He quickly guided the tender out through the shallows – so much for nice dry trainers! The possibility that James' blood might be on their soles entered Michael's mind and suddenly the dousing in saltwater didn't seem such an imposition. He rowed out to the L'Amour Vrai, whose white outline slowly emerged from the night. She was bobbing unconcernedly on her anchor rope, oblivious to the traumas that had occurred during the day. Michael climbed aboard over the stern and heaved first the bike and then the tender up onto the motor cruiser. He secured the tender and propped the bike against it and the stern. He pulled the fuel can and the screw drivers from the rucksack and set to opening the cap to the fuel tank. He grabbed the funnel from the deck locker by his feet and poured the diesel into the tank. He took his rucksack below deck and put it on the helmsman's seat whilst he ducked into the forward berth and switched on the boat's electrics. He turned on the external lights and the one in the wheelhouse. He stepped back through and took his food supplies, iPad and anti-bacterial wipes from the bag and popped them on top of the console. He pulled out a fresh pair of latex gloves and exchanged them for those he was wearing, which had developed several small tears. He put the rucksack on the bench seat opposite and leant back to press the engine start button. It coughed into life. Michael moved back out of the saloon and navigated his way to the bow where he operated the motor to pull up the anchor cable from its sandy resting place. As soon as it was stowed, he returned to the cabin and manoeuvred the L'Amour Vrai to face back out to sea and pushed the engine throttle forward. As the cruiser butted out of the bay Michael decided not to hug the coastline but to strike out directly for Cherbourg. There was a strong north-westerly wind at his back, which he knew was often the case in the channel in March, and the tide was also with him. He dared to hope that fuel wasn't going to be an issue. He looked at his watch, it was just after midnight. He turned on his iPad and checked the Cherbourg to Saint Lazare train times before he pulled up Google Maps to plot his course. Michael settled into his seat, sipped at the Diet Coke and began to work his way through his provisions, biting into the egg and cress sandwich first. He kept his focus on the inky blackness of the night and on the automatic identification system. He was relieved that the stiff breeze meant that there was no fog but it was bitingly cold. He hoped he would see the lights of the other vessels and or their signatures on the AIS long before they became a danger to him. Despite having to concentrate so hard on sailing, the cruiser James continually invaded his thoughts and guilt gnawed at him. The vision of James dying in front of him would not go away. Macbeth's reaction to Banquo's ghost came to mind

'Thou cans't not say I did it; never shake thy gory locks at me.'

But he hadn't done it and actually he knew now that he would never have done it. Sitting there in the wood watching the snowfall he had realised he could not do it, William's influence had ultimately prevailed, whatever James had done he cared for him too much ever to hurt him. He hadn't known what he was going to do but he had known that he wasn't an executioner, an angry, foolish man definitely, but not a killer. What he had to do now was to find a way of ensuring that Vines was held to account for James' death, but not by Michael. He had no idea how that might be accomplished, he needed to think. In the dark hours of the crossing, Michael began to rationalise what had happened. He didn't forgive himself for how he had behaved but neither did he blame himself for James' death.

Chapter Forty-Two

When he was about an hour from the French coast Michael cut the engine and allowed the boat to wallow in the swell. He had avoided feeling seasick up until that point, but he knew that if he spent very long sitting there, he would become ill. When the boat wasn't underway its motion became irregular and immediately uncomfortable and the impact upon him, he knew, would be unpleasant if he gave it time to take hold. Quickly he took his spare fuel cans and threw them over the side. They bobbed away into the darkness. Then he took the knife out of its carrier bag and tossed it over the side. Finally, he stuffed the black bin bags from the forward berth into the rucksack along with the spare latex gloves, screwdrivers and detritus from his snacks and plunged it all over the side. He had a bottle of Diet Coke and one apple left for the remainder of the voyage. He returned to the cabin and got the boat moving, relieved to be feeling a cessation to the rocking motion. The AIS showed a couple of ships to the east coming towards the L'Amour Vrai so Michael steered slightly to the west of his ideal course and pushed the throttle slightly further forward, bringing the boat's speed up to twenty-six knots and moving it away from the possibility of a close encounter as soon as he judged it to be safe he reduced the speed and returned to his original course as he remained vigilant about the boat's fuel consumption. He looked again at the gauge and felt reassured that he still appeared to have well over a quarter of a tank of diesel left.

The lights of Cherbourg soon appeared on the horizon as he closed in on the French coast. He finished his Diet Coke and, feeling embarrassed about the negative impact on the environment of this crossing, threw the empty bottle and apple core overboard. He closed quickly with the shore and was soon faced with the wall of the outer harbour. He slowed down the vessel to a crawl as he passed into the harbour's embrace. He knew he had to ditch his iPad. Even a cursory viewing of its activities would show exactly what he had been doing as it would detail; boat research, train times, and navigation of the Channel and he was pretty sure the GPS could be tracked too. He took the iPad out onto the deck and held it over the side, letting it slide into the depths. The moment he let it go he realised he had no note of Francesca's mobile number or email. She would not be impressed by absolute silence; she was most definitely a woman who demanded attention but it was too late now, there was nothing he could do to remedy the situation. He stepped back into the wheelhouse and steered for the marina entrance. Michael switched off the running lights and proceeded the rest of the way with the boat in darkness. It was five fifteen local time as he drew into Chantereyne and scoured the nearest pontoons for a spare berth. He did not radio the Harbour Master to announce the L'Amour Vrai's return as he hoped it might go unnoticed at this hour in the morning. Clearly there had not been too many boats toing and froing during his absence as the berth he had vacated, D thirty-four, remained empty, and it was of course, a good distance from the Harbour Master's Office, it was the perfect destination.

He brought the boat in bow first and cut the engines so that it drifted in to gently nestle against the dock. He hurried to the bow and secured the L'Amour Vrai to the jetty, then he returned to the cabin and packed his shoes, cap and jacket into his remaining carrier bag. He took the anti-bacterial wipes and hurriedly cleaned the surfaces. There shouldn't have been any fingerprints, but he wanted to be doubly sure. He turned the isolator switches and electrics off and then took most of his remaining French bank notes from his wallet. He cleaned them with a wipe and placed them on the helmsman's chair. One thousand two hundred and fifty euros, he hoped the boat owner could fill his tank and repair the door without being too much out of pocket. It would be ironic if Michael's attempt to ameliorate the negative impact on the boat's owners led, somehow, to him being apprehended but he couldn't see how it could. His 'Robin Hood' style act of 'generosity' actually made him feel very slightly better about the whole sordid affair, but only very slightly. Michael also harboured the faint hope that the owners might not even bother to report their losses if they weren't out of pocket. He came back out onto the deck and looked towards the Harbour office, nothing seemed to be stirring there. He grappled with the bike and manhandled it onto the dockside. He then fetched the carrier bag and slipped the remaining wipes inside. As he climbed over the low rail and onto the pontoon Michael reflected that whilst this trip had been a pretty shabby affair, at least he could take some pride in having sailed single handed across the Channel. Of course, the person who would have been most impressed was probably lying stone cold in a Devon mortuary.

Michael climbed on the bike, popped on a mask and pulled his hood tight around his face. He cycled slowly down the dock towards the quay. He rode out onto the quayside, turned right and stopped to lift the bike over the low gate onto the path across the park. He allowed himself a second to pat himself on the back for managing to get ashore undetected. A classic pride before a fall moment as he then saw a uniformed figure appear from between two parked cars on his left. He didn't think that the port officer could have seen that he had come from dock D but he certainly didn't want any sort of interface with him. His heart sank as the officer put up his hand and called out for him to stop.

"Monsieur, Monsieur, arretez vous s'il vous plaît."

Michael panicked and put his head down, pushed hard on the pedals and pumping his legs accelerated towards the officer.

"Monsieur arretez vous," the officer shouted again.

Michael rode straight at him and then tried to swerve to the right of the officer at the last moment. The man lunged to his left in an attempt to block Michael's escape. They collided with a sickening crunch and Michael's left shoulder ploughed into his adversary's chest. The officer was thrown backwards and after tripping on the kerb landed heavily on the pavement on his back. Miraculously Michael managed to stay on the bike and righted it as it wobbled further to the right careening across the road as he regained balance and control. He had managed not to fall from the bike but could feel the impact of his shuddering collision with the officer as a sickening pain began spreading through his left shoulder and screaming down his left arm. He glanced back and saw the prostrate figure scrabbling for his radio. Michael turned sharply left through the park and raced across the Place Napoleon and into the built-up area behind. He headed up the Rue d'Eglise and then swung left up the Rue des Moulins to bring him back onto a parallel track to the road towards the station. In the distance he heard, what he presumed to be, police sirens wailing. He knew he needed to get off the major road and swung to his right down the Rue d'Espagne which appeared to narrow into a small alleyway. The alleyway was partially blocked by a large commercial bin with the words 'gaspillage alimentaire uniquement' stencilled on its side. It sat outside the restaurant Grill Pantegruel. Michael braked to a halt next to the bin and dismounted. He threw up the lid with his right arm as his left arm hung throbbing at his side too painful to move. He tried to pull his hoody over his head and almost cried out with the resulting shocking pain. He gritted his teeth and kept tugging at the material, eventually managing to get it over his head and slide it down his immobile arm. The large bin was full of waste food. Michael took the hoody and shoved it deep into the glutinous mass. He opened his carrier bag and pulled the cap from its interior and put it on his head. He took some of the anti-bacterial wipes out and wiped down the handlebars, frame and seat of the bike. He had wanted to return it to the rack from where he had taken it, but the authorities would be looking for a man with a black hoody on a bicycle. The hoody was gone, and it was time to part company with the bike. He hoped it would be reunited with its owner who would have absolutely no idea about the journey it had taken over the past few days.

He walked swiftly on; keeping his eyes peeled for police cars, very aware that there were very few people about as it was barely six a.m. and so he was likely to still attract attention. His shoulder was excruciating and his arm seemed incapable of movement, even walking was almost unbearable. He shambled up Rue au Ble and then the Boulevard Robert Schuman, keeping in close to the buildings in case he needed to find refuge in a doorway. He picked his way towards the station with the pain in his shoulder worsening with every step. At the top of the Boulevard, he turned left and felt a wave of relief as his destination came into view. As he crossed the road to the entrance, a police car came into view travelling slowly in his direction from the vicinity of the marina. He tried to cross the road purposefully without drawing attention to himself. He forced himself not to look back but headed straight for the ticket machine. He purchased his ticket and took the couple of euros change from the machine. This was all he had left from the fifteen hundred euros he had originally withdrawn. His train was due at six fifty-eight; he made the involuntary movement to look at the watch on his left wrist and was met with a graunching wall of pain. He stood still gasping and trying to ride out the waves of agony throbbing from his shoulder. Gradually a degree of equanimity returned, and he glanced up at the station clock. He had cut it fine as the clock read six fifty-four. Michael eased his body the few yards to the edge of Platform B and allowed himself a glance over his right shoulder to check if any members of the gendarmerie were following. Only a couple of men, who looked like construction workers as they were dressed in blue overalls with yellow high visibility vests over the top, came through the entrance to join the scattering of individuals on the platform.

Chapter Forty-Three

Michael was thankful for continental efficiency as the train pulled in a minute early and he clambered on relieved that he had sanctuary at last. Before taking a seat, he stepped into the toilet cubicle at the end of the carriage and caught a glimpse of his face as he stepped towards the toilet bowl. He looked grey and sweat was prickling his forehead. After struggling with his one functioning arm to undo and then do up his trouser zipper to allow him to urinate, he then doused his face with water from the tap. He felt slightly more refreshed and as the train pulled out of the station he walked gingerly through the carriage, taking a seat that allowed his right shoulder to be against the window and to allow his left shoulder some protection from any buffeting from the train's movement. He soon realised this was a vain hope. He had had some aspiration to find some respite from his rasping distress in sleep, but he struggled to find a comfortable position and was continually wrestling with his posture. When he did finally doze off, he was almost instantly awoken by the guard checking tickets and that left him fully conscious for the remaining hour of the journey. He could not blank out the pain and found himself bending forward and breathing heavily as every bump and vibration of the journey shocked through him. The pain was so overpowering and all-consuming that Michael could only think about getting to a hospital, his physical distress completely overwhelming the turmoil of his emotions.

Finally, after the most physically excruciating three and a

half hours of Michael's life, the train pulled into the station at Gare Saint Lazare. He heaved himself out of his seat and onto the platform. He almost crawled his way to the taxi rank outside. The queue was short, and he was soon gasping out his need to get to the nearest hospital to a driver who seemed less than impressed with his efforts at communicating in French.

"Le service des urgences de l'hôpital le plus proche d'ici, s'il vous plaît."

The driver replied with a gruff monosyllabic, "Okay."

Michael manoeuvred himself into the back of the taxi and slumped uncomfortably into the seat. Unfortunately, Michael had chosen a taxi driver who seemed determined to fulfil every negative feature of caricatures of the profession and proceeded to jerk his vehicle toward the hospital in a series of accelerating dashes punctuated with tyre screeching halts and torrents of abuse gesticulated out of the taxi window. Michael battled to survive the journey without crying out in pain. After a manic ten minutes in the taxi they reached the Hopital Saint Louis but at this point Michael realised there was a further challenge ahead. His wallet was in his left rear pocket, he did not have enough cash left in his other pocket and so he would need his card from his wallet. The driver proffered the contactless machine and Michael contorted to pull the wallet out with his right hand, leaning forward and simultaneously trying to raise himself slightly out of his seat. The driver watched him with undisguised contempt on his face and muttered his impatience as Michael agonisingly slowly retrieved his wallet.

"Vite, vite, vite monsieur".

Michael snapped a retort and considered exiting without paying but that was hardly likely to help him keep a low profile,

"Attendez, monsieur-j'ai une mauvaise épaule".

Michael clearly filled the cabby's expectations of a crazy Englishman! Eventually he managed to grip the wallet between two fingers, loosen it from his pocket and take out the card which stimulated an approving beep from the machine. He extricated himself from the rear of the taxi using the doorframe to lever himself upright and with gaelic sighs ringing in his ears and slammed the door shut behind him with as much force as he could muster. Michael turned and lurched towards the hospital entrance as the taxi driver gunned his engine and screeched away into the Parisian traffic saluting Michael's retreating figure with a raised middle finger.

Chapter Forty-Four

Michael picked his way gingerly into the hospital reception area carefully protecting his left arm from any collisions with the building, its furniture, or its other occupants. He was met by a nurse in the waiting-area, and he tried to explain that he had injured his shoulder. She examined the injury without removing his sweatshirt and then made a note of the medication he took before she spoke to a colleague at the reception desk who emerged to ask Michael in fluent English for his insurance and credit card details.

"Sorry," she said, "the English are no longer European so no more EHIC cards and no more free medicine. The nurse says you need an x-ray and then to see the doctor. Wait here and they will come for you very soon. For my form how did you injure yourself?"

"I fell on the stairs in my hotel and struck my shoulder on the banister," Michael replied without hesitation having used some of his waking hours on the train to establish, what he felt would be, a plausible explanation.

He eased himself back in his chair to wait. He had had several visits to Accident and Emergency departments in the UK for a variety of cricketing injuries, broken fingers, a cricket ball in the mouth and a broken wrist. He had always found that a lengthy wait at some point in the process was a feature; before the x-ray, before seeing the doctor, or waiting for the agreed treatment. He tried to prepare himself mentally for a similar experience, despite his desperation for instantaneous relief. There was no wait for the x-ray as two porters arrived, almost immediately, with a wheelchair and took him through a double door to a radiographer. The radiographer asked him to stand up and took several images of his shoulder from a variety of angles, gently positioning Michael as he felt appropriate. The porters returned and wheeled him into a small room with a bed and various pieces of medical paraphernalia. A couple of minutes later a young woman in a white coat arrived with a packet of x-rays in her hand, Michael realised he must be getting old if doctors were beginning to look young. She had long blonde hair tied back in a single plait that ran down the centre of her back and was tied off with a small blue velvet ribbon just below her shoulders. She was a pretty woman, but her face had a serious set to it, she was clearly very aware of the responsibility that came with her role and did not waste time or effort on such frivolities as smiling. She was accompanied by the nurse he had seen earlier.

"Monsieur White, I will try to speak English, but I don't practise very much. Your shoulder is dislocated, it has gone behind. This is unusual, you must have hit it very well. We need to put it back. If you relax, I can pull it back, it is possible. If you do not relax, we will perhaps use anaesthetic, okay? You want to try?"

Michael was not convinced by the thought of a manipulation without anaesthetic,

"Will it hurt?" he asked.

"If you relax it will be okay. If you do not it will be difficile," replied the doctor with a light frown that Michael interpreted as meaning either, of course it will hurt what a foolish question, or why are you asking are you a coward?

Michael felt embarrassed into trying the manipulation

without anaesthetic; he had some pride and did not want to appear frightened in front of four strangers.

"Right, let's give it a go then," he affirmed; trying to show rather more assurance than he felt.

"Monsieur if you will lay back please?" the doctor asked nodding towards the head of the bed.

Michael perched himself on the edge of the bed, the sweet antiseptic smell of hospitals in his nostrils, and tentatively laid back onto the firm mattress. One of the porters came around to his right side and rested his hands on Michael's shoulder and bicep. The nurse stood on his left, above his shoulder, and placed one hand on his left shoulder by his neck and the other below his left bicep. The doctor took a firm hold, her right hand under the bicep next to his elbow. With her left hand, she gripped his forearm.

"Now Monsieur White, relax please," she stated, it was said with an authority that indicated it was an order and an expectation, not a request.

Michael took an involuntary breath and tensed but the doctor did not hesitate and pulled his arm forcefully outwards at right angles to his side. His shoulder screamed its protest, but Michael gritted his teeth and then, with a palpable clunk, the searing pain stopped and was replaced immediately by a dull ache. The doctor probed the area around the joint with her fingers and nodded to herself seemingly satisfied with the outcome.

"Bon Monsieur, we are done, you wear a sling, yes, and take pain killers. The nurse will give them to you. You must take it easy for a while," instructed the doctor.

Michael smiled, hardly able to believe the excruciating pain had gone almost as quickly as it had arrived.

"Thank you so much."

"De rien," the doctor nodded, almost smiled and then left to deal with her next case.

Within twenty minutes, Michael was leaving the hospital with painkillers added to his carrier bag's load. He had also completed a couple more forms which the receptionist told him would allow them to deal directly with his insurers whom they had already contacted. He hailed a taxi and was soon heading back to his hotel and, he mused in wonder that it was not even midday yet.

Chapter Forty-Five

Michael entered the Hôtel Liège Strasbourg and climbed the stairs to his room, he had been distracted from the horror of James' death by both the pain and the miraculous recovery of his shoulder, but now his grief crowded back in on him. He opened the door to his room walked in and lay on his bed. He knew he had to see through the rest of his plan to ensure that he did not end up paying for Vine's crime, which would be hugely ironic, and therefore he needed to be back at the conference that afternoon and try to give the impression that he had been there throughout. He tentatively removed his clothes, being particularly careful with his sweatshirts, and headed for the bathroom. He showered, shaved and cleaned his teeth. He got dressed into a pair of clean trousers and a fresh shirt and tie. He pulled his sports jacket and shoes from his carrier bag. The jacket was rather crumpled, he shook it and pulled it on gently, easing it over his left shoulder. He slipped on his shoes and sling and headed for the Conference.

Michael arrived back at the Hotel Rocroy during the lunch break and managed to join the back of the queue for the buffet. He selected some pizza and added a green salad. He took a glass of water and some cutlery, put it on a tray and went and sat at a spare seat on one of the circular tables that accommodated four people. He introduced himself to the two women and one gentleman who were already eating their meals at the table. The three were educationalists from Holland and, being Dutch, spoke

English that rivalled Michael's. He listened carefully to their discussion about the previous day's sessions and tried to glean as much insight about the content as he could. All three were elegantly dressed, in sharp contrast to much of the English teaching brigade who seemed to have abandoned all professional dress codes. That was a reflection not just of how English teachers dressed at conferences but so often in schools too, there seemed to be an acceptance by many that if the general public and media had a low opinion of them they would dress down to meet it! When the group's discussion moved to that morning's lecture one of the women turned to Michael and asked him for his opinion. He was ready for such a question and tilted his head to indicate the sling supporting his left arm and said,

"Unfortunately, I dislocated my shoulder in a fall at my hotel this morning and I had to go to the hospital to have it put back, not an experience I recommend, so I missed the talk I am afraid. I would certainly have rather been here than where I was!"

The group expressed their sympathy for his misfortune. Having finished his meal, Michael accompanied his new acquaintances to the Conference's closing keynote after lunch. The purpose of the lecture was to summarise all the main points from the previous two and a half days, which Michael felt was a focus that was probably more useful to him than to anyone else. It was delivered by the Conference Coordinator who had obviously worked hard to read all the submitted papers that had accompanied the talks and to turn them into a homogenous delivery. The lecture finished at two thirty p.m. and Michael took some time to bid his newfound friends farewell. Hopefully, he could rely upon their memories if he needed to produce witnesses of his attendance at the conference, he scribbled down their names for future refence – should it be needed. Michael walked out into the hotel reception area and asked the member of staff at the desk where he might find a local, good quality, jeweller. The young man beamed at him,

"Ah, you could try Maison Artaner on Rue de Paradis. My sister is the manager there, she will look after you."

He showed Michael the directions to the shop on a Paris street map that lay on the desk. Michael left the hotel and headed south. He emerged onto Rue de Paradis and spotted the shop frontage which proclaimed 'Maison Artaner' on a banner that protruded from the building at right angles to the wall. It was clearly visible to anyone walking down the road. Flowers cascaded from two planters in front of the shop's grey framed windows. Michael had to admit that the place dripped class; he just hoped that his bank account could cope with a purchase from here. It was important to him to find a gift that Francesca liked. He wanted to cheer her up and whilst he understood that a trinket would in no way undo the vile, life changing, abuse it might just bring a smile to her lips. He knew that he wanted to move away from the relationship and grow old with his memories and not with Francesca, but he did not want to hurt her. In hindsight, he could see just how shallow his behaviour had been over the last few months. The attraction of Francesca was certainly physical but more ashamedly having such a beautiful girl on his arm had massaged his ego. It had clearly said '*look at me, I may be nearly sixty, but I am still desirable*'. He knew that there was not a deeper connection, and whilst he had enjoyed spoiling her with expensive presents and meals out, he could not be the man Francesca needed or wanted. Frankly, he struggled to conceive why she had looked twice at him, but now he needed to set a new course, or perhaps it was more return to an old one. He did not know how he was going to achieve this. She had been treated abysmally. Now was not the time to add to the savage blows that she had already suffered but he knew he had to be true to himself. He could not live in a long-term relationship which rested squarely upon his vanity. He had to think clearly about what he could do about the situation with Francesca, and he needed to think about what he could do about James' murder. However, he wanted time and space to do that. Right now, he needed to focus upon his purchase and get it right.

Chapter Forty-Six

Michael pushed through the glass door of the Maison Artaner and a buzzer sounded within the store. Michael was faced with a room that was furnished rather like a chic lounge. There were two blue armchairs, occasional tables, and a sideboard with a mirror above it. Potted plants and vases of cut flowers were sprinkled around the interior and two beautiful garlands hung on the inside of the shop's windows. To the left of Michael there was an internal glass screen through which he could see a workshop, where a middle-aged man sat at a workbench crafting bespoke jewellery. The work looked intricate and taxing and the craftsman's attention did not waiver from the silver bracelet clenched in the small vice in front of him. The ache in Michael's shoulder spread to his wallet. There was no jewellery on display, and he didn't have the time, or quite possibly the money, to wait for a piece to be fashioned specifically for Francesca. He was not sure that a piece of bespoke handcrafted jewellery sat very comfortable with the direction of travel he wished to take with their relationship. Just as he considered beating a retreat from the shop, a young lady entered the room from a door behind him and to his left.

"Monsieur, puis-je vous aider?" the young woman ventured.

Michael had not thought about what he was going to say and mumbled his request, immediately aware that it was hardly helpful or specific.

"Des bijoux pour ma copine?".

Asking for jewellery in a jewellery shop seemed somewhat clumsy. He knew he did not want a ring that could lead to misunderstandings and more hurt and he never seen Francesca wearing a brooch or earrings so perhaps he should be asking for a necklace or a bracelet? The saleswoman looked at him appraisingly,

"You are the gentleman that my brother sent from the Hotel Rocroy aren't you, how can I help?"

Michael was relieved the situation had just become far more straightforward.

"I want a necklace or bracelet for my girlfriend, I don't know if you have them already made?"

His saviour smiled, "Yes Monsieur, we do, now what sort of stones do you want in the piece?"

"She has beautiful blue eyes; I would like something in Atlantic blue, I think." Michael detailed his request in a halting voice as his thoughts gradually crystallised.

"Okay we have a few options, would you like silver or gold or white gold for the setting?"

"Silver in colour please", he responded.

"Right I suggest a pendant in a silver mounting, would you like to see some?"

Michael nodded his agreement. She disappeared back through the door from which she had come and after a couple of minutes re-emerged with a velvet tray held out in front of her. On the grey velvet nestled four pendants all with blue stones and silver mountings. Each had a little white card attached to them by a short thread. Michael presumed that the tags listed their prices, but they were too small for him to be able to read without craning forward and making his anxiety about the cost of the purchase obvious. They were all exquisite pieces but the one sitting on the right-hand side was most reminiscent of Francesca's bewitching eyes. With a feeling of trepidation, which he tried to keep out of his voice, Michael asked how much the pendant was, his request felt almost vulgar in such a place where beauty clearly triumphed over such base considerations as money.

"Ah Monsieur, this is a beautiful choice, it is a pear blue topaz, and the tear drop cutting sits well in the silver mounting. She must be a lovely lady to be receiving such a gift," the shop manageress answered without actually giving him the crucial information. He knew he was being ensnared.

"And the cost?" Michael repeated feeling rather crass and cheap.

"Oh Monsieur, c'est moin cher, it is only three hundred and twenty euros," she smiled at him, but he could see the question in her eyes, *was this too much for the Englishman and was the intended recipient worth it?* Michael put her out of her misery and returned her smile,

"That is perfect, thank you."

The manageress returned to the rear of the shop and came back with the pendant draped inside a grey box, lined with velvet. The jeweller's name was embossed in silver on the lid. She slipped the box into a similarly coloured paper bag which also carried the shop's name. Michael pulled out his credit card and completed the transaction. It was a lot to pay but given the circumstances not too much and probably the very least he could do. He did feel a pang of guilt that perhaps he was trying to buy himself out of the responsibility, that he clearly held, for putting Francesca in harm's way in the first place but his options were limited. He had misjudged James, he and no one else was culpable, and a piece of jewellery wasn't going to give him absolution. Michael had planned to stay in Paris on the Thursday night and travel back to Pra Loup on Friday but as he walked back to his hotel, he resolved to pack up and catch an evening train. He could stay in Grenoble overnight before driving home first thing in the morning. He knew he should not ski but he was desperate to stand at the top of Le Lac, soak up the sunshine, drink in the views, and, perhaps, find some sort of peace and calm to salve his wounded soul.

Chapter Forty-Seven

The receptionist at the Hôtel Liège Strasbourg was the same one who had been on duty when Michael had arrived and she patiently explained that, unfortunately, as Michael was leaving so late in the day, he would still be liable to pay for his full stay. Michael paid his bill and asked for the train times from the Gare de Lyon to Grenoble. The receptionist flicked them up on her computer screen and surveyed the information before swivelling the screen so that Michael could see the listings. He appeared to have two options; he could catch the five fifty-two which would arrive in Grenoble at nine thirty-nine, but which included one change of train, or get the direct service at six forty-three which was due to get in at Grenoble at nine forty-two. The latter seemed the better option and would allow him some time to grab some food at the Gare de Lyon. Sadly not at Le Train Bleu, which would have required a reservation some time ago, but at one of the proliferation of snack bars and cafés at the station. He asked the receptionist for the details of the Novotel near Grenoble Station. She printed off the information for him and she then allowed him to use the phone at her desk to make a reservation before she used it to call him a taxi. The Metro bore little appeal as his shoulder was throbbing insistently and he certainly did not want to provoke his damaged nerve endings further by having to jostle with the crowds of passengers on busy underground trains. Michael left the hotel and waited on the kerbside for his taxi to arrive. A silver Peugeot drew up and Michael slid into the back seat of the car. The driver turned to him and confirmed,

"Gare de Lyon Monsieur?"

"Oui, merci beaucoup," Michael responded.

The car pulled smoothly into the stream of traffic and eased its way forward towards the station. In contrast to his experience earlier in the day, this taxi driver seemed almost languid in his approach as they progressed serenely towards his destination. Whilst it may have taken a little longer, Michael was appreciative of the much more tranquil journey. Perhaps the driver had noticed his sling but, in any case, Michael took the opportunity when it was presented to add a tip when the option appeared on the card machine. The taxi dropped him in front of the external facade of the Gare de Lyon, which Michael had not seen previously as the Metro was accessed from inside the station. The front of the station was dominated by an extensive piazza over which towered a massive clock. Michael spotted a burger restaurant, King Marcel, and made his way towards it. The black canopy over the external seating area declared its name but then, alongside, was written the message; My Burger is French. With his curiosity pricked Michael entered the restaurant and ordered a 'French Cheeseburger' with chips and a Coke. When it was served, Michael acknowledged that this was far more of a gastronomic experience than he had expected in a burger restaurant. The burger was stacked high with; cheese, bacon, onions, tomatoes and at the base sat the beef patty. It was delicious and whilst Michael tried to savour every mouthful, he was fighting against the fact that he was very hungry, so ultimately, he wolfed it down. Having finished his food and despatched his Coke, Michael ordered and drank a large cappuccino before paying and heading towards the concourse of the station, pulling on his facemask as he went. As soon as

Michael boarded the six forty-three train, he walked down through the carriages to the buffet car and bought himself a bottle of water. Following a short reconnaissance, he found an empty seat facing forward, put his bag in the overhead rack and sat down. He unscrewed the cap of the water bottle and put the bottle and cap on the table in front of his seat. He then took two of his prescribed painkillers from their foil wrappers and popped them into his mouth, manoeuvring them to the back of his throat with his tongue. He swallowed them with the assistance of two gulps of the refreshingly cold mineral water which not only facilitated their passage but also removed their chalky bitter taste. Michael was exhausted. He sat back in his seat and allowed the rhythmic swaying of the train to take him to a place where there was some respite from his shoulder and his constant self-inquisition. He was soon rocked into a deep sleep. He was fortunate that the guard did not request his ticket until the train was past Lyon Exupery, which allowed him not only a decent rest but just enough time to be fully awake before he reached his destination. Grenoble station was quiet as Michael walked out across the concourse, only a couple of other passengers had alighted from the Paris train and like him moved away quickly keen to bring their journeys to a close. Michael pulled his sheet of directions to the Novotel from his pocket and set out on the short walk to the hotel. He stepped into the lobby at ten o'clock and felt grateful that the hotel had a twenty-four-hour check in. He was also grateful that his room was on the ground floor and only a few steps away from the reception area and restaurant. The receptionist informed him that breakfast would be available from seven a.m. He set his alarm for six thirty as he wanted to be away early and back in Pra Loup as soon as possible. He wanted this nightmare far behind him, but he suspected that for both himself and for Francesca a full recovery would be impossible. He reflected that at least the horror of James' murder would be geographically distant. It was an experience that he knew he could never talk to anyone else about, it would be a secret he would have to take to his grave. *A problem shared may be a problem halved,* he thought but this was awful and all his own. He would have to cope with his feelings, the horror and guilt, in total isolation. His turmoil could not be eased by the understanding or sympathy of anybody else.

Breakfast at the Novotel was, as usual, extensive and impressive. Michael drank several cups of coffee and ate a bowl of fresh fruit as well as a couple of croissants. Feeling replete, and to an extent reenergised, he headed back to the station car park. During the hours of darkness there appeared to have been a significant snowfall and even at this low altitude several inches of white fluff lay on the undisturbed surfaces. It had a cleansing effect on the urban landscape, giving the grubbier buildings a crisp white coating like a thin layer of icing on a cake. Michael was relieved that he had left the Volvo in a covered car park, the task of digging his vehicle out of the snow and clearing the windscreens was one he was very happy to have avoided given his physical state. He reached the car and stomped the snow from his shoes which were now damp. He unlocked the car and slung his holdall and jacket onto the back seat. He walked over to the pay-station and put first his ticket and then his debit card into the appropriate slots. He punched in his pin number and then pressed the green knob so that both could be returned to him. His bank account had been further diminished by one hundred and thirty-six euros and seventy cents. This had been a horrifyingly expensive trip, but it was nearly over, and he could feel the mountains calling him. He got into the car and started the engine, immediately the front windscreen fogged as warm air hit the cold surface. He sat for a couple of minutes allowing the heater to do its job and also flicked the windscreen wipers on to try to hurry the process of clearing the front window. Little mounds of cleared glass appeared at the bottom of the windscreen and gradually grew and extended upwards. As soon as he could see out without having to crane his neck, Michael put the car into gear and drove to the exit. He presented the ticket to the barrier machine which sucked the white card through the slot and into its internal workings and an automated '*Au Revoir*' appeared on the small plastic screen. The barrier swung up and Michael drove out of the car park and swung left onto a deserted road setting out on his journey back to Pra Loup. The main roads had been ploughed and the snow had churned into mini drifts on the hard shoulders and the central reservation. The lanes were narrowed but the traffic, what little there was of it at this time of day, still passed fluidly. The vehicles were gradually converting any remaining snow laying on the carriageway into a dirty brown slush, punctuated occasionally by a patch of snow that had dislodged from a car roof and fallen heavily to the ground.

Chapter Forty-Eight

Michael drove out of Grenoble and up into the mountains. He drove carefully. He was keen to get back to Pra Loup but he was also acutely aware of the challenges driving on a snowy and potentially icy surface presented. The sky was battleship grey and occasional flutters of snow issued forth; sometimes becoming heavier and consolidating into large flakes that settled into a fresh crust on the road and surroundings. The mountain routes were being continuously cleared to ensure they remained passable. Michael found himself behind a large orange snowplough which belched dirty diesel fumes as it toiled its way up the mountain road. It boasted a sizeable blade at the front, which was clearing the path before it, whilst it had a trailer section at the rear which was full of grit that it was scattering with an attached spreader. If Michael drove too close to the rear of the plough the grit bounced against the Volvo's body work and peppered the windscreen like a hundred baby woodpeckers stinging the vehicle, so he hung back a short distance. The only difficulty with this approach was that it seemed to be an open invitation to some pretty reckless individuals who used the gap in order to overtake him and position themselves to pass the plough which they often seemed to do on blind bends. It brought to mind the comments of the English coach driver on a school trip Georgie and he had taken many years ago. Every time cars had overtaken the coach on blind bends on the mountain roads, which was often, the driver turned to his co-driver and would grumble,

"I wish I went to their opticians… must have glasses that can see round corners".

Michael allowed the plough to escort him to Gap. It slowed his journey, but he felt secure in its wake and he did not have to put snow socks or chains on the tyres of the Volvo. Once past Gap Michael lost his escort, and he followed the road along the valley next to the river and then swung past the Lake *Serre Ponçon* and began to climb steeply back into the mountains. After just a few hundred yards he realised that, although the skies were clearing ahead of him, significantly more snow had fallen here than in Gap and rather than being scraped to the side of the road it had become rutted and compacted where it had fallen. Several vehicles ahead of him appeared to be losing traction as they tried to negotiate the slope. Michael felt the Volvo's tyres slide, spin and snatch at the surface. He knew he could not put off the inevitable. He pulled the Volvo into a lay-by on the opposite side of the road. He got out of the car and picked his way around to open the tailgate. Despite his care the snow swallowed his socks and soaked down into his shoes. He pulled the tyre covers from the back of the estate and eased them out of their plastic container. He took one and slid it over the top and sides of the left-hand rear wheel. Once it was in place he went back to the tail of the car and took the second sock and passed that over the right-hand wheel. He returned to the driver's seat and drove the car a couple of feet forward. He stopped, took the car out of gear and put the hand brake on. Then he got out and went back to the tyre socks. He pulled the remaining sections of material over the rear wheels, shut the tailgate and got back into the car. With freezing hands, he turned the key in the ignition and drove steadily back onto the opposite carriageway. He had driven a number of times with chains on the tyres previously but only once with the newer fashioned socks. They seemed to provide a good grip, although Michael did not really understand why. Chains obviously dug into the snowy surface, whereas he presumed the socks functioned due to friction. He concentrated hard on the road surface and drove on up the incline. The sun was breaking through and finally the snowfall was easing off and looked like it was stopping all together. It would be a beautiful day on the slopes and Michael yearned for the clear air and white expanses of Pra Loup.

As he drove his mind began to play with the options, he had for holding Vines to account. He knew, without much consideration at all, that he could not put himself in the position of executioner. Sense had finally seeped into his fevered brain and his moral code and principles had re-emerged. He knew he could not have killed James, no matter how heinous his crimes had been. It was not because James was his closest friend, it was because he was a fellow human being and Michael was no Macbeth. Whilst Vines' crime was horrendous, he too was a man and Michael would be as bad as him if he proceeded with the Old Testament approach of 'an eye for an eye, a tooth for a tooth'. Vines had to face justice, but the question was, how? Michael pondered. He could tell Tim that he had been there and had seen what had happened. Tim was a soldier, he was used to the concept and, if his stories were to be believed, the reality of taking a life for the greater good. This idea was fraught with problems. Did Michael really want to demean the memory of James by telling his brother about the rape? Perhaps James deserved that, but Tim would be in enough pain without this devastating knowledge, and he didn't deserve to suffer further, after all Tim was not guilty of anything in this affair. Ideas churned around in Michael's mind, his brain was a tumble drier full of anxiety and self-doubt. He concluded that if he brought Tim into his confidence it would be no different to him putting the bullet in the gun himself. He would be responsible for Vines' death just as surely, as if he had stuck a knife in him and Tim's life probably would be destroyed. The best option, and probably the only option, was for Vines to feel the full weight of the law but the problem remained how was that to happen? He drove on admiring the beautiful sunshine glistening on the fresh snow, a blanket of miniscule twinkling stars in the morning light. The shining contours of the mountains bedecked in their lustrous covering was in direct contrast to the dark malaise that rested in Michael's chest. Maybe he should just go to the police and lay his whole story bare. Would they believe that he had not killed James when he had gone to such extraordinary lengths to get into the UK undetected? Would they want to interview Francesca and put her through further pain? Would he end up spending a large chunk of his life in prison? His reputation would be destroyed and whilst that seemed a fatuous concern given the magnitude of the events; he knew himself well enough to know that he really struggled with any unfair public criticism that impacted upon his reputation. That was why he had struggled to deal with Vines' Facebook attacks and the negativity they promoted. He was frightened by the idea of being at the centre of a murder trial and the ensuing media storm. He was shocked to think that he had ever conceived of killing James, nothing about that decision made any sense now. Eventually he dismissed the option of going to the police. In reality, he had dismissed that option when he had knelt next to James' body and he realised that that impulse was the one he had to stand by. He supposed he could just do nothing. He hated that thought, but was that because he hated Vines? James would have paid for the rape, but had he deserved to die for it? Vines would have killed a local headteacher for no comprehensible reason and if he could kill James what else was he capable of? Michael needed to do something; he was certain about that, but he did not yet know what. Crime Stoppers might be a viable option. He could give an adjusted account of the evening, anonymously of course. It would not be able to be used as evidence, but it might direct the investigation to focus on Vines. Crime Stoppers was a charity and independent of the police. They handed on information in confidence. You could just fill in a form online and submit it. Michael wondered if he did that from France would his location come to light and put him in the cross hairs of the investigation. He pondered this and came to the conclusion that he was being ridiculous. A national charity that guaranteed anonymity was not going to change or break its policy just because the information related to a murder case. Crime Stoppers might just be his best option. It wouldn't give him the opportunity to provide hard proof that Vines was guilty, but it might be enough to focus the police investigations. He resolved to send the email once he had access to a computer or a phone. Whilst it would not be a smoking gun, it was the best he had. The road wound down to Barcelonnette and he drove through the last couple of villages all covered in snow. Michael glanced at the clock on the car's dashboard. The journey had certainly been slower than usual, but it was only just midday. He would have time for a ski when he got back. As he skirted past Barcelonnette and turned right over the bridge onto the Pra Loup road Michael decided to break his silent reverie and switched on the car radio. It was tuned to ninety-nine-point seven megahertz and Nostalgie was broadcasting. He drove up the mountain road and the tones of Matt Munroe filled the car. Michael could not help but smile at the timing. It was one of his favourite songs which played at the beginning of one of his favourite films; The Italian Job. It was the soundtrack to the orange Lamborghini Miura, being driven by the unfortunate Becherman, sweeping through the Alps on the Great Saint Bernard Pass. The road climbed and Michael looked out to his right to see Barcelonnette and the Ubaye valley stretching out far below him. The disc jockey introduced the next record, which was very current for this station, and Tim Minchin's voice replaced that of Matt Munroe. The ballad of 'The absence of you' drew Michael into its lyrics and the singer seemed to Michael to be talking directly to him.

Chapter Forty-Nine

Michael drove through Pra Loup 1500, past the Godille Ski Store, past the small supermarket situated in what had been the petrol station and on past the flat landing site for the helicopter. Pra Loup lay a few hundred metres further on and Michael slowed the Volvo as he drove amongst the parked cars, heaps of snow and occasional skiers. He passed the Gendarmerie to his right and followed the road as it bent around to the left. He slowed to a crawl and signalled right, pulling in in front of the Loup Immobilier. He just hoped Francesca was there and not out with a client, otherwise getting into the apartment would be impossible and his dreams of skiing that afternoon would disappear. He climbed stiffly out of his car. His shoulder was rather sore, and his legs were suffering from such a long journey. He stretched and walked into the estate agents. Francesca's desk was empty, but Pierre was there. Michael had met him back in the autumn when he was signing his papers.

Recognising Michael, Pierre moved forwards,

"Monsieur White. How are you? Can I help you?"

"I am not sure you can," replied Michael, "I was looking for Francesca, is she here?"

Pierre's downturned mouth told Michael he was not going to get the answer he was hoping for.

"No. I am afraid she went skiing for the day. We are not very busy, and the snow is wonderful."

"Damn," whispered Michael and then to Pierre he said, "She

has the keys to my apartment and I need them. Any chance you could ring her?"

"Of course, Monsieur White, no problem. But first we could try her drawer, she often puts keys in there."

Pierre offered a glimmer of hope and waved his arm across to Francesca's desk before walking to stand with Michael next to it and sliding the left-hand drawer out to its fullest extent. It was full of a plethora of bits and pieces; phone chargers, nail files, pens, paper clips, hairbrushes, a mirror, elastic bands – an Aladdin's cave of essentials for modern day office life! There were also two sets of keys. Michael was relieved to see that one was his own. He could go skiing after all, a wave of relief swept through him. He reached down and picked them up knocking a mobile phone that was partially obscured by a pack of post-it notes with his knuckles. Recognition lit up his eyes, it was his lost mobile. Francesca must have found it. She was a star!

"My keys and my phone. Excellent job Pierre, thank you."

"Oh," said Pierre looking surprised, "I thought that was Francesca's old phone. When she popped it in there, she said it was an antique and she would be sending it to 'Quick Mobile Fix' who will buy old mobile phones."

"I think," smiled Michael, "that was your colleague's warped sense of humour! Thanks again. I must go and sort myself out to go skiing. Au revoir et merci Pierre."

"Good-bye Monsieur White, have a good day."

Michael left the estate agents and walked across to the gallery, heading for the chemist at the far end. As he walked, he tried to turn on his mobile but, unsurprisingly, the battery was completely flat. If he were to ski, he would need some sort of support for his shoulder. Driving had been hard work and the movement involved in that was minimal compared to planting a pole whilst skiing. He entered the chemists and found an array of supports for all different parts of the anatomy. This was obviously an area of great demand for the shop, he was clearly not the only fool who wanted to ski when injured. He stood and tried to read the information and advice on four different types of shoulder support. He was struggling to work out which one would give him the protection he needed whilst still allowing him some degree of movement. He was on the edge of a decision when he felt a hand on his right shoulder and a familiar voice in his ear. Jean Paul was standing behind him, his tanned face crinkled into a smile.

"Hello my friend. How are you? Why are you not skiing in this fresh snow?"

"Hi Jean Paul. I've just returned from a conference in Paris, and I dislocated my shoulder falling on the stairs in the hotel."

Jean Paul looked at Michael sympathetically. "Disloqué, that is not good. No skiing for you Michael."

"Well actually," Michael replied, "I'm buying a shoulder brace so that I can have a gentle ski."

"Michael, the snow is great today, but it is not worth hurting your épaul, err, shoulder more. You told me you were always careful; this is not careful Michael." Jean Paul looked at Michael, his mouth turned down at the corners in mock disapproval.

"I will be very careful on the slopes, but I have to ski. I have to be on the mountain today. My soul needs the mountain." Michael smiled wistfully. "Anyway, why are you here Jean Paul?"

"My wife has a gorge iritée,"

"Sore throat," interpreted Michael.

"Yes, yes, a sore throat. So, I must collect some medication before my lesson at one o'clock."

"But Jean Paul, isn't génépi the cure for a sore throat?"

Michael replied, smiling.

"Yes, you are right, and I have told her this, but she still makes me buy expensive medicine." Jean Paul grimaced and shrugged his shoulders seeming to imply that his wife was a complete mystery to him. The two men laughed and proceeded to the checkout. Michael then headed to his apartment and Jean Paul headed to the ski school meeting point shouting back a parting comment to Michael

"Be careful Michael, the mountain won't make the pistes easier just because you are hurt."

Michael smiled to himself, touched by Jean Paul's concern, but still hurried back to his apartment to prepare for skiing. He opened the front door, went in and drew back the curtains to allow the daylight back into the interior. He plugged the phone in to charge and then went to his bedroom to get changed. His shoulder slowed the process, and it was further complicated by trying to work out how to put the brace on and then actually doing it. Finally, he put his boots on and he was ready to go. He picked up Francesca's gift and slipped it in his pocket. It was unlikely, but if he did see her on the mountain, he wanted to be able to give it to her. He pushed through the front door and tried to manage his skis and poles while causing as little discomfort to his shoulder as possible. He ended up scooping the entire load under his right arm and struggling to the Clappe lift. Next to the lift he dropped his load to the floor, clipped on his skis and then grasped both poles in his right hand. He made his way through the barrier to be lifted up by the chair and transported up the mountain. He looked up at the blue sky and white peaks which stretched up above the tree line and drew several deep breaths of the cold clear air. For a moment he felt uplifted by his surroundings, but only for a moment.

Chapter Fifty

The last time Michael had ridden the Clappe chair James had been on one side and a radiant Francesca on the other. Even the blue sky and the pearly snow could not offset the great sadness lying deep within him for long.

At the top of the lift, he peeled off to the left and began to ski down towards the Pegieou lift. It only took him a couple of jarring left turns to realise that Jean Paul's advice, as in all things, had been very wise. Each turn to the left and subsequent pole plant resulted in his shoulder being forced up and away from his body. It was unbearable. He stuttered to a halt and changed his grip on his poles so that he was holding them both together in front of him and parallel to the slope. He swung gentle turns without the poles touching the snow and, whilst it felt a little odd, it was far more comfortable and just about manageable. It was almost like having a steering wheel in front of him to guide his turns. The turns lacked any dynamism but were still effective. He would have to keep to the gentler runs but that didn't pose too much of a problem as the viewpoint at the top of Le Lac was his target and he could ski most of the route there and back down again on fairly gentle and forgiving blue pistes. At the top of Pegieou he bore right down the blue road that began the Cabone du Berger run and crossed over the Le Lac drag lift. He descended to the bottom of the lift down the red run which, apart from a short depression, was not too challenging to his newly adapted style.

At the bottom of the drag he decided he would be able to manage the lift best without his poles and decided to leave them by the chair's entrance and pick them up again on his way back down. He felt confident that he would be able to manage the runs fairly comfortably without carrying the poles at all. He shuffled up to the buttons of the drag lift and as he reached the front of the short queue, he took the button from the lift operator in his right hand. Holding the metal shaft in his mittened hand he allowed himself to be pulled steadily up the mountain. His left arm remained hanging by his side as its movement was constrained by the brace. It was a long lift, but Michael looked up to its summit where it would eject him onto the plateau below the Seolan mountain. The whole region would be spread beneath him in all of its beauty, forests, valleys, peaks and towns. He took a sharp intake of breath in anticipation. He really hoped this place might afford him some feeling of peace and serenity. He knew of no reason why it should, but he always felt the arm of tranquillity around his shoulders when he stood here and looked in wonder at the panorama that would still be there long after he was gone.

Michael struggled to dismount the lift without his ski poles and ended up almost sprawling to the ground. He removed his skis and walked with them under his right arm to stand looking out towards Les Agneliers and the Mercantour National Park beyond. The deep snow lay in swathes across the landscape, resting in the branches of the larch trees far below and blunting the contours of the rockier slopes above them. The old Quartier lift was groaning its passage up the mountain and beyond it a couple of skiers arced their way down the red piste in long lazy turns. Directly below him, running down under the lift were two beautifully regular tracks in the deep fresh powder. Whoever had left their marks on the steep area of off-piste snow must be wonderful skiers mused Michael. The legacy of their descent may only be transient, but for now their tight linking S curves were a thing of beauty.

The mountains would be here for ages to come but the weather, the seasons and the people visited themselves upon the landscape in an ever-changing perpetual motion and Michael was determined to enjoy fully his flash in eternity in this beautiful place.

The peaceful vista belied an underlying dynamism and Michael was only a momentary part of it, like a snowflake in the sunshine. He did feel calmer, but not truly at peace with himself. Even here, James' glassy stare found a resting place in his thoughts and feelings of guilt washed through him. He hoped time would be his ally and gradually lighten his dark thoughts but for today, he determined to enjoy this wondrous place.

His eyes panned down the old lift, seeing a few skiers perched in the slatted seats, embraced by the creaking arms of the safety bars. A few hundred metres from the top his gaze tripped on a jacket he recognised. He looked closer at the figure seeking affirmation. There was no doubt it was her. She was skiing with someone, which was hardly a surprise, even in such a well-managed resort as this, skiing alone was not a safe option. He watched the chair clicking towards him and he patted his pocket to check the pendant was still there. He felt the contours of the box through the down of his jacket. This may be a relationship that he needed to gently cool but when one gave a present there was always the excited anticipation of the receiver's reaction. Michael imagined her eyes sparkling and her lips curling as she opened the box. He shook himself. He must be careful. She may be beguiling, but she was not his future and he must not be hers. Her life, her desires and her expectations were so different to his.

He was secure in his past and wanted to be comfortable and relaxed in his future and he now knew that was not possible with Francesca.

The pair on the lift were coming close to the top of the lift and were engaged in a deep conversation, their faces turned inwards to each other so that their observer's existence remained unnoticed. Michael watched as the pair swayed towards each other and entered into a lingering kiss. As he watched them kiss Michael became aware of who was with Francesca, it was Marc. The anger of cheated pride flared in his chest and he fought to rationalise what he was seeing. He should be feeling relieved that what he was seeing would make what he had to do far easier, but his feeling of betrayal was very real, and it was an emotion that he had become only too accustomed to in the past week. The kiss lingered on and was only brought to an end by the urgent necessity to lift the safety bar and descend into the snow. The laughing couple emerged from the lift's disembarkation area their happiness was in stark contrast to his utter misery.

Michael wanted to shrink into the shadows and avoid being seen but bright sunlight surrounded him and there were no hiding places. He hoped that their exclusive attention on each other might mean that he could go unnoticed. He did not want to see the smirk of victory that would surely trip across Marc's face. He needed time to shape the words he could deploy in the conversation that would now assuredly end the relationship between himself and Francesca. He needed time to understand what had happened here. How could he have misjudged the situation so appallingly? Francesca threw back her head to laugh at something Marc had said, and they hesitated as Marc pulled his phone from his pocket and showed her something on the screen. Michael stood stock still vainly hoping that if he did not move, he would somehow remain invisible to the couple, as if by being frozen to the spot he could disappear into the winter landscape. As Francesca looked up from the mobile phone, she looked straight into his eyes. For a moment the world seemed to pause, taking a breath to consider what might happen now on the mountaintop, what confusion may ensue from the deceits of these characters.

Francesca looked shocked and Michael knew the look that crossed her beautiful visage. It was one he had seen a thousand times in his career, that of the schoolchild getting caught out when lying about their homework or what they had been doing. He glanced towards Marc and was surprised to see not a smirk of victory but a frown of worry – not at all what Michael had been expecting.

Francesca turned to Marc and spoke urgently to him. Her voice was hushed as she clearly did not wish Michael to hear what was being said. Marc nodded in compliance and pushed off on his skis to take the blue link run back down into Pra Loup. Francesca pushed with her poles and skated effortlessly up the slight slope to stand a few feet from Michael on the lip at the edge of the piste, below which the mountain dropped away towards Les Agneliers. For Michael the view and the sunshine had lost their lustre and any reprieve from the chasm of his dark thoughts that he had felt had quickly evaporated.

He knew he did not want to be with Francesca, and there was now an easy way to end their affair, but he had trusted her, and he felt so let down. He knew she had suffered unimaginable hurt and perhaps turning to her childhood sweetheart for security was an understandable response. Did he need to be sensitive to this? He was sure that he and Francesca had established a real rapport. He believed that their relationship extended slightly beyond the bedroom so he hoped that, at this painful moment, they would be able to hang on to the ability to communicate without falling into a vitriolic confrontation that would mar any possibility of friendship in the future. Francesca's opening salvo made Michael realise that his hopes were going to be challenging to achieve.

"So, Michael," she spat, "You are spying on me. You don't tell me you are back and then you sneak up on me."

Her comments came in a venomous aggressive wave and Michael almost felt the words assault him as a physical force; he took half a step back. Leaving this conversation with a friendship intact was going to be a herculean task. He knew he had to calm the situation. Francesca had suffered enough, and he would not, could not, respond to the expression of her hurt by hurting her with his own vitriolic words.

"I'm so sorry Francesca, I lost my iPad, and I couldn't contact you."

Francesca's reply was swift and ferocious.

"You lost your iPad, you lost your phone, you are losing it old man. You will be pissing yourself soon."

Michael bit back an acid defence and repeated his apology.

"I'm very sorry Francesca I didn't mean to embarrass you. I was just coming up for a gentle ski this afternoon. I had hoped to see you, but I didn't want to, or mean to, upset you."

He suddenly felt as if he was behaving how a father would, trying to calm a tempestuous teenager, and he bridled at the thought. Why should he behave like a doormat? But he took a deep breath and strove to maintain some level of equanimity and didn't allow himself to become assertive. Francesca calmed slightly as her barbs were met with pacifying comments and not antagonism. Michael noticed an almost negligible droop in her shoulders and interpreted this as his opportunity to de-escalate the conversation further. He had spent hours of his professional life learning how to have difficult conversations with colleagues, parents and students and how to diffuse high emotions in these conversations. Somehow, it was so much more testing to apply the same skills when it was your personal life.

"Francesca it is okay I understand that I have caused you great hurt and so you don't want to be with me anymore. I do understand. If you want to be with Marc that is fine, it is okay, it is my own fault. I let you down. I failed you. I don't deserve to be with you. I have no desire to do anything that will upset you further. I have been lucky to have you as a friend and I am deeply sorry about what I allowed to happen."

Francesca was taken aback at such an approach, but she was not to be dissuaded from her full-frontal assault on Michael that easily.

"Michael if you really cared for me you would have brought me back something beautiful from Paris, not just sneaked up here trying to catch me out."

Even Michael was shocked at her brazenness but made a momentary decision to indulge her; perhaps the pendant would allow hostilities to be brought to a close and for some sort of friendship to remain where passion had once sat.

"Francesca, I have brought you a gift and you may have it if you wish because all I wanted was to bring you a little happiness, all I want is for you to be happy and that hasn't changed and won't change, no matter whether we are together or not."

He pulled the grey jewellery box from his pocket and took a couple of steps towards Francesca. The glacial stare that had been fixed on him warmed slightly and her lips upturned fractionally at the corners of her mouth. She took the box from Michael and opened it. The pear-shaped blue topaz glinted in the sunshine.

Francesca lifted the pendant from its box and ran the chain through her fingers. Then she held the topaz teardrop up and studied it as the sunlight fractured and flickered through its myriad of facets. The jewel's beauty seemed to blunt her anger and she spoke in a more conciliatory tone.

"Yes, it is beautiful Michael and thank you. This has been a bad time for me, and I have been struggling to cope. I am sorry." Suddenly a moment of realisation flashed across her face.

"You have been to your apartment for your skis. How did you get in?"

"Oh," Michael replied, "I popped into your office and Pierre was really helpful and got the keys for me from your desk along with my phone. Where did you find it?"

The brief truce came to an abrupt end and Francesca erupted.

"You went into my desk. How dare you take things from my desk without asking. You bastard. You absolute bastard, I thought I could trust you."

Michael recoiled in surprise at the renewed hostility. He had no idea what he had done to provoke it.

"Francesca, I didn't go into your desk Pierre did and I am really grateful that you found my phone."

Francesca was not to be soothed and the icy stare returned to her eyes. Her lips straightened in disdain the tone of her voice became almost malicious as she berated Michael again.

"Your phone is dead. You take things from my desk. You let your friend rape me. All you want to do is make me sad and you have succeeded you nasty old man. I am sad now. I suppose that makes you happy – it is what you wanted."

Finally, Michael bit at the injustice. This woman was being so unreasonable, so unfair when he had tried to be so understanding and supportive, when he had risked everything for her.

"You didn't look very sad on the chair lift with Marc and if the pendant makes you sad, I'll take it back."

He took a step towards her with his hand outstretched. She responded with a poisonous look,

"If you want your cheap jewellery old man you will have to come and get it."she snapped, shoving the necklace in her jacket pocket.

With that, she flicked her skis one hundred and eighty degrees and pushed herself over the lip of the piste and down the steep off-piste slope that ran below the Quartier chair. Michael regretted allowing himself to rise to her angry words. Any longer-term friendship had disappeared and any ability he had to support Francesca following the rape had gone too. He stepped to the edge and watched her waist deep, bouncing through the powder. Michael had no intention of following her. His shoulder was sore, he had no poles, and the slope had a very steep pitch. In any case, he was not sure there was any point in continuing the conversation as he did not believe there was any coming back from the angry words, they had both spoken. Too much hurt had been caused and too much antipathy had been exposed. Despite his burning frustration and anger, Michael could not help but watch in awe and wonder as Francesca danced through the powder making the incredibly steep slope her plaything. He would miss skiing with her, on snow she was a thing of true beauty, and he had to admit off the snow too.

Chapter Fifty-One

He heard the crack before he saw anything move. Suddenly he realised that the mountain appeared to have split in two and the slope, a hundred metres below, began to move very slowly. Michael shouted a warning, but Francesca remained oblivious to the quickly accelerating mass of snow above her and continued her balletic turns directly into the path of the avalanche. After a few moments, she glanced over her shoulder and immediately changed course arcing to her right to try and avoid the tumbling snowpack. Whether she had heard, sensed or felt the avalanche Michael did not know. For a moment, he thought she was going to find safe ground beyond the path of the tumbling waterfall of snow but its fingers reached out and tugged at Francesca's legs and skis and then she was being somersaulted out of control as the full body of the barrage of snow caught her. She was tossed like a rag doll, crushed and battered by the avalanche from all sides and then she was gone, devoured by the mountain. The snow piled to a halt in a deep gulley well below where it had ensnared Francesca. Other than the transitory blizzard that flickered over its final resting place, all was still. Michael stared at where she had been but there was no sign of the Atlantic blue jacket, no movement at all. No skis. Nothing. Michael turned to his left and saw two of the piste security team running towards him. They knew only too well what the thunderous crack had meant. They spoke to him urgently as they stood and scanned the slope below

"Quelqu'un a-t-il skié en hors piste?"

Michael understood that they were asking if someone had been skiing on the off-piste and answered in two devastating words,

"Francesca Riehl."

The two men exchanged a look of grave concern and were galvanised into action. One grabbed his radio and spoke hurriedly into it. The other turned to Michael and asked

"Où était elle?"

Michael pointed as he answered.

"She was over there two hundred metres down on the right, à droit."

The two members of the ski patrol team ushered Michael to follow them as they plunged forward running down the slope. Michael struggled to keep up and found the uneven terrain difficult to manage. The nearest of the two men called back to him

"Avait elle un transceiver Monsieur?"

Michael's reply of 'non' stimulated a groan from the man. As they arrived at the point where Francesca had last been seen Michael called to his two companions,

"Ici, here, ici."

They immediately took off their jackets and lay them in the snow to mark the beginning of their search area. Each pulled a probe from their bag and they began to probe across the slope, covering a width of about twenty metres before they then moved down a step. Michael had no probe and wasn't sure that his shoulder would cope with thrusting one into the snow anyway. He did not know what to do and just stood there and watched the methodical but almost frenzied search. Time was not on their side and they had a huge expanse of snow to cover. It seemed to take forever for more of the ski patrol team to appear but, in reality, it was probably only about five minutes before two more men and a sniffer dog joined their colleagues and they were followed by a steady stream of others. Some appeared on snowmobiles, others on skis having had to take lifts to reach the search site. There were soon upwards of a dozen people working in line probing the slope with the dog working its way backwards and forwards across the snow. Michael heard the distant sound of the rescue helicopter's rotor blades beating the air and soon it was churning the air overhead and dipping down to land on the piste at the top of the slope. It disgorged another three rescuers and who were also joined by several ski instructors answering the call for help at Le Quartier. Jean Paul appeared at the top of the slope and Michael watched him pick his way down.

"Michael, are you OK?"

"Yes Jean Paul. It's Francesca."

Jean Paul gave an audible sigh, the air releasing from him as though he had been physically punched in the stomach.

"Oh no." was all he said before turning to join the search. The rescuers were now stretched across the piste probing the snow shoulder to shoulder. A couple of times a shout went out and frantic digging began but on neither occasion was there a successful outcome. Time was ticking on. Michael looked at his watch to find that nearly an hour had passed since his heated words and Francesca's escape down this treacherous slope. Even if she had not been killed in the original horrific fall her chances of survival were fading. He felt utterly useless just spectating on the rescue effort but there was little else he could do. He had seen too much death recently and he prayed that Francesca was going to be lucky. If only he had managed to keep his temper, he would not be standing here now begging to hear the cry of discovery and exultation of survival go up. The sun was beginning to dip in the sky and Michael became aware that he was getting very cold. He berated himself for even allowing the thought to emerge. He was cold but Francesca was quite possibly freezing to death. Where was she?

The dog appeared to be particularly interested in a spot thirty yards below Michael. The dog's handler called to a couple of his colleagues and all three began to probe the area. A shout went up from one patrol member who was probing slightly to the right of the dog. He began waving to the other team members and within moments, a coordinating pattern of diggers was in place. They dug furiously, swapping the lead digger frequently to ensure there was no slowing down when tiredness took hold. The team were creating a swathe of snow back away from the growing hole. Michael ran down towards the diggers, desperate to see some affirmation that they had indeed found Francesca. The shovels scooped the snow away from just behind where the probe still marked the spot amongst the avalanche debris where they thought they had found evidence of a person buried. The probe had been driven deep into the snow, probably two metres of it was below the surface. Michael moved below the diggers, keeping out of their way, to a position where he could see up into the channel they were cutting. A shout went up as a glimpse of blue appeared. Two more members of the ski patrol joined the lead digger and all three pulled snow away frenetically from the emerging figure. Michael stretched and moved to his left to try and glimpse more of Francesca's torso emerging from the encasing snow. Her head was twisted back at an unnatural angle. Michael was drawn closer, like a moth to the flame, but he needed to be sure. Her blue eyes stared out, but her wintry tomb had stolen their lustre. Francesca, the town's favourite daughter, had gone; the smile, the laugh, the electric blue eyes dulled by the power of the mountain. Michael sunk to his knees. The ski patrol team and instructors fell silent as the realisation of what had happened spread through their ranks. Every one of them would have known the broken figure in the snow. Every one of them would have been entranced by her skiing – a Goddess on the slopes but a Goddess who lacked immortality. Jean Paul came to Michael's side and put an arm around his shoulders pulling him close and holding him for several seconds. No words were shared; there was just a profound silence. The blue sky above reached down to the white mountain peaks. The beauty of their surroundings was an absolute contrast to the grotesque scene that held the gazes of the entire rescue team, a scene that seemed to transfix them. They were all willing a slight movement, a flicker that would alter their reality and allow joy to return to the mountainside. Finally, instructions were shouted, and the digging continued revealing the entire body which was then lifted from its frosty cavern and laid gently on a rescue sled that had been dragged across the slope. An orange tarpaulin was secured around Francesca's frame and the sled was dragged across the Quartier piste and attached to one of the parked snowmobiles. Its driver mounted the vehicle and gunned the engine before pulling away from the group of defeated 'rescuers' and following the run back up to the summit and the waiting helicopter. The helicopter soon rose up and took her away. *Electric blue eyes… if you should go.*

Chapter Fifty-Two

The ski patrol team began to pack away their equipment and leave the scene. Some made their way to the piste and skied down but others, like Michael, slogged their way back up the uneven terrain to the plateau at Le Lac. Michael struggled with the climb. His shoulder was unaware of the tragedy of the situation and continued to demand the attention of some aspect of his consciousness. The snow did not want to support his weight and with each step forward, he sunk through the alabaster surface up to his knees. Sweat dripped down his back and the altitude gripped at his chest. One of the ski patrol noticed his plight and came to his aid. He was a big man with a bronzed face and several days of dark stubble flecked his chin. He put an arm under Michael's right elbow and levered him forward. Eventually they clambered over the lip and back onto the piste. Michael thanked his saviour profusely in a staccato series of gasped words of gratitude

"Monsieur… merci beaucoup...merci beaucoup...vous êtes très gentil…merci."

A faint smile came to the man's lips but did not reach his eyes; too deep a sadness rested in them

"De rien Monsieur, you are welcome," he replied.

Michael clipped on his skis and skated towards the blue link road which would return him to Pra Loup. He picked his way down Le Lac red and across to the Cabane du Berger blue and finally followed the liaison Pegieou blue to collect his ski poles.

With his poles grasped in front of him, he slowly lumbered down the La Clappe blue which deposited him at his apartment. He stood there, bereft. He did not know what to do, where to go and even how to react to Francesca's death. He took off his skis and manhandled them back to his apartment. He went in and took off his boots and jacket and poured himself a large brandy. He sat sipping the fiery alcohol and staring out of his window utterly numb. There was a loud knock on his door and Michael, somewhat surprised, moved to answer it. The door swung open to reveal Marc looking pensive and pale.

"Marc?" was all Michael could manage.

"Michael, où est Francesca, where is she? Elle n'est pas revenue," stuttered Marc.

Marc clearly knew nothing of the events of the afternoon. Michael grappled for the right vocabulary.

"Elle a skié hors piste, Il y avait une avalanche. Francesca a été prise dans l'avalanche. Marc I am so sorry she is dead...elle est morte."

Marc gave out a wail like the sound of a wounded animal. His face crumpled, utter devastation racked every sinew of his body and tears swept down his cheeks. Michael stepped forward, tears pricking his eyes, and held Marc in his arms. The enmity that he had felt towards him dissipated in their mutual grief. Marc's body heaved as he gulped in a great lungful of air. Eventually Marc stepped back from Michael.

"Michael, I am sorry I must go to her parents," he croaked as he wiped his eyes and stumbled away.

Chapter Fifty-Three

Michael walked back into the flat and returned to his brandy. He picked up his phone to see if it had charged and was working. He pressed the button on the side for several seconds and miraculously the Google screen appeared – there was some hope! After thirty seconds or so, Michael pressed the button on the side again and then flicked the photo of Georgie upwards and the security number display appeared. He entered his code – one, nine, six, six – and the home phone screen popped up. He scanned it quickly; there were missed calls as well as unopened WhatsApp messages, texts and e-mails. He decided to start by checking the calls and possible voice messages but before he had a chance to begin his interrogation his mobile rang, and Tim's face appeared. Michael took a deep breath and answered the call. He needed to get this right. Tim's voice appeared in his ear, taut with tension.

"Michael, Michael, why haven't you been answering your phone?"

Michael tried to answer but Tim rushed on. "Michael, have you heard? James, it's James. He was murdered on Wednesday evening in the school car park."

Hearing the news from Tim of what he had seen with his own eyes underlined its reality and Michael gave an involuntary groan.

"Michael are you okay? The police don't know who did it. Nothing was taken so it probably wasn't a robbery gone wrong." Having shared the information Tim appeared to be engulfed with grief and Michael could hear him sobbing on the other end of the phone quite incapable of speaking, the two friends were a thousand miles apart but were welded together as one by their desolation.

Finally, Michael spoke,

"Tim, Francesca was killed in an avalanche today; my phone has been lost so I haven't heard anything about James. I'm really struggling here Tim," he gulped.

"Oh Christ Michael, do you want me to come out?" Tim responded fighting to control his emotions.

"No, thank you Tim. I think that I want to come home. I think I need to be at home."

The realisation dawned for Michael that what he was saying to Tim was indeed true, although he had not thought of it before the words came out.

"I am coming home in the next few days and I'll ring you when I'm back in Devon," Michael continued.

"Okay Michael. Ring me if you need anything, or if you just want to talk. See you soon buddy. Be strong."

It was just like Tim to battle to control his emotions and to be offering Michael support when he clearly needed it himself. Tim was no stranger to violent, sudden death, but Michael knew just how close Tim was to his brother and how deeply he would be hurting. A huge wave of regret washed over him and over the whole sorry affair. At least now he had a plan for the immediate future, he would need to get on with packing up the apartment and booking a crossing if he was to travel shortly.

His attention wandered back to his phone, but no sooner had he flicked back to the home screen it rang again. Michael answered the call, recognising the name of the Chair of the Governors as it appeared on the display.

"Michael, it is William here. Have you heard the dreadful news?"

Michael replied, appreciating the fact that William had thought to check that he had been told about James,

"Hello William. Yes, I do know the news. Tim, James' brother, rang me to let me know. Do the police have any idea who did it? That Vines is a nasty enough piece of work."

"No, they have no idea. They think it might be a mugging, but they're, what's the phrase?... 'Pursuing all avenues'."

"And how is the school community coping?" enquired Michael.

"Well," William paused for a moment, "I wanted to talk to you about that. We, the Governors that is, wondered if you would be able to do a caretaker job for the last couple of weeks of this term and next term so that we could appoint a new headteacher in September. We would pay you on the same salary you finished on and we'd be happy for you to take the odd day off if you wanted to. The school team is rocked and we need a calm headteacher that the students, staff and parents have confidence in."

"Wow," responded Michael, "I didn't see that coming. Can I have twenty-four hours to think about it William? I have had some other tragic news here as well."

"Yes, of course. I realise that it has come right out of the blue, but we'd be very grateful," the Chair of Governors conceded.

"Okay. I'll ring you tomorrow with my thoughts. It was good to talk to you. Bye."

Michael hung up with a thousand thoughts exploding in his mind. Did he want to do this? Would Vines be a danger to him? James would have wanted him to, but did he owe him anything at all after what he had done? The school needed him, but he had moved on and so much had happened in the last week. Would he be able to cope? He fiddled with his phone as he tried to rationalise all the things that had happened and what it all meant for him. He looked down at the phone and navigated to the list of missed calls. Unsurprisingly there were a number from James and more recently from Tim. He opened the messages and saw that he had voicemails to listen to. He pressed the number on the first message to open them. The automated voice on the line informed him that he had six new messages and then moved to play the first one. It was the voice of his dead friend; the man who had betrayed him.

'Michael ring me!'

The voice sounded anxious and upset. Michael saved the message. The second message was the same voice.

'Michael, I've tried to find you, but I can't. I have to go and get the plane, please ring me as soon as possible.'

Again, Michael saved the message. The third message was James again, but this time it lasted rather longer

'Michael it is me again. I wanted to tell you this in person, or at least speak to you on the phone, but I can't get an answer. Mate, I am really sorry, but I forgot the Felix Francis book, so I went back to the apartment to get it. Francesca must have thought I had already gone because when I walked in she was having sex with Marc. I am so sorry, but you need to know the truth about her. Please, please ring me."

Michael sat open mouthed. He replayed the message twice more and then saved it. His emotions were in compete conflict. If James was telling the truth he was the man, he had always thought him to be. If Francesca had been lying that would explain what he had seen on the mountain and would also explain her reaction to him and her absolute rage when she realised, he had his phone. On the other hand, she had looked so downtrodden and distraught when he had found her, surely that couldn't have been the face of deceit. Michael moved on to the fourth message which was James again imploring him to call. He saved it and moved on to the fifth. The fifth was quite different. It was James again but an excited happy James.

'*Michael, I want you to be the first person to know I met someone before Christmas and, well, she is the one. It's very quick but I have decided to ask her to marry me. If she says yes, will you be my best man? Her name is Alice. She's lovely and I am sure you'll like her. I can't wait for you two to meet....*'

A cry interrupted James' announcement. It was a cry that Michael had heard before. It was followed by a crash and then one clearly enunciated word *'Vines'* followed by a crunch and a silence. Michael replayed the message listening attentively to the time of the call. The message was left the previous Wednesday night at eight twenty-seven. James had been on the phone to him when he had been murdered and he had identified his killer. Michael had tears running down his cheeks, hearing James' voice and what he was saying was just too much to bear. He sat and sobbed. Guilt, relief, frustration and anger percolated up through his body. He wanted to phone Tim, but he was aware that he had to regain some level of control of himself so that he would be able to speak coherently. He knew that Marc must know the truth about Francesca's accusations. He needed to speak to Marc and that would not be an easy conversation. There had been a momentary cessation of hostilities, but the questions Michael needed to ask hardly seemed like ones that were going to fall on receptive ears. He had first-hand knowledge of Marc's temper and aggression. First things first though he needed to phone Tim and tell him about the voice messages from James. Michael picked up his phone, selected Tim's number and pressed it. The phone rang three or four times and then Tim's familiar voice came on the line

"Hi Michael, are you okay?"

Michael replied, fighting to keep a grip on his emotions,

"Not really Tim but I have some new information. I don't know… Look… I've just been through the messages on my phone which hadn't been picked up whilst I had mislaid it. Tim, what time did James die? Do they know?"

Tim hesitated,

"The lead detective, who I know quite well, said it was likely to be between eight fifteen and eight forty-five… Why?"

"I received a message from James at eight twenty-seven," Michael replied. "I can hear the attack and James names the attacker. It was Vines; there's no doubt. We need to tell the police. Tim, he left another message… he had met someone. He was going to propose to her. Her name was Alice."

Tim was silent on the other end of the line for several seconds. The all-action hero was struggling just like Michael.

"Okay," Tim finally replied, "I'll phone the detective. His name is Carl Collins. I will give him your number and get him to ring you. Do not wipe that message Michael and don't lose your bloody phone again! I'll ring him now. I don't know if he'll ring this evening or tomorrow but keep your phone close."

"Okay Tim… And Tim… I'm so, so sorry," Michael gulped and ended the call.

Chapter Fifty-Four

Michael poured himself another brandy and sat in a depressing gloom, his mind wrestling with how he could approach Marc. He needed to know the truth. He thought he had meant something to Francesca but did that mean she had been honest with him? A glimmer of an idea entered his head. Maybe Jean Paul could help as a translator and intermediary and perhaps he had some leverage over Marc. The idea grew into a plan and Michael felt a glow of hope. He took hold of his mobile and scrolled through his contacts, selected Jean Paul and rang him.

"'Allo Michael, ça va?" the French man's soulful voice answered.

"Jean Paul, I need to talk to you and ask you a favour. Can I come and see you?" he gabbled.

"Oui, oui, yes of course. I am at home; come and eat with us Michael and we will talk."

"Thank you thank you, tu es très gentil. I will be with you in half an hour, a tout à l'heure, see you shortly."

"A bientôt Michael."

Michael ended the call and went through to his bedroom. He stripped off and showered and shaved before dressing to visit Jean Paul and his wife. He took a bottle of wine from his depleted stocks and headed for his car. He climbed in and drove slowly down to Pra Loup 1500 where Jean Paul's farmhouse sat at the edge of the village. He parked outside and made his way to the front door. He knocked tentatively and the door was opened by

Jean Paul with Dominique standing at his side. They moved forward to Michael as if one and hugged him. The three of them stood on the doorstep in an emotional embrace that felt like a silent protest against human mortality, an affirmation that in the reflection of such a tragic day they still survived. Dominique ushered Michael in to sit by the roaring fire, a light in the darkness of this terrible day. Jean Paul joined him handing Michael a large glass of wine that matched his own. The two sat looking into the flames, neither seeing the intricate orange and blue flickering of the fire but instead a pair of unseeing beautiful blue eyes in the snow on the mountainside. Dominique came back from the kitchen with three plates piled high with poulet fermier on a tray. The roast chicken with onions, baby potatoes and peas cooked in a white wine and gruyère sauce smelt delicious. Michael and Jean Paul moved to join Dominique at the huge oak table and Jean Paul refreshed all their glasses.

Michael had thought that he was not hungry but Dominique's wonderful cooking and the fact that he hadn't eaten since breakfast in Grenoble soon convinced his stomach otherwise. As they ate, Dominique chatted about her son in her charming 'franglais', which Jean Paul regularly interrupted to translate. They had had him later in life but he was clearly a source of great pride to the pair. He had just qualified as a doctor and was starting his first permanent job the following week. Michael had always hoped for a child, Georgie would have been a great mother, but it was not to be, and it was just one more element of his life that added to his isolation – no Georgie, no James, no Francesca. He resisted the temptation to wallow in self-pity. Look where he was, with people who cared about him and he lived between two of the most idyllic places on the planet. He needed to dig deep and move forward. To do that he needed to know the truth, he needed to know what really happened that afternoon in his apartment.

One of the people who had been close to him had lied, and that was awful. However, if he could identify which one at least his memories of the other would be unfettered. Ignorance just meant that his memories of both were tainted and his memories were one of his greatest sources of joy. Dominique stood up from the table and cleared the empty plates. She retreated to the kitchen where they could hear the noises of dessert preparation. Michael suspected that this was a tactical withdrawal to allow him the time and space to talk to Jean Paul. On cue Jean Paul turned to him and with eyebrows raised questioningly he asked,

"So, Michael, how can I help you?"

Michael hesitated, his hand travelling automatically to stroke his chin, not quite sure how to start,

"It is complicated."

"Okay you explain and I will listen," Jean Paul smiled encouragingly.

"Here goes, I warn you it isn't pleasant."

Michael's eyes were cast down and he studied the table surface as though it might help him to articulate what he had to say.

"Last week after my lesson with you I went back to the apartment. I walked in and Francesca was there very upset with a bruise on her face and only half dressed."

Michael glanced up at Jean Paul who was listening intently but showed no emotion.

"She said that James, my friend, had raped her but she would not go to the police. However, James told me that he had found Marc with Francesca in my apartment. I cannot find out the truth from Francesca and James was murdered in England on

Wednesday by a parent in his school. I need to know who was really telling the truth or I cannot remember any of them happily. I know the truth will stain the memory of one of them, but at least one will be untarnished. The only person who knows the truth is Marc. I need to speak to him. Can you ask him to speak to me?"

Michael paused studying Jean Paul's frowning face.

"Michael you are living in a tragedy. I understand why you want the truth. I will speak to Marc tomorrow and see what is possible. I hope I can help you my friend."

He refilled their wine glasses and left the table briefly to fetch another bottle of wine from the fridge and, Michael suspected, to let Dominique know that she could return to the meal without interrupting the confessional. Michael took a long swallow of his wine whilst his hosts returned to their seats Dominique placed three dishes of tarte tatin and a jug of cream on the table between the three of them. She smiled

"Crème Anglaise."

Even at a time like this it was difficult to resist Dominique's cooking and Michael ate the sweet apple tart feeling a sense of relief that he had not only unburdened himself of his dark secret, but that Jean Paul was willing to help. As the last spoonful of the meal was eaten Jean Paul poured three more large glasses of white wine before clearing the table. Michael sat with Dominique enjoying the chilled liquid making its crisp journey across his taste buds and down his throat. Dominique began to tell Michael about growing up in the mountains and meeting Jean Paul. Michael had to slow her down on occasions but understood most of what she said. The host was gone for several minutes but on his return, he emptied his wine glass in seconds and then enquired of Michael,

"A digestif by the fire?"

"By a digestif I presume you mean your génépi?" Michael smiled.

"Yes of course," Jean Paul confirmed, "Only the best for our friend."

Dominique and Michael moved to the fireside and sat on the sofas surrounding it. Jean Paul then joined them with a bottle of his magic liquid and three small glasses which he proceeded to fill and pass around. When they all had a glass in their hand Jean Paul raised his and toasted

"To better tomorrows!"

The three threw the shots back in a single gulp and Jean Paul refilled the glasses. Michael held up his génépi and followed the lead set.

"To friends in times of need!"

Again, the glasses were replenished, and Dominique took her turn.

"To Francesca!"

Jean Paul's eyes met Michael's but all three raised their glasses repeating the toast,

"Francesca!"

The toasts were over, but Jean Paul clearly saw no reason to put the stopper back in the génépi bottle. Michael was becoming aware of the impact of the alcohol upon him and the fact that it was getting late.

"I must go home whilst I still can," he said quietly.

"No, no," Jean Paul insisted "It would not be safe for you to drive Michael, even if you are very careful. You must stay here we have plenty of room."

Michael did not insist and allowed Dominique to show him upstairs to a large bedroom with huge, wide larch beams overarching it. The room was dominated by an enormous double bed that was covered with a beautiful hand-stitched patchwork quilt. A rather antiquated sink sat against one wall. Michael poured himself a glass of water from the tap and dragged off his clothes. The alcohol had blunted the ache in his shoulder, but he disturbed it slightly getting undressed. Wearing just his boxers he pulled back the bedspread and quilt and climbed wearily into the welcoming bed. The mattress was obviously very old and stuffed with feathers. It wrapped itself around his exhausted form, the pillows moulding comfortingly to his head. He was asleep in minutes, a deep dreamless sleep, held secure by his farmhouse cradle. His inner turmoil marginalised by génépi and friendship. He eventually awoke to Dominique's voice calling up the stairs.

"Michael, Michael, le petit déjeuner."

Chapter Fifty-Five

As he emerged from his slumber it took Michael a moment or two to remember exactly where he was. He sprung from the bed a little too energetically and his shoulder protested. After washing as best he could he pulled his clothes from the night before back on and made his way down the creaking staircase. Breakfast was laid out on the oak table and as he sat down Dominique brought through a basket of warm croissants which she placed alongside French bread, butter, jams, fruit juice and a pot of coffee. Michael smiled up at Dominique.

"Salut et merci beaucoup."

She returned his smile, "Bonne journée Michael et bon appétit."

Michael could hear muffled voices in the kitchen, but his real focus was on the coffee pot, he really needed the curative powers of its contents after the previous night's excesses. The hot black coffee coursed through him. He bit into a warm croissant which flaked in his mouth, allowing its buttery laminations to play moistly on his tongue. He gradually became aware of movement behind him and he turned to see Jean Paul entering the room with Marc at his side. Marc looked utterly defeated, no longer the strutting peacock spitting spite but rather crumpled like the discarded wrapping paper on Christmas day. He had been ground down by grief and Michael could only feel sympathy for him. They both sat down and joined Michael at the table. Marc nodded acknowledgement to Michael who replied.

"Good morning."

Jean Paul spoke as he poured a coffee for himself and another for Marc.

"Michael, I phoned Marc last night and he came to talk this morning. He thought, perhaps you had had something to do with Francesca's death, but I have explained to him that the pisteurs saw her ski off on her own and that it was nothing to do with you. So now, we have also talked about what happened in your apartment and he has told me everything. I will explain to you what he has said and then you can ask anything you need. Is that okay?"

"Yes, thank you… Merci," replied Michael.

"First Michael," Jean Paul continued, "There was no rape. Marc and Francesca have been in a relation marche et arrêt, an-how do you say- on and off relationship, since school. Last Wednesday Marc saw Francesca go into your apartment with James. He saw James leave and he went and knocked on the door. He was very upset that he was not with Francesca and that she was in your apartment; he thought you were in there too. She opened the door to him and they went in. She saw how upset he was, and she told him that she would always love him and they kissed. Then, though they hadn't intended to, they made love Michael. Francesca had not meant to hurt you, but it just happened. Your friend came back into the apartment and found them. All he said was 'No Francesca, no' then he left. Francesca was very cross; with Marc, with James, with what had happened. Marc stayed for a while to try and calm her but in the end, she just told him to go. He came out of the apartment and began to walk back to his truck when he saw you skiing down to Pra Loup, so he made sure you didn't see him and then went back to Barcelonnette. He saw Francesca again when you were at your meeting in Paris, and they seemed to be getting on better together again. That is what Marc has said."

There was a long pause whilst Michael digested all that had just been said. He reflected that there was one detail that seemed to have been missed and so he asked,

"Jean Paul, can you ask Marc how Francesca got the bruise on her face?"

"Yes of course. Marc, Michael veut savoir comment Francesca a eu l'ecchymose sur son visage?"

Marc drew a breath and then replied,

"Quand James est entre elle s'éloigne de moi et s'est cogne le visage sur l'etagère pres du canape. Elle a été choquée de le voir."

Jean Paul interrupted to translate.

"She banged her face on the shelf by the sofa because she pulled away from Marc when James came in, she was so shocked and upset at what she had let happen."

Michael sighed; he knew what he needed to know. He turned to Marc.

"Merci beaucoup Marc, je suis désolé."

Marc nodded, tears welling up in his eyes, "c'est fini?" he enquired.

Michael nodded. Marc stood up and groped his way out of the room, his shoulders bent and his chest heaving in lamentation. His coffee remained on the table untouched. Jean Paul looked at Michael assessing the impact of Marc's words upon him.

"Michael, Francesca was an étoile filante, a shooting star. She came from the heavens, but her beauty was best seen from a distance. It was always dangerous to be in her path. She was not like other people. She took risks. She did not obey the rules. I am sure she loved you but in her own way."

286

Michael appreciated the sentiments of the soothing words, but he knew he had been a fool. It was the ultimate self-deception of the older man; to believe that a younger woman actually loved them! He felt like Alan Rickman's character in the film Love Actually – the classic fool. What would Georgie have thought?

"Jean Paul, thank you, you have done so much for me and you have been so kind. Tomorrow I will go back to England, but I will return next winter if you can put up with me!"

"Michael, you are our friend, you will always be welcome in our home and Michael the mountain will always welcome you too".

Dominique re-entered the room having been hovering just beyond the door, she had heard most of what had been said. Her eyes were damp with sorrow as she walked towards Michael with open arms. The three of them embraced, holding on to each other tightly seeking reassurance in each other's arms that they might recover from their despair. Eventually Michael broke away from their comforting arms and with repeated thanks left the farmhouse and returned to his car. He drove slowly back to his apartment, competing emotions filling his head.

Chapter Fifty-Six

As Michael parked his Volvo his mobile rang in his pocket. He pulled it out and looked at the screen. It was not a number he knew. He swiped up the green circle to answer the call.

"Hello Mr White, Detective Inspector Carl Collins here. I have spoken to Tim Piper and I believe that you have some information for me that might help us with the James Piper case."

In the tumult of yesterday evening, Michael had completely forgotten that he was expecting this call.

"Yes, yes I do Inspector Collins, I have a voicemail message from James Piper which was left at eight twenty-seven p.m. on the day he died and it sounds like he was being attacked. He identifies the person that I presume was the attacker by name, a parent from the school named Vines."

"All right Mr White," the Detective Inspector said seriously, "Do you still have the message on your phone?"

"Yes, I do," Michael replied, "And I think it will stay on there for quite some time."

The Detective continued, "Mr White it is very important that we do not lose that message. I would like you to play the message over a landline to this number. I will take a recording, then as soon as possible I need you to bring that phone to the station and make a statement. When are you expecting to be back in the UK?"

"I shall be back in Devon tomorrow evening," answered Michael, "When do you want me to phone you and play the recording?"

"Just give me twenty minutes and then ring this number and we'll be ready. If you can ring me tomorrow and let me know when you are an hour away from Exeter, I can arrange to meet you at the Police Station, and we can get the real thing. I'll hear from you shortly. Goodbye."

Michael walked back into his apartment and sat down on a stool. His eyes travelled from the sofa to the bookshelf. He took his phone and went to his voice messages. He carefully deleted the early messages from James. He did not want to hand a phone to the police that might raise any questions at all, and he certainly did not want to make the same mistake that Francesca had. He listened again to the message from Wednesday evening and felt a lump in his throat. He wasn't sure where he could access a phone to ring Detective Collins from, the days of public phone booths had long since vanished, but he hoped the Tourist Information Office might be able to help. He walked across the gallery to the Tourist Office and made his unusual request. The receptionist at the Tourist office listened attentively to what he said. Luckily, the inquiry was met with the usual desire to be of service and he was shown, without further ado, into an office behind the reception desk. He pulled up the policeman's number from earlier in his mobile's call history and used the land line to ring it. The now familiar tones of the detective came down the line.

"Thank you, Mr White. If you could just play the message now, on loudspeaker on your phone would probably be best."

Michael played the message and then confirmed that Detective Collins had heard and recorded it.

"Yes, I did hear the message Mr White. We are just checking that the recording worked… Yes, it has, that's good. And just to confirm the time of the message was eight twenty-seven p.m.?"

"That's right," Michael affirmed.

"Thank you for your help Mr White. That should give me enough evidence for a search warrant and to arrest our Mr Vines. I will see you tomorrow; have a safe journey and thank you."

Michael confirmed his appointment at the Police Station for the following evening and put the phone down. He left the office and thanked the Tourist Office staff profusely for their help, the receptionist shrugged and smiled finding it amusing that someone should be so grateful to her for doing her job, and he then left to return to his apartment and pack. It took him a surprisingly short time to get ready to travel as he was leaving almost everything in the flat. He was coming back, despite everything that had happened he knew Pra Loup would always be special to him, not even the avalanche could take that away, nor Francesca, nor Marc. He loved these mountains, he loved to ski and he loved his apartment, he would be back.

He decided to make his journey rather less of a marathon slog and leave immediately, allowing him to break up the drive with an overnight stop. He had one last task to compete before he set out and that was to phone William, the Chair of the Governors, and tell him his decision regarding the caretaker headteacher post, there really had not been a decision to make. The number rang and William picked up almost immediately.

"Hello William, it's Michael here," Michael began, "I have decided that I would like to help out. I will be back in the UK tomorrow and I can be in school on Monday morning so we can sort out all the details next week if you are sure that is what you want?"

Michael could hear the relief in William's voice as he replied,

"Yes Michael, yes Michael we are absolutely sure, thank you we are so grateful."

Michael was surprised at how gushing the response was, but he supposed that was the impact of the awful shock everyone at the school had suffered and now they were clutching at any passing debris to keep themselves afloat.

"Can you let my colleagues know that I will be helping out William? An all-staff email is probably your best bet."

William was effusive in his thanks and clearly relieved but Michael thought to himself that it was what James would have wanted and he was not going to let him down again. It was his duty to support the school and he was going to fulfil his duty. He took his bags to the car and then spent a moment looking up at his beloved mountain. He had experienced such joy and such sadness here in the space of a few short weeks, but it still felt like home. What had happened was not the mountain's fault but that of the flawed humans who chose to play their games on her beautiful slopes. He climbed into the Volvo, turned on the ignition and began his journey, leaving the enchanting Pra Loup behind –for now.

Chapter Fifty-Seven

Entering the United Kingdom legally was far less angst ridden than skulking across the Channel in a stolen motor cruiser. He almost enjoyed the familiarity of the traffic jam on the A303 at Stonehenge and busied his brain with the challenges of leading a school which had just had its much-loved headteacher murdered. How could he best support the staff, the pupils, the parents and the wider community? Any death in a school was difficult, losing pupils was always awful and Michael had experienced that twice but losing a member of staff in such a violent manner put him deep in uncharted waters.

Michael phoned Detective Inspector Collins at eleven a.m. to let him know that he was about forty-five minutes from the police station in Exeter.

The Inspector was waiting for him on his arrival; he did not fit the mental picture Michael had subconsciously created of him following their phone conversations. He was much shorter than Michael, he was probably only five foot eight inches tall, and was slight in stature. His tired, crumpled suit, hung from his shoulders with folds of loose material curtained around his body, the sleeves were slightly too long, and the impression given was that it was the suit of a significantly larger individual. Perhaps it had been bought from a charity shop, Michael thought, because even if the inspector had been on a serious diet his arms would not have shrunk. The inspector's face was even more crumpled than his suit, wrinkles proliferated across his forehead and reached out like a tracery of spider's web from the corners of his eyes and mouth. His chin bore what appeared to be a couple of days of stubble adding further to the impression of a man who had no interest in his own appearance and the old brown leather belt that was keeping up his oversized trousers looked incongruous against the scuffed black shoes that cried out for a coating of polish. In sharp contrast his hair was jet black, not a grey hair in sight and if any other aspect of his dress or looks had given any hint of pride, or even vague nuances of self-interest, Michael would have thought that it was dyed. Michael concluded it was his natural colour. As it was the hair colour made it difficult to make any sort of guess as to the age of the detective. His dishevelled appearance gave the impression that the man himself was disorganised and haphazard but one glance at D.I. Collin's eyes belied that conclusion. Michael found himself looking into a gaze that seemed to be searching deep into his being, trying to read his every word or hesitation for hidden meaning. After just a short conversation Michael realised that he was dealing with a man who had a mind which was razor sharp, everything else was purely window dressing. He took Michael's phone and apologised that, as it was a key piece of evidence, it would not be returned to him for some time. He then took Michael's statement, stopping him occasionally to ask clarifying questions- one or two of which forced Michael to tread very carefully with his answers. Having taken the statement the inspector told Michael that he couldn't update him on the investigation as forensics were still working on a variety of materials removed from the Vines' home and car. Michael took the opportunity to furnish Collins with as much background information about Mr Vines' previous behaviour as he could remember and also mentioned James' conjectures about the broken windows and the CCTV. The inspector's eyes held him in a steady stare as he listened attentively, the man may not take care of his appearance like Poirot but Michael was quite sure he would be a similarly challenging adversary if you were a suspect. He needed to make sure that he never became a suspect but ultimately he knew he hadn't killed anyone and that Mr Vines had.

It was well over an hour later before Michael was finally signing his statement and receiving the receipt for his mobile. Michael made one request before he left, that one of the police tech. team download and email him all the contact numbers on his phone so that he could get in touch with anyone he needed to. On leaving the police station, Michael went to the local Curry's PC World and purchased a new laptop and a cheap pay as you go phone with an adequate level of technology. Then he headed home to the South Hams.

He had a few contact numbers in Georgie's address book and so he was able to ring Tim when he got back into the house – this time using his keys at the front door. Tim was keen to hear Michael's update about his trip to Exeter. Tim, like Michael, had had no feedback about the police search or any progress that they had made.

The week at school proved to be every bit as tough as Michael had feared it would be. A team of psychologists had been deployed by the local authority to work with individuals and small groups, but while walking the corridors Michael often found children or teachers crying in corners, unable to manage their grief. He took strength from the knowledge that James was the man he had known and that it was him who had been a fool for doubting his friend. Every single one of these tears was earned by a great teacher and a great man. Somehow, Friday arrived and Michael hoped that the school community would find some peace when the pressure cooker effect of all being together in a shared space, James' space, could be released a little. He knew, probably more than most, that grief became more manageable over time. It never went away but you could find ways to cope.

On Friday evening, Tim phoned to talk about James' funeral arrangements. His body had been released and the following Friday had been identified as a possible date by the undertaker.

"Okay Tim. I plan to close the school so that all staff can attend. I will inform the parents on Monday. We already have a list of students who would like to attend. I have spoken to the church and we will be able to have an overspill by video link in the church hall and another outside in the churchyard. Hopefully it won't rain." Michael explained.

"That all sounds fine Michael. At the end of the service the coffin will be taken to the crematorium which will be attended by just a few invited people, mostly family and you, of course."

"Thank you, I do appreciate that thought. Do you want the school to do anything as part of the service?" Michael asked.

"It would be nice to have the school choir sing as James arrives but most important of all I want you to do the eulogy before his coffin leaves. That is what he would have wanted."

"Tim," Michael interrupted, "Are you sure you don't want to do it?"

"No Michael. He idolised you, he loved you, he would have thought it a huge honour for his friend to speak at his funeral."

"Of course, I'll do it Tim. I would be honoured. I'll keep in touch during the week to finalise everything."

Chapter Fifty-Eight

The day of the funeral was a 'Pra Loup' day Michael thought; bright blue clear skies welcomed the mourners. Every seat in the church was taken, as were all the seats in the hall and the churchyard. Detective Inspector Collins stood just inside the churchyard as Michael walked in amongst the mourners. He was almost unrecognisable as he stood observing the despondent throng, he wore a smart dark blue suit with polished shoes and he had shaved, Michael presumed and hoped there was nothing more to the Detective's presence than a desire to pay his respects, he made a mental note not to stroke his chin as he approached the officer. Michael paused to say hello, his hands firmly by his sides, but as he did so, the sharp eyes read his thoughts,

"It is my wedding and funeral suit, unfortunately it gets far more outings for the latter than the former. Good luck today Mr White, this isn't going to be easy", he nodded towards the stricken assembly.

"No... thank you," Michael replied and with a nod of the head turned and walked into the church.

James had been much loved and respected and that was very clear from the sombre mood and the sheer number of mourners. James' parents stood just outside of the Church door, to one side and away from the growing mass of people. The Colonel stood, as if at attention with his wife by his side. The only sign of emotion they displayed was the surreptitious touching of their fingers. Michael stopped and spoke to them briefly offering his condolences. The Colonel nodded his acknowledgement and James' mother offered a calm, "Thank you."

Tim was already inside the church when Michael entered and was standing near the font with a very lovely blond woman who looked to be in her early thirties. She wore a plain black dress that had a collar at the neck and a simple string of black beads. Despite her attire being so understated, she looked beautiful although the grief that played out across her face made her look pale and strained. Tim waved Michael over as he entered the church,

"Michael, please can I introduce you to Alice."

Michael grasped the young woman's outstretched hand and found only a husky whisper rasped from his mouth as he said

"Alice, hello. I am so sorry."

Alice smiled at him, she was quite unable to speak, and tear drops laced her cheeks. Tim put a strong arm around her shoulder and hugged her. He showed Alice to her pew at the front and then returned to Michael's side.

The church managed to maintain an atmosphere of hushed reverence even though its pews were steadily filling up with row upon row of the bereaved. There were so many people that had been touched by James' life and a great number were here although, Michael suspected, they would rather be anywhere else, doing anything else.

"I spoke to Carl Collins earlier," Tim began in hushed tones.

"I saw he was here," Michael briefly interrupted inclining his head towards the graveyard to indicate where he had seen him.

"He thought we would want to know, even though this morning hardly seems the most appropriate time, that apparently the forensics from Vine's house are back. He seemed to think that it is very good news and from what he said I have to agree. Firstly,

297

they have found fragments of James' phone in the sole of Vines' trainer. Secondly, they found microscopic splatters of James' blood on a black sweatshirt and finally the cameras on the A38 picked up Vine's car registration at the exit by the school at five p.m., and then again going in the opposite direction at eight thirty p.m. So, they can place him at the scene at the time of the murder and the blood spatters tie him directly to the stabbing. He has been charged with James' murder and remanded into custody."

Michael exhaled "Thank God, the bastard is going to pay."

"He'll struggle to explain away such strong evidence that is for sure," said Tim. "Now let's concentrate on James. The hearse will arrive shortly. Are you ready?"

"I am ready," said Michael nervously, "But whether I can actually get through this I don't know."

"I'll be right by you if you need me to take over. Courage Michael, this is for James."

The coffin entered to the strains of the school choir singing Abide with Me and was set down on the trestles at the front of the church. Michael stood transfixed by the sight; he was transported back to when he had stood with James by his side looking down at Georgie's coffin. He was vaguely aware of the vicar speaking, hymns being sung and heads bowing in prayer. Then there was silence and all eyes turned to him. The vicar stood to one side and invited Michael to take his place at the lectern. Michael fumbled for the typed sheet in the inner breast pocket of his jacket, pulled it out and walked forward to the lectern. He smoothed his script against the flat wooden surface and looked out at the congregation and cameras in front of him. He caught Alice's eye and she smiled supportively. Michael's eyes dropped to his script. He paused and then began. Keeping his eyes either on the script or a point above everyone's heads at the back of the church he read.

"All of you will have known James Piper in different ways; to some he will have been your boss and colleague, to others your teacher and headteacher, to some the headteacher at your child's school, to some a friend, to others a loved one. You will all have known this man differently and you will all have your own memories of him. Some of those memories you will share with people here today after the service, other memories may be more personal and private, but I defy you to be able to remember this man without smiling. Smiling about a favour he did for you, a joke he told. Smiling about one of his mad cap assemblies or his fancy dress on world book day. Smiling because he inspired you to be more than you ever thought you could be or smiling because he was there for you. James Piper loved his school, loved being an educator and loved life. There was nothing he wouldn't do for his students, his staff, his friends, his family. We all know that he has been taken from us too soon, when he still had so much more to give, but I also know, just as I am sure you know too, that he would want all of us to remember him with a smile and honour his death by making the most of our lives, working hard and playing hard. James Piper was a great man, a lovely man, a funny man and he was my friend. He was a man you could always rely on, a man of honesty and integrity, a man you could trust."

Michael turned to James' coffin and bowed his head, tears spilling from his eyes.

"Goodbye my dear friend."

The four pallbearers moved forward, lifted the coffin on to their shoulders and began to carry it from the church. As they walked slowly out, their faces set in the preoccupied frowns of their profession, the choirs' voices sang out to accompany James on his final journey.

"Above me hangs the silent sky;
Around me rolls the sea;
The crew is all at rest, and I
Am, Lord, alone with Thee"

Michael, Tim, Alice and James' parents followed the coffin from the church, their lives changed forever.